A Broken Us

A Novel

Amy Daws

A Broken Us

Copyright © 2014 Amy Daws
All rights reserved.

Published by Stars Hollow Publishing
ISBN 978-0-9903252-4-6
Editing by Heather Banta www.linkedin.com/in/heatherbanta/
Cover design by Amy Daws
Cover photography by Megan Daws
Author Photograph by Megan Daws
Cover models Rachel Lausen and Eric McLaughlin
Cover shoot location Mary Ellen Connelly residence

This book is licensed for your personal enjoyment only. No part of this book may be reproduced in any form or by any electronic or mechanical means including information storage and retrieval systems, without permission in writing from the author. The only exception is by a reviewer, who may quote short excerpts in a review. If you would like to share this book with another person, please purchase an additional copy for each recipient. If you're reading this book and did not purchase it, or it was not purchased for your enjoyment only, then please go to your favorite retailer and purchase your own copy. Thank you for respecting the hard work of this author.

This book is a work of fiction. Names, characters, places, and incidents either are products of the author's imagination or are used fictitiously. Any resemblance to actual persons, living or dead, events, or locales is entirely coincidental.

To my husband, Kevin.
Thanks for being the best Mr. Mom I've ever seen.
I couldn't do this without you.

CHAPTER ONE

Brody aggressively paces the hallway of our tiny split-foyer house. I cringe as he rakes his hands through his curly brown hair and lets out a frustrated sigh. Anger and tension are radiating off his body like blurry lines surrounding a campfire.

I turn away from him because I can't stand seeing him like this. So hurt. So broken. A sadness creeps over me as I look around our home we built together. I painfully take in my last moments here. I can't believe this is the last time I'll be sitting on this very couch. Four years ago, we picked it up off the side of a curb. Sure, we may have been one step away from being labeled dumpster divers, but we knew it was nothing a $40 carpet shampooer couldn't fix. We were senseless like that together, and it was great.

Every flat surface in our house is littered with picture frames. Brody didn't mind my obsession. I'm infatuated with finding the wackiest frames I can. I frequently receive them as gifts from friends, family, and even coworkers. I love putting unconventional pictures in frames. There's a photo of Brody sleeping on the couch, and one of me with my three nieces, eating mashed potatoes. My favorite is a mustard-colored pleather frame with tiny black seahorses glued around the edges. Inside the frame is a picture of Brody and me on a four-wheeler. I'm facing backward, straddling him while his arms grip the handles. He's biting my neck as I laugh. We were so happy. So innocent. So perfect.

Candid photos show more about one's life and personality than posed pictures. My heart sinks as I realize none of these pictures will be going with me.

"How can you do this, Fin?" he barks, spinning back on his heels to stride down the hallway again.

Still sitting on the couch, I stare at my hands in stony silence, swallowing big gulps of air while he adjusts to the news I just dealt him.

"How can you need time?" he throws at me in a mocking tone. "Away from me?" He trudges swiftly across the living room. In only four paces, he's on his knees, directly in front of my face, gripping my cheeks between his soft, large hands.

"You can't mean this, Fin. You can't!" his voice cracks as he says my name and his expression melts from anger to desperation.

"Brody, don't." I state, pragmatically. "I have to. I told you I can't do this anymore."

"THIS IS US!" he booms, loudly, while turning my face back to look into his eyes. "You can't do *us*? That kills me, Fin—it kills me!"

"This is what I need, Brody. I've explained everything. There's nothing more to say. I told you this isn't up for discussion."

I've been practicing these very words in the mirror for the past week, fixing my expression to look strong, and not insecure. The last thing he needs is to receive mixed signals from me.

Brody looks down and appears to be collecting his thoughts. As his gaze comes back up, his eyes rove quickly over my whole face. I know he's searching for any glimpse of reservation in my decision to leave.

"Please, Finley," he says, with shaky breath. "You love *us*, you can't do this to *us*."

I knew he'd use *us* against me. I knew he'd say this, and I'm prepared for it. *Us* has the potential to be my kryptonite. But I can't let it get to me.

When Brody and I first started dating, we were incredible together—like two peas in a pod. We were goofy, stupid, funny, and playful. We were all the things that made a person laugh a lot in life. We both lit up inside when we made our relationship official.

One night, back in college, after a rousing and playful wrestling match in my apartment, we'd been laughing so hard we had tears in our eyes. In that moment, I let out a large exhale and said, without thinking, "I love us."

Brody froze and looked at me in shock. My eyes widened as I realized the intensity of the proclamation I'd just made to him. I'd known I loved him for nearly a month, but we'd only been together for two, and I sure as hell didn't want to be the first one to say *the L-word*. But my big, fat mouth blurted it out like it was just a normal Tuesday!

As I realized he wasn't responding, I awkwardly tried to get up off the floor and think of a quick excuse to get him the hell out of my room. I silently chastised myself for scaring the crap out of him, and therefore ruining the best thing that had ever happened to me. He grabbed my wrist before I stood all the way up, and unceremoniously pulled me down on top of him. He sweetly said, "I love us, too."

The only emotion I remember feeling in that moment, was giddiness. I felt giddy! As my heart pounded happily beneath my chest, Brody appeared to be contemplating something. He had just reciprocated my feelings, so I couldn't fathom what he could have been pondering.

As he tucked my hair behind my ears, he spoke softly, "Actually, I think I love *us* more than I love—you—does that make any sense at all?"

It made perfect sense. Brody and I fit together so naturally, in a way I didn't even know was possible. It was like I'd evolved into a better version of myself I didn't even know was inside of me. I'd never met anyone I could laugh with so often and be my complete self with. It was Brody who brought that out in me. And I did the same for him. It was *us*. Ever since the day we first declared our love, we never said, *I love you*, we always said, *I love us*. I was so excited in our early days of love. I'd been transformed into a hormonal teenybopper. I was like a 14-year-old girl talking with my bestie about my first kiss with a boy, squealing the last word of my sentences because I couldn't contain my excitement. *Good Lord, I was a goner.*

Brody and I made it five years and still said, *I love us*. It was strange to others, and probably sounded a bit egocentric, like we were announcing to the world that we thought we were this hot power-couple everyone should strive to be, but that couldn't be further from the truth. We were simply in our own bubble, playing by our own set of rules. It was *us,* and it was perfect.

"It's *us*, Fin! I love *us!*" Brody repeats, snapping me out of my memories of a much sweeter time. Our love was so much easier when we were in college.

As I look into Brody's deep, navy-blue eyes, my heart begins to break and bleed inside of me. Brody and I had so many dreams together. But they were made when life was so much easier. I squeeze my eyes closed, trying to erase the beauty of his face and our love. Tears quickly escape down my cheeks. As I attempt to turn my head away from his grasp, he grips my face harder between his two hands, forcing me to face him. I feel his warm, soothing breath on my lips, panting with desperation. My lips betray me and part ever so slightly; with that, he attacks my lips with fervor.

Brody works passionately on my firmly closed mouth—begging, pleading for a return in gesture. I sniff back a gasp of air through my nose as his hands drop from my face and wrap around my lower back, binding my arms against my sides.

I have to hold out, I can't give in. I can't show him I still love *us*. He won't want me when he learns the truth. This is the best way—the easiest way.

But deep down, I know that this is Brody. I love him. I don't just love him; I love *us*, which means more in our weird, remote world. He's kissing me and begging me to stay. *Why the hell am I doing this to us?* I want to give in and let us be us, in whatever capacity that may be. *No, no!* I've thought this through; I can't let him sway my decision. He might not love us if he learns the truth, and I can't stomach that. In the long run, he will be much happier without me. He'll find someone new and she can receive his passion—*his kiss*.

And Brody doesn't just kiss, he *commands*. The man has a technique I have never experienced, and I have kissed my fair share of guys in my wild college-girl phase. His hands touch my cheek in a way that makes me feel cherished and consumed with one simple touch. I swear I've come close to orgasm multiple times from Brody's incredible kisses.

I contemplate one last kiss, one last goodbye to take in, so I'll never forget—*us*.

I slowly turn my palms out to feel the sides of his denim clad thighs, so muscular and familiar. I move my head slightly, giving him better purchase of my mouth. As my lips begin to move against his, Brody's hands move up my back, releasing my arms to roam. His right hand reaches the nape of my neck and threads through my long brown hair. He gently pulls my hair tightly, just how I like. I know exactly what he's doing.

This is a reminder kiss. This is Brody's way of making me remember how great we are and how hot we make each other.

My reserve breaks as I feel gentle flutters in my lower belly. I'm past the point of no return. I can't help it. I'm needy for Brody. I always have been. His total package is completely irresistible.

Brody has gorgeously thick and curly brown hair. He cuts it short, leaving just enough length for me to comb my fingers through. His navy-blue eyes contrast perfectly with his creamy complexion. Brody has an unexplainable look about him that feels comfortable and undeniably sexy. It's not only his appearance that draws me to him, it's the comfort I feel with him. Brody feels like home to me. When we made love for the first time, he commanded my body with the deeply intense emotions he had for me—it was simply profound.

It's amazing how hot finding your soulmate can be; to find someone who truly gets you, and encourages you to be yourself by just being who he is. When the physical aspect of our relationship took off, it was everything I could do to keep my hands off of him for any extended period of time. We were always touching each other and being complete goofs at the same time. It worked for us.

Some of our hottest sex sessions escalated when we talked in ridiculously stupid voices, laughing obnoxiously. We relentlessly made fun of each other and called each other out on the stupid stuff we did. It made us feel connected and safe. We understood each other. We'd be laughing at something ridiculous, then with one glance, we were all over each other. It was as though our happiness and sex drive combined tracks on a railway and ignited us into a frenzy.

I feel that frenzy now as my fingertips brush the side of his bare skin peeking out of his soft, fitted t-shirt. The skin-to-skin contact zaps Brody into action. He quickly breaks away from my lips and pulls my t-shirt up over my head.

As he begins to come back for my lips he pauses and looks down at my breasts. I'm ashamed to see I am wearing his favorite bra—a sheer, teal brassiere that covers nothing. My nipples harden under his hot perusal.

I don't know why I wore this set of underwear today. I wasn't planning on things escalating like this, but my mind betrayed me when I got dressed for work that morning.

A frustrated grumble rises out of Brody's chest and he commands my mouth again. His hands run down the backs of my thighs and lift me up. My legs wrap around his waist in response. Brody is strong. He's not what I would call bulky but he's tall, lean, and toned.

I'm nearly six-foot tall myself, so he towers a good four inches over me, giving him the caper for these types of antics. I'm not blessed with the willowy runway model frame. I have an hourglass figure with a plump behind that Brody seems compelled to touch every time I pass him in a room. It doesn't matter if we are in a crowded restaurant or at a family function. He has no shame. He doesn't like being referred to as an Ass Man though; he says my eyes are his favorite feature. My eyes are blue, according to my driver's license. The blue is so light that my surroundings are reflected in them and they change from blue to grey, and sometimes green. I'm told aqua is the best color description.

Brody's one free hand begins roaming over the top of my full B-cup breast as he carries me down the hallway into our bedroom.

He lays me down on our familiar and comfortable bed we've

slept in together for the past three years. I feel an ache in my heart, knowing I'll never be back in this bed. I thoughtfully watch him as he undresses me—and then himself. He kisses me tenderly up my leg. When he reaches my belly with his lips, I close my eyes and will the pain in my heart to stop. *Not there, don't kiss me there.*

I quickly roll him onto his back and take control of the situation. I don't want to have that conversation, so before he sees the pain in my eyes, I connect our bodies and we begin moving together in perfect synch.

Brody strokes my hips and thighs, and my hands wrap into my hair as I ride him into a state of oblivion. Brody loves me on top. *This is a good farewell position. He deserves this—it's the least I can give him.*

As if sensing something in my demeanor, he sits up. While still inside me, he places his ear against my chest. His hands caress my back while we continue gyrating against each other. I'm desperate to focus on our bodies and not what this means. He pulls back to look into my eyes and I quickly look away.

"Look at me, baby. I need to see us," he says, in a raspy, aroused voice.

My eyes instantly crash into his and we stare deeply at each other until our bodies can't hold out any longer. I cry out loudly and Brody kisses me passionately, swallowing the pleasure coming out of my mouth. As we come crashing back down together, he pulls me down on top of him and turns us on our sides, tucking me into him.

When my body settles back down, I can't stop the tears from pouring out of my eyes. We didn't use protection and it doesn't even matter. We haven't used protection for nearly two years...and it doesn't freaking matter. Sex with Brody is always incredible, but the sick, doomful feeling afterward is more than I can bare. It is utterly painful to feel so incredibly amazing one minute, and be slammed with crippling depression the next. I can't give *us* what we want. My body is broken. Barren. *Us* is broken.

This is why I have to leave.

How can I force Brody to be stuck with someone like me? Someone who can't give him all he deserves in life? Am I expected to get over the idea of never being able to see a tiny, pink, cuddly bundle of *us*? As narcissistic as it might sound, not making a mini-us is not what I signed up for. I'm in love with *us* and loved the idea of seeing a tiny person who had a little bit of me and a little bit of Brody.

And what if Brody decides he doesn't want me? How can I possibly live with the horror of being dumped for not being able to do the most important thing a woman's body is designed to do? I am in baby-making hell with a man who gets me so innately well that it physically hurts to continue being with him. Brody and I have had an incredible connection for years, but this feels like the *one thing* that he just might not be okay with.

We never married, so there's no fuss to it other than moving my stuff. Brody and I never wanted to get married. We were so confident and content with *us*, that marriage seemed irrelevant. To us, it felt like an archaic thing to do to make other people happy. We knew we had something above the normalcies of other couples; getting married and putting rings on our fingers would sully the commitment we had to each other.

Our families were uneasy with our arrangement. We both come from traditional families in the Midwest. *Get married, have children— blah, blah, blah.* We assured them we were just as committed to each other as any legally-married couple—even more so. They gave up arguing about it so fervently, but still made small, snide comments here and there.

When we finally revealed we were going to try to have a baby, they were excited. I think they thought if we had a baby together, we'd eventually decide marriage would make things easier as parents because then we'd all have the same last name. And maybe they were right, but Brody and I didn't feel that way, so we were just taking things in stride. I guess they'll all have a good laugh when they hear about this.

I turn over and hug Brody as tightly as I can. Burying my face in the crook of his neck, I breathe in his musky bar-soap scent.

"That wasn't goodbye," he softly whispers into my hair.

I pull away and look into his eyes, and I finally see it. *Defeat.*

"It was, Brody," I whisper back, my eyes welling with tears.

"I don't understand. Why won't you at least tell me where you're going?" he croaks as his eyes become red around the edges.

I rub the pad of my thumb along his cheekbone and thread my fingers into his hair. "You don't have to understand. Just know it's what I need."

I kiss him one last time with all the passion I can muster and he doesn't even respond. His lips form a hard line against mine and I know it's over.

I creep out of the bed and quickly grab my clothes before dashing into the bathroom to clean up. I'm quiet as I step out, nervous Brody will be waiting for me in the hallway, attempting to prevent me from leaving. When he's nowhere to be seen, I tiptoe down the hallway then step outside into a blast of unseasonably warm air. The last days of summer don't appear to be leaving Kansas anytime soon.

As I settle into the driver's seat and glance at the suitcases in the backseat, I breathe a sigh of relief. He's letting me go; this is what I want. To reassure myself, I reach into my purse and pull out my boarding pass, passport, and the British pounds I had transferred from American dollars. I glance at the time on my boarding pass and check the clock on my dash.

In four more hours, I'll be on a plane to London. Well, New York first for a layover, then on to London. I take one last look at the place Brody and I have called home for three years. This place used to be full of happy, magical memories—now it stares back at me with an ominous threat of disappointment. I can't stay here and live this life. Not like this. London can be my new lover.

CHAPTER TWO

My best friend Leslie gave me the courage and motivation to make the big trip over the pond. Leslie lives in London, in a flat with two or three other roommates. I can never keep track because it always changes.

I'm sure Leslie fits right in in a big city like London. When we were kids, I always felt she was destined for something bigger than our small hometown of Marshall, Missouri, just two hours east of Kansas City. Leslie lived on a big family-run dairy farm and I lived on a small acreage, so we had a lot in common growing up around livestock and farmers. Together, we would get into all sorts of mischief, but we always managed to stay out of any serious trouble. Sometimes we would hang out in my parents' cozy basement watching movies, eating junk food, and being ridiculous together. I remember one time Leslie and I laughed for hours about how her nostrils flared when she talked. She had the wackiest sense of humor and I was always along for the ride.

In fact, I never laughed as hard with anybody as I did with Leslie, until I met Brody. That was one of the first things I told Leslie about the new, hot guy I met at college. I said, "Leslie! You won't believe it! He's one of us!"

She understood exactly what I meant and was genuinely happy for me. So a few weeks ago, when I called her crying on the phone about another negative pregnancy test, it was her idea I come to London to get away for a while. She didn't want me to break up with Brody, she just wanted me to relax and get my mind off things for a bit. But Leslie didn't know all the facts. I was too scared to tell her I'd actually broken it off with him and planned to move to London indefinitely. I'd be damned if I let her change my mind. If there wasn't room for me to live with her, I'd find a place on my own. She did it; so could I.

Leslie moved overseas on her own and was a legitimate, proper, freelance designer. She is currently working on a big project for *Nikon* designing a camera-bag line. She's been living in London for a few years now, traveling back and forth between London and China, teaching factory workers how to create her designs. What an amazing life. She was seeing the world and thriving, she wasn't worried about babies and fertility cycles.

I'm full of nervous energy as I board my international flight at JFK. I find my seat and recline. There's no turning back now. I try to convince myself I've ruined Brody's sweet and perfect idea of me, and even if I wanted to go back, I'm certain he wouldn't accept me.

I can do this, I can be alone. I can be without us. Brody is the love of my life, I know and feel it in my core, but I will find happiness elsewhere. Maybe even with another guy. At the very least, I can find someone to have a fling with—someone to take my mind off *us*. Maybe I'll find a nice Brit to settle down with who doesn't want children. But first I want to be wild and crazy and forget about getting serious with anyone for quite some time. London can be my lover.

I've dreamed about living in London ever since I developed a huge love for British Chick-Lit novels. I never used to be a big reader but my sister, Cadence, handed me a book and said, "Just try it, you'll like it! When you finish, you can watch *Debra Messing* in the movie version!"

I immediately asked her the name of the movie, because I was an avid movie watcher and I loved *Debra Messing*. When she said *Wedding Date*, I couldn't believe it. One of my all-time favorites! *How could the book ever compare?*

It didn't compare. Not at all. It was a thousand times better! It gave me so many more details about a story I'd already loved. The book was called *Asking for Trouble* by *Elizabeth Young*. Her funny, quirky British sense of humor and writing style resonated so strongly with me, I immediately purchased paperbacks of all of her novels. They were all wonderfully fun and romantic; they are now my most prized possessions in my book collection. They are books I frequently reread; it's like visiting an old friend each and every time. I know I love a book if the moment I read the final page, I quickly turn back to reread all my favorite parts again—which are almost always the romantic scenes. My novels are an escape for me when I need it most; a great distraction to ease the fear of being barren; and so began—and continues—my love affair with British Chick-Lit. For years, I've been reading *Elizabeth Young*, *Sophie Kinsella*, *Jill Mansell*, *Marianne Keyes*, and *Samantha Young*. It's all so interesting to me, being from the boring old United States. Anything across the ocean is a place I have never seen. The UK is a country with fascinating history and vibrant fictional characters I instantly fell in love with. What better place to run and hide from a life I'm scared to live?

I can be a new version of *us* with my pal, Leslie. She doesn't want to make a baby with me! Thank God, because that'd be an awkward conversation to have.

I know she can show me a world that will make me forget all about babies, marriage, and *us*.

CHAPTER THREE

I feel butterflies in my belly as the plane finally hits the tarmac at Heathrow Airport. I nervously tuck away *A Girl's Best Friend*, my favorite *Elizabeth Young* book, into my oversized carry-on. The flight has been long and arduous, with a three-hour layover in New York. I have been traveling for fourteen hours and I feel like crap. I want to brush my teeth and change my clothes. But holy shitballs, I'm in London!

Just hearing the different dialects of British accents on the plane gets my blood pumping. The flight attendant is giving her final directions to us in this gorgeously posh tone that simply melts in my ears like butter.

As I make my way over to luggage claim, I turn my phone on and a slew of texts begin popping up on the screen.

Leslie: What gate are you at?

Mom: Did you land safely?

Cadence: George and I picked up your car. I can't believe you are flying to London right now! Call me and tell me everything when you get settled.

The last one from my sister makes me smile. I'm really going to miss her. She's married with three daughters and a baby boy on the way. She's totally living vicariously through my adventures. She is settled down now with kids; she knows this is an adventure she could never take.

Not to mention, she is one-hundred percent *Team Brody*. Regardless, she's happy for this big change in my life and feels a large sense of pride being the one to spark my love affair with London by giving me that book so many years ago.

My heart drops in my chest as I see Brody's name pop up.

Brody: Not that I give a fuck, but I hope you're alive and shit. I have no clue where you are or who you are staying with. Hope you're having a ball. I'm in hell.

A lump forms in my throat as his obvious pain and anger exudes through the text. That does not sound like my Brody. Yes, he is candid and curses frequently, but he's always treated me like a prized possession he would forever love, adore, and protect. *I did this to him. I brought out this ugliness.*

I quickly open Leslie's message and text her my gate number. After what feels like an hour, my four gigantic luggage bags come rolling toward me. I struggle to grab them, then realize I'll need a cart to carry everything. After some finagling, I'm able to roll all four pieces of luggage at once with my carry-on purse draped over my shoulder. *I'm a big girl, I can handle these without a man.*

I slowly and carefully make my way outside, searching the crowds of people, taxis, and buses, looking for my long-lost childhood friend. I swear the people here even *look* different. They all have a different style of dress than I'm used to seeing in the Midwest. In Kansas, you see plenty of people with cute style and clothes, but it's not common. The majority stick to classic jeans and tee shirts. Here, nearly everyone is wearing different colored pants, leggings, or slacks. Even the facial features here seem different than the people I grew up around.

A loud, obnoxiously long whistle overpowers the noise of the traffic and people. I scrunch my brow and look over to see a flamboyantly dressed redhead sauntering toward me.

"Leeeeeez?" I screech, hardly able to contain my excitement. "Leslie!" I finish loudly before I let go of my four suitcase handles. She bounds into my arms animatedly. I am so freaking excited I lift her off the ground.

"Fin-fin!" she declares fondly, smiling at me with tears in her eyes. "You made it, you lil' world-traveling-whipper-snapper, you!"

"Me? A world traveler? Schyeah, right—Miss Big-important-worldly-designer, dashing between London and China to big important meetings," I goad, in a smug British accent.

"'Tis true! 'Tis I! I am designer extraordinaire, straight outta' London, love! Why, I oughta...aww, crap! I think I went Australian there. My roommates would kill me if they heard me talking like this!" she laughs at her own feeble attempt at a British accent.

As I take Leslie in, I see that while her clothes, style, and hair have changed dramatically, she is still the same old Lez that used to pedal her bicycle down the gravel roads to meet me in my sister's car. I was easily a good year younger than legal driving age, so I'd make her ride her bike; I was too chicken to cross the highway and pick her up. We never did anything particularly bad. We would stuff her bike in the trunk—make a failed attempt to close it—then cruise the gravel roads with the windows down and our hair blowing wildly. We just savored in the rebellious act of driving without a license.

Back then, our clothes were pretty standard: jeans, flip-flops, and t-shirts. But standing before me now is a stylish, artistic creator. Leslie's thick, auburn hair is chopped short into a bob with short pixie bangs. The Brits call it fringe. She's wearing loud-print leggings with multi-colored swirls all over and a deco-checkered sleeveless blouse with a collar. It doesn't match by any standard, but she's rocking it with ferocity.

I feel rather plain in comparison in my black leggings with my loose, cream-colored, off-the-shoulder top.

"Oooo, God, that's ceeeeuuute!" Leslie drawls as she gently touches the Native American-style statement necklace around my neck.

"Oh, thanks," I reply, my hands touching the same place, "I bought it at the airport in Kansas before I left. I knew I'd need to dress this outfit up somehow with you coming to pick me up at the airport. I feel like Humpty Dumpty next to you right now!" I tease, while playfully smacking her ass.

"Don't be ridiculous, Fin!" she states, with a huge wave of her hand. "You couldn't be more fabulous if you were carrying *eight* suitcases. Speaking of which, what the bloody hell are you thinking, bringing four ginormous suitcases for a one-week vacay? I told you to pack light!"

Her eyes bore into me with indignation. I know she's not really pissed, but I also know I need to explain my plan for staying here longer. I decide to avoid the question; telling her at the airport is not ideal.

"What can I say? I have to have options to keep up with you!" she laughs and reaches around me to drag two of the suitcases behind me.

"This is so unlike you, we'll have to take a cab now, you know. We can't bring this kind of luggage on the tube. We'll get mugged, raped, and sold into international sex-trafficking," Leslie says, deadpan.

My eyes bug out of my head as I take in what she just said.

"Kidding, Fin! Good Lord, you better brush up on your British dry sense of humor or you'll never have any fun here!" she laughs as we make our way over to the next available cab driver waiting at the curb.

The driver stows away three suitcases in the trunk and sets one in the passenger seat next to him. Before I know it, Leslie and I are out on the streets of London in a proper, historical-looking, black, English taxicab.

CHAPTER FOUR

After I get over the initial odd feeling of the driver being on the opposite side of the car, and driving on the wrong side of the road, I take in the scenery. I'm even checking out the small pubs located on every other block, daydreaming about what those people do for a living that allows them to be in an old English pub at this time of day. It's all enthralling to me! Sure, there are bars in Kansas and Missouri, but they are more extravagant here—more excitement, more hustle and bustle—there's an overall charm to everything.

Leslie turns to me in the back of the cab, "So, my neighborhood isn't real posh or exciting, but it's cool. It's located in Brixton, which I suppose you would say is like South Central London. It's a pretty diverse community. There are definitely some sketchy areas but the house we live in is cool. It's a large Victorian townhouse. It reminds me of the brownstones you'd see in, like, Brooklyn or something—but older."

I have no idea what brownstones in Brooklyn look like, but I can imagine. I've watched *Sex in the City* for Christ's sake! I'm not a complete loser. Or should I be saying wanker now? Tosser?

"We could never afford it on our own," Leslie continues, "One of my flatmate's parents own it, but they never stay there anymore. They live in some villa in Italy almost year-round. Occasionally, they come back to the city, but thankfully, they get a hotel so there's enough room for all of us!"

I'm floored. Villas in Italy, Victorian mansions in South London, I have no clue where the hell we're going; I don't care. It's new and different. *Exactly what I need.*

The cab driver pulls up alongside a big beautiful brick house on the corner of a busy narrow street. Traffic whizzes by as I take in the Rapunzel-type tower on the corner of the block. "Is this it?" I ask Leslie as we clamor out of the cab.

"You bet yer ass it is! We're gonna rock this house the whole week you're here! Get ready, sista', I'm getting you naked-wasted tonight!"

Leslie heads to the back of the cab to grab the rest of the bags while I take in the grandeur of the home. Even the door handle looks exquisite. I can't help but notice the entry; the door is painted a bright purple with ivy vines growing all around it onto the beautifully shaded patio area to the right. The rest of the house looks old and important—maybe a little ominous, but this vibrant-colored door practically screams, *WELCOME!*

I help Leslie with my bags as we make our way up the steps into the old house. It even smells British. What the hell does British smell like? Like I have any freaking clue. Jesus, I better not say that crap out loud or people will think I'm mentally deranged. But if I had to guess what *British* smells like, I'd bet it would smell just like this house—old and interesting.

I glance up the staircase just past the foyer, and see what looks like three stories. The main floor consists of a tiny living room on the left with a neat fireplace. Connected off of that room is a long hallway leading toward the back of the house. There's a big dining room to the right of the foyer, with ten plush chairs seated all around it. The greatness of the large expensive-looking table is a bit lost amongst the clutter scattered all over it. Covering almost every surface are various books, papers, pens, CDs, and mail, right next to two large packing boxes with packing peanuts spilling out of them.

"Gotta run to the loo. Sit tight, Fin!" Leslie squeals as she dashes past me to the hallway off of the living room.

"Fucking magazines. Magazines! Can you fucking believe it?"

A tall and uncomfortably skinny redhead ambles into the dining room from the kitchen and looks at me pointedly.

"The cow sends me boxes of fucking magazines when all I bloody-well want are my damn clothes!" he barks and gives a box a shove across the table.

"Are you talking to me?" I ask, confused.

"I don't see anyone else in the room, so yeah, you'll do." He roughly tousles his bright orange hair. I'd never seen hair like his. It was cut short along the sides and sat high on top of his head with a natural frizz, seeming to help it stay afloat without product. Almost like…a rooster. I conceal my smirk as a side-by-side comparison pops into my head.

"Oi, Frank! Stop being a bitch to Finley!" Leslie shouts, coming into the foyer again. "For Christ's Sake, she just got off an incredibly long flight. She doesn't give a fuck about your ex-whore's magazines."

"He *was* a whore. The bitch. Probably wiped his arse with these magazines, too. I can't imagine what it cost to post these bastards. What a bloody waste of money. Money that could have been better spent on booze! Speaking of which, who's up for a drink? I've about had it with this bollocks all day," Frank looks at us expectantly with his hands on his tiny hips.

"Sounds great to me," Leslie replies. "You're up for it, aren't ya, Fin? Only way to beat the jet-lag!"

"Um, okay!" I answer, excitedly. Was this really how my first night in London was going to be? Leslie's roommate, Frank, seems a bit out there, but I have a feeling I'm going to have a lot of laughs with him.

"Fuck your kit and let's roll," Frank says, coming out of the dining room and into the foyer. "Christ! How many bloody bags did you pack? Are you moving the fuck in?"

"I know!" Leslie adds, "I still can't get over it, Fin. What the hell? It's so unlike you. I've traveled with you before and you've never even needed to check a bag!"

I know I can't let this question slide again, so I decide to get it over with and see what happens. "Actually, yeah," I say.

"Yeah, what?" Leslie replies, curiously.

"I'd like to…um…move the fuck in, if that's okay." I query, self-consciously, adjusting my necklace and looking around the house to see if any of the other roommates are around to hear this request.

"Blimey," Frank replies, "I thought you were trying to get up the duff with your bloke back in Chicago."

"Chicago? What?" I question.

"FRANK!" Leslie bites, "Shut the fuck up, you loud cow! Sorry,

Fin. Frank knows everything…he's my gay boyfriend. We talk—it can't be helped."

"What does he know, exactly?" I question, still totally confused.

"He knows you're trying to have a baby with Brody," she says, glaring at Frank. "Back in Kansas—*not* Chicago, Frank!" Leslie finishes, looking at me, apologetically.

It's like a cold bucket of ice-water has been dumped on top of my head. I'm not prepared for this conversation. I knew I'd have to have it eventually, but I feel sideswiped. I'm still trying to decipher the odd jumble of words that came out of Frank's mouth. Even if he is Leslie's gay boyfriend, a little word of warning would have been nice.

Frank interrupts my shock and says the only logical thing anyone could in this moment, "This seems like a chat best had over drinkies. Come along, loves!"

Frank grabs my arm and pulls me out the door and down the concrete steps. I follow them around the corner to a pub just two blocks away. The pub is dark, with old wood and hunter-green carpet all over. It smells like musty beers have been spilled on it for centuries and never been properly cleaned.

"Zoey, three pints of our usual, please. On the double—we got trouble over here!" Frank states, grandly, to the room full of strangers. No one appears to give a damn what this lanky redhead is talking about, so I don't lose much thought over it.

"Spill, Fin. Now!" Leslie demands, looking at me with earnest eyes.

"Christ, Lezzie, at least let the bitch have a drink first," Frank replies.

Frank is like no one I've met before. His sharp tongue and dry wit are extremely appealing to me. I find people with no filters refreshing; I always know where I stand with them. I think I've heard him say more curse words than anything else so far, and I've only known him five minutes, but he has a way about him that makes me feel comfortable.

The waitress brings over three large glasses of dark beer; I grab mine, nervously. *Do I like dark beer?* I'm not sure I've ever tried it.

I sip it gingerly at first and immediately taste the chocolaty-coffee richness to it. *Yes. Yes, I like dark beer.* I take three large gulps, wincing slightly at the lack of coldness as it travels down my throat. Beer in America is ice cold, which makes it so easy to drink. Maybe dark beer isn't served cold?

Leslie and Frank's eyes are glaring at me with anticipation.

I can already feel the effects of the beer in my head, so I know it's time to spill.

"I've left Brody," I say, before losing my nerve.

"What. The. Fuck?" Leslie asks, slowly, her auburn bob framing her face closely as her jaw drops.

"It's over, we're done. I'm done. I can't do *us* anymore," I reply, taking three more large gulps of my beer as Leslie and Frank gape at me.

"Wait, you dumped him, or he dumped you?" she asks.

"I don't know why that matters," I reply.

"Just fucking tell me, Fin!" she throws at me, angrily.

"I ended it, okay? But it doesn't matter; it would have ended anyway. There's no point in continuing things," I say, as I take another gulp.

Frank clears his throat, "So you're moving here—to London? You want to live with us?"

"I mean, yeah, if you'll have me. Er, I mean, if there's room. But if not, I'll find another place if I need to."

"What about your job, Fin? You love your job." Leslie asks, with a hint of alarm in her voice.

"Well, technically, I'm just taking a leave of absence right now. I have four weeks of paid vacation banked, and then I'm on my own. Val's company has a sister agency here I'd like to get involved with, but I don't really know anything about them yet, and I really don't want to bring it up to her. She'll probably lose it on me."

I work as a creative director's assistant for an advertising agency. They do TV, radio, web, and literary marketing for high-profile clients. I was in the process of being primed to be creative director and take over for my boss, Val, so she can fill the shoes of the vice president who is looking to retire in a few years. It's an incredible opportunity, and I've networked my ass off to get it.

"Well, no shit she'll lose it on you, Finley! You're blowing the opportunity of a lifetime by leaving! You're lucky she hasn't fired you!" Leslie spits out.

"Val's fine with it. She understands." I reply back, "She hired two interns for the fall and is demoting one of the sales executives to help her out for the next couple months. She said I can do copy editing and write from here, and she'll pay me as a freelancer until I come back." I pause, "She still thinks I'm coming back. I didn't have the balls to tell her I'm not."

Frank looks to Leslie, gauging her reaction. Leslie's face is covered in disappointment. *I can't stand it.*

"You're a fool for leaving that job, Finley," she says, shaking her head.

"I can't fucking stay there, Lez!" I croak, a sudden onset of tears filling my eyes. "I can't be *that girl* for him anymore. It was killing me, Leslie! *Killing me.* I can't walk around anywhere back in Kansas or Missouri without a baby. You know what it's like there!"

Leslie makes a motion like she's going to interrupt me, but I don't give her the chance, "I can't give him what he wants, and he won't want me without it. I know him, Lez, I know *us*. It won't be *us* anymore without creating a mini-us. We are wrecked. I refuse to sit there waiting for Brody to wise up and leave me for somebody more…more…fertile." I turn my face away and wipe the tears off my cheeks, quickly. "It was only a matter of time, I'm just beating him to the punch. I'm not sure it's even the life I want anyway."

"Fuck me. Don't let the old blokes at the bar see you blubbering, they'll get all awkward and call a doctor. Brits don't like emotions," Frank says, trying to lighten the mood.

I look back at Leslie and see her eyes welling with mine.

"Fucking Americans," Frank whispers under his breath, looking at the two of us.

Leslie sniffs and reaches her hand across the table, "I wish I knew how to fix this, Fin. I'm ill-equipped!" she says, her voice trembling. "This is a lot different from our problems as kids."

"I know," I groan, tipping back the remainder of my beer, savoring the feeling of numbness crawling over my skin.

"Well, fuck it! The flat is yours if you want it," says Frank. "You'll get the shit room because it's all that's bloody left. But who knows, you're American, you might think it's quaint."

I look at Frank, wide-eyed, as realization sets in that he's offering a room to me, indefinitely. *Thank God.* This is a huge load off my mind, knowing I at least have an affordable place to live while I figure my damn life out.

Suddenly Frank stands up on his seat and shouts, "Zoey, another round! We've got a new roommate to toast."

"Get the fuck off that chair er I'll rip your bloody arse off there myself!" Zoey shouts back at him with a thick dialect I barely understand. Maybe Irish?

"My arse hasn't bled in years, you wench!" Frank shouts back.

Leslie and I burst into a fit of laughter at Frank's announcement in a room full of strangers.

I think I'm going to like it here. I think I'm going to like it a lot.

CHAPTER FIVE

As the sun creeps in through the white lacy curtains, I grab my head. *Ugh. My head. My head hurts really bad!* UK beer must be a lot stronger than American beer; I've never felt so crappy. I check the time and see it isn't even 6:00 a.m. Damn it, why can't I ever sleep in with a hangover? I should be exhausted after all the travel and drinking yesterday.

I look around the room that is to be my home for the foreseeable future. Frank told me I was getting the tiny room and he wasn't joking. It is super tiny, but has its own personal charm. The room is situated alone on the third floor in the Rapunzel-style tower overlooking the corner. Half of the room is a semi-circle with three large bay windows covered with sheer lace curtains. An old-fashioned radiator that's been painted white adorns the flat part of the wall. *And lucky me, no closet.*

This room would be a perfect little art studio. Anything but a bedroom. But all the other rooms are occupied, and the master bedroom on the first floor is off limits for Frank's parents, so this is what I'm left with. Beggars can't be choosers. And I would have desperately begged for anything at this point, so long as it gets me away from home—and Brody.

Brody. Just thinking his name hurts my heart. I sit up on the twin mattress plopped unceremoniously in the center of the room. No bed frame, just a lavender fitted-sheet and a big purple comforter. This is what I'm running to? Sure, we had a curb couch, but it was definitely a step up from a tiny circular room with a mattress.

I stand up and look out the window to remind myself to stop moping. I'm in London, for crying out loud. *Stop being a pansy ass, Finley. You flew across the ocean to start a new life and now you're sulking? Enough already.*

A skate park with various ramps and rails is located diagonally from the corner. Even with the excessive amount of trash around it, it still manages to look quiet and peaceful in the morning light.

A buzzing sound echoes in my small room. I rush over to check my phone and see my sister's name pop up on the caller ID.

"Cadence, hey!" I say, excitedly. I slightly wince at the tone of my scratchy morning voice.

"Oh my God, Fin. How is it? Tell me everything! How was your flight? Where are you staying? How's Leslie?"

"Leslie is good. Different, yet the same. We're staying in this big old house that Frank's parents own."

"Frank, huh? Is he a hottie?"

"Um, not really my type. I'm afraid I'm not really his type either. But he's a lot of fun."

"Awesome, awesome. So, what time is it there? I was supposed to be in bed hours ago, but I got interrupted."

"It's just after 6:00 a.m."

"Crap, did I wake you? I need to get a London clock or something!"

"No. Actually, I woke up right before you called. It's fine. So, what interrupted you, is the baby kicking?"

A slight pause on the other end spiked my curiosity.

"Is everything okay?" I ask, slightly alarmed now. "Is the baby okay?" I feel tension rising in my chest. This is my first time realizing how difficult it will be for me to be so far away from family. If something goes wrong, I can't be there right away. Booking an international flight isn't cheap. Most likely, I'll have to endure my helplessness here by myself.

"Chillax, oh my God. Everything is fine. Mini-George is still baking away in there."

I release a relaxed sigh. *Stop being so dramatic, Finley.* I think my nerves are still on edge because of the whole Brody situation.

"I was calling because I had a late-night visitor tonight."

I pause, waiting for her to finish.

"*Brody.*"

My heart stops. It literally stops beating for two whole seconds, then I breathe really fast and heavy for a few seconds while attempting to regain my equilibrium. Brody lives in Kansas City, nearly two hours from my sister's house in Marshall. What the hell was he doing there?

"He's heartbroken, Fin. He showed up drunk and angry. Seriously angry. George nearly threw him out twice because he wouldn't lower his voice and calm down. At one point, I thought George was going to punch Brody!"

"Oh my God," I reply, my heart breaking into a million tiny pieces.

"Yeah, George is protective of his girls. He didn't take kindly to a belligerent drunk yelling at his pregnant wife, I'm afraid. Luckily, the girls were asleep and didn't see any of this."

My heart continues racing as the drama plays out in my head, "Oh my God."

"At first, he demanded I tell him where you moved, who you were living with, whether or not you were sleeping with someone else. Like, he was angrily shouting and stuff. George stepped in and was able to settle him down. Then he just got really sad. He kept saying, 'It's *us*, it's *us*. How could she do this to *us*?'"

"Oh my God."

What the fuck is wrong with me? Why did this all have to happen like this? Maybe I should have told him I was moving here.

"Then he just kept begging me to tell him where you are, Finley. I could hardly stand to look at him. He looks so miserable. So incredibly miserable."

Tears immediately form in my eyes.

"He's sleeping it off in the living room right now. I told him he was a freaking moron for driving here drunk. He got really nasty again and said I shouldn't give a fuck about him because *you* sure as hell don't. He's being a total dick, but I can't help feeling bad for the guy!"

"Oh my God. This is all my fault," I say.

I curl into the fetal position on my tiny mattress as tears run freely down the side of my temple onto the pillow. I can't stop picturing him sleeping on their couch with his curly brown hair all rumpled and his big long legs falling off the side. Maybe I should have just told him where I was going? That way he wouldn't have harassed my family.

But he won't leave this alone if he knows where I am. He'll come after me. He loves me. He loves *us*. An ocean wouldn't stop him from getting to the bottom of what's going on, and I refuse to tell him about my infertility.

"You can't tell him, Cade. You can't. He won't let it lie. He'll come here and demand answers. Right now, I'm the bad guy and that's okay. It's my fault we can't have kids anyway, so let me be the villain. Brody is way too good of a guy to be stuck with someone like me. If he learns the truth, he'll feel guilty for wanting to end us and he doesn't deserve that. It's my fault. My body. My issues. All mine."

"You have a warped-ass view of this situation, Finley. But I'm tired of trying to convince you otherwise. I promised not to, so I'm keeping my mouth shut. Anyway, everything is fine. I'm sure he'll leave in the morning before the girls get up, so we won't have to explain anything about Uncle Brody."

Uncle Brody. Ugh. Those two words slice into me like a dagger through the heart. My sister is the queen of passive-aggressive comments. She may not be actively trying to talk me out of my decision, but she sure as hell is going to make back-handed comments to get her point across.

"Anyway, this international call is costing me a fortune. I'll message you on *Facebook* later and we can talk more, if you want. I need to take my pregnant booty to bed."

"You can't message me. I deactivated my account," I say.

"You did? Why?" she asks.

"Just to be on the safe side, so Brody can't contact me."

"You are so messed up, Finley," she says, flatly.

"I know, Cadence…and hey," I reply, before she hangs up, "I miss you."

"I miss you, too," she responds with a little more sincerity. I can tell she is angry with me, but she promised to let me figure this out on my own.

I hang up my phone and curl up under the thick comforter, sobbing as quietly as I can while my thoughts continue on Brody. This is my worst freaking nightmare. My barren body has turned an incredibly beautiful man into a mess of anger, resentment, and sadness. All because I can't have kids. *Thanks a lot, God.*

Over the years, my sadness has turned into resentment of this world around me. It pains me to see so many people have children they don't deserve. Why can't I get a teeny tiny break? That's not too much to ask. If God could just give me one little baby *us* with Brody, I would want for nothing else the rest of my life.

The sobs seize me again as I think back on each negative pregnancy test. My eyes would play tricks on me as I'd stare at the strip, imagining the second line was popping up to tell me I was pregnant.

Walking the streets of Marshall, or even the neighborhood Brody and I live in, would be littered with constant reminders that my body isn't good enough to do the natural thing most women's bodies can.

Going to London maybe looks like I'm running away from my

problems, but I don't care. I need a fresh start away from everyone. Away from Brody.

Brody was it for me; I know I'll never find anyone better. Deep inside, I know that if I told him the truth, he would love me through it. The truth is, I can't love myself through it. Looking into Brody's eyes would be a constant reminder of what I can't give him. I can't let him stay with me and wonder when he'll begin to resent me. I can't handle the idea of *us* turning into something ugly.

I sigh as memories of how Brody and I met flutter into my head. I had noticed him on campus before, but never had a chance to talk to him. When he finally approached me in the parking lot of our apartment complex, I was a smitten kitten. We were together nonstop after that. We managed to go out and have fun with all our friends and enjoy our senior year, but the reality was, we were both itching to graduate and start our lives together, away from the college scene. After graduation, we found a house in Kansas City and moved in right away.

Brody landed a great job with a well-known contractor after his awesome recommendation from an internship with the city. Now he's a commercial construction estimator. He's outdoors most of the year and drives around to different job sites putting estimates together. His company is always building the next best thing in town and surrounding areas. I got hooked up with Val at the agency, and Brody and I had life by the balls. We knew exactly where we wanted to go with our future. It was easy.

After living together for a couple of years, we decided to stop using birth control and let Mother Nature decide when the right time was for us to get pregnant. Even though we were acting like we didn't care when it happened, I couldn't help but get my hopes up every time we made love that nine months later, a piece of *us* would arrive.

When nothing happened for nearly a year, I became a little obsessed with finding ways to help it along. Brody humored me with acupuncture and psychic visits, herbal treatments and abdominal fertility massage. He about cut me off when I told him I wanted to talk with a shaman healer, but it was nothing a little sexual manipulation couldn't overcome. Never mind the crazy shit that lady told me! "Bury a piece of your hair with a piece of his hair in the oil of the ellipsis and chant this chant to the Gods of the Moon every night for a fortnight." Holy balls, even I knew that sounded crazy! But those were the acts of a hopeful woman with her head in the clouds.

I became increasingly worried there was something seriously wrong with my body, preventing us from conceiving. I'd always had irregular periods and heavy cramps, so nothing felt natural to me down there.

Without telling Brody, I scheduled an appointment to have a private consult with a fertility specialist. I didn't want Brody to know. I was embarrassed and ashamed. I hated the idea of him sitting with me in a waiting room full of other reproductively-challenged women. I was perfect in Brody's eyes. I didn't want him to see me as anything less if I could help it.

And he was always so optimistic. He never seemed concerned with the fact that we hadn't been preventing pregnancy for over a year and achieved no results. He knew I took a lot of pregnancy tests…*probably way too many*. He'd always put on a happy face and do whatever he could to cheer me up. If I had to hear "Maybe next month" one more time from him, I was going to scream.

I wanted the cold hard truth from a specialist. After a couple months of exams, tests, blood draws and procedures, the doctor scheduled a consult with me. As soon as the nurse placed me in the doctor's office, instead of an exam room, I knew I was done for.

The words *infertile* and *adoption* tumbled out of his mouth. I was seized with panic. I wanted to run out of his office right then and there, but I sat there and listened to him talk about my hostile uterus and how I will never be able to carry a baby and blah, blah, blah. I was sick to my stomach. I couldn't contain the trembling in my hand as he passed me an adoption agency's pamphlet. To think about adopting an unknown child, when our whole love story is based on this crazy *us* theme, seemed unfathomable!

I decided I couldn't handle a life with Brody and no *us* baby. So when Leslie asked me to come out and visit her for a week, it seemed like fate was telling me my next move. I knew there was no way I could break up with Brody and continue living near him, in the same town. The temptation would be too much. I loved *us* way too much to trust myself to do the right thing and stay away.

So I shattered his heart instead. I moved as far away as humanly possible. I tried to prepare him by pulling away a few weeks before my flight. He picked up on it and tried to pull me back into *us* by being goofy and playful, like we always were. But I couldn't get past all the issues of my new diagnosis. Even surrogacy sounded terrible to me. I couldn't fathom using some other woman to carry *our* baby.

The fundamental gift a woman can give a man is a baby. It's the ultimate evidence of love. The longer I stuck around with Brody, the less like a woman I felt. I made arrangements with my sister to help me by picking up my car at the airport and storing it at their acreage in Marshall. The rest of my belongings I'd deal with later, once Brody moved on maybe? I don't know. I didn't think it all through.

Brody didn't know until the day I left that I was ending us. I honestly thought he'd fight harder for me to stay. Sure, he tried, but he still let me go. Maybe he was ready to call it quits, too? If that were the case, I don't think he'd be showing up at my sister's house drunk and cantankerous. He'd be moving on.

I hugged the blanket closely to me, aching for the warmth of his familiar arms around me, and I eventually drift into a restless sleep.

CHAPTER SIX

I awaken later in the afternoon and hear voices below me. Holy crap, its 2:00 p.m.! I can't believe I slept this long. I'm bursting to pee, so I crawl up off my mattress to make my way out the door. Looking down when I open the door, I am surprised when I slam right into Frank's chest. He smells strangely like cinnamon.

"Morning, love!" he announces, brightly.

"Uh, hi?" I reply, rubbing the sleep out of my eyes and inspecting his outfit. He is covered in denim, head to toe. Tight, Skinny Jeans, a denim button-down shirt and a denim jacket. He even has a denim ball cap on with the bill tilted up high, revealing his frizzy orange hair.

"The Lezbo went to a meeting with the gods of photography and requests our presence at Shay Nightclub promptly at 10:00 p.m. tonight," he says, with a curt nod of his head. "I've been instructed to escort you there and make sure you don't look like a dopey Midwestern hussy. Her words, not mine, love."

"Okay, so…the all-denim look," I lean back to examine him more fully. "Is this considered fashionable here in the UK, or are you headed to a hoedown later?"

"Oooo, what's a hoedown? I want one!" he asks, eagerly.

"Never mind," I say, moving past him toward the bathroom across the hall.

"For your information, there's a denim surplus here in London and I'm just doing my civic duty to help the community. It's a real epidemic!" he remarks, seriously.

I squint my eyes at him, speculatively.

"Not as gullible as the Lezbo when she came to town. Pity. We had a ball feeding her full of crazy crap." He begins walking down the creaky wooden staircase. "Food and refreshments in the kitchen if you'd like to refuel that juicy ass of yours!"

I laugh as I walk into the bathroom. Frank is definitely going to keep me on my toes.

After a long, sort-of-hot shower, I dress myself in a pair of comfortable leggings and a college hoodie. It's a chillier fall here in London than it is back home. I glance down the hallway of the second floor, wondering who occupies each room, since I still haven't received a grand tour of the house. Leslie, Frank and I were a bit too buzzed to care when we got home last night.

They had both noisily, and albeit a bit drunkenly, pounded their way up the narrow staircase with all my suitcases to show me to the only room on the third floor. I had flopped straight down onto the thin mattress and passed out within minutes, in the same nasty clothes I'd been wearing for more than 24 hours.

In the light of day, I'm able to see more of the home and appreciate the beauty of the old finishes and woodwork.

As I make my way through the dining room and into the kitchen, I walk in on a couple in the midst of what looks to be an intense conversation.

"Oh! Sorry, I can leave," I state, annoyed at myself for interrupting them.

"No, no. You're fine! Don't leave," a small Asian girl says, looking over her shoulder and extracting herself from between the man's legs where he sits perched up on the wood countertop.

The girl looks back to the guy and whispers something incoherent, he looks back at her, angrily. I avert my eyes because I feel like I've interrupted either a fight or a make-up session, I'm unsure. I look out the front window behind the small kitchen-nook table and notice the cute patio set surrounded by a wrought-iron fence covered in ivy. It looks like the perfect place to sit and read.

"You're Leslie's mate, right?" the girl asks, widening her slanted eyes at me in question. "I'm Julie, and this is Mitch."

Mitch is in the process of inspecting his shoes, apparently deep in thought. Or perhaps he is contemplating buying a new pair? He's cute in a petite skater-boy sort of way. He has chin-length blonde hair tucked neatly behind his ears.

"Our room is the first door on the right, upstairs," Julie offers.

"Cool. Yeah, I'm Finley. Er, Fin, er, whatever you want to call me. Nice to meet you guys." God, I'm a moron. I loathe that whole uncomfortable hand-shaking moment. Do I shake their hands or don't I? It might be a bit too formal. Oh crap, now it's too late. If I shake their hands, I'll look like an idiot. *A dumbass wave of the hand it is!*

"Right. Well, let's bail then," Mitch says, sullenly. He's obviously pissed about something; I hope it's not my presence. Maybe he's mad about his shoes.

"Okay. Well, nice to meet you! We'll see you around a bit, I hope," Julie announces apologetically on her way out. Mitch drags her tiny frame out of the kitchen.

I make my way over to the counter and see an assortment of pastry items next to a plate of tiny sausages. My stomach is churning at the smell of it all. I nibble on a piece of what looks like a sweet roll when Frank pops his head in.

"Thank the Lord, you've showered! I didn't want to be the one to tell you this, but I could literally smell your pitties last night at the pub. I nearly vomited in my lager. It was a travesty!" he says, popping the top off the can he just grabbed out of the fridge.

My reaction must be a good one, because in the midst of his drink he busts out laughing, spraying pop all over himself and the refrigerator door! "Bloody hell, Finley! I'm only messing with you!" he says, wiping his mouth with the sleeve of his denim jacket. "Had to get back at you for the denim crack upstairs, ye bitch!"

My shocked reaction turns to scorn. I look him hard in the face and say, "You have pop boogers coming out of your nose."

"Fuck me!" he shouts, turning into the stainless-steel fridge door to get a look at himself.

"Now who's the gullible one?" I ask, with a sneaky smirk spreading across my face.

Frank looks me up and down, "I think you might be a bit of fun after all, Finley, my dear."

"You're not so bad yourself, Frank and Beans," I reply.

"What. The. Fuck. Are frank and beans?"

"A Midwestern delicacy. And in your denim outfit, I think that's exactly what I'll be calling you from now on. I can see you sitting around a campfire right now with a horse tied up to a tree behind you, munching on your frank and beans."

"As long as it's a fire on Brokeback Mountain, I'll be any kind of Frank you want!" He looks at me proudly for a moment, "Fine, fine, Finny. Let's go explore some sights while Lezbo is off doing God knows what. Maybe we'll even find you something to wear that's not so…university. Blech."

***

I look down at my hoodie I've been wearing for the past five years, and frown. I love this hoodie. I loved my college days. They gave me Brody. *Brody. Damn.* I was just starting to feel a little better.

Frank and I have an amazing afternoon together. He walks me around the neighborhood and shows me all the best local places to shop for groceries, clothes, and typical odds and ends stuff. We walk by the pub we went to last night and he informs me they spend the majority of their time there because they keep the old geezers in check for poor little Zoey.

The city is beautiful. It's a huge juxtaposition of different architectural structures from centuries long gone. Definitely not something I'm used to seeing in Missouri or Kansas. Everything here seems so much greener, too. Lusher, despite the constant grey overcast sky. There are also tons of parks dotted around the place. I've never seen so many tiny parks all in one place.

I'm taking it all in with wide eyes full of wonder. I can't help but mourn this experience a tiny bit because I'm not doing it all with Brody. Brody would have loved this stuff. He never spoke much of travel like I did, but he loved pretty much everything I loved. If we were together, he was happy.

We pass a couple of women with tiny babies in strollers. My heart hurts just looking at them. I wonder how they got their precious little miracles. *Was it easy? Was it hard? Do they know what a true gift they have? Do their husbands know how lucky they are to have fertile wives?* The more I look at them, the angrier I get because it's quite likely they don't appreciate all they have been given, and I would!

Frank must have picked up on my wandering thoughts because he quickly rushes us to the next street over to show me the tattoo shop where we can watch artists tattoo people in the window. It's cool, so we purchase a basket of fries. Chips. *Whatever the hell they call them.* We watch a guy getting a huge eagle tattooed on his back for nearly an hour. Frank is easy to talk to; he says the most outlandish things. I laugh and feel happy that I like my new roommate so much.

We make our way back to the house and Frank rummages through my four suitcases until he finds an outfit he thinks is passable for our evening ahead. By the time he starts rifling through the fourth suitcase, I'm beginning to fear he won't find anything suitable. I sure as hell won't fit into Leslie's clothes!

"This will do. Now, tart yourself up so I can escort you to the club and make all the men envious of my new bitch," Frank says, with flair, as he exits my room.

Frank has selected a long red high-waist skirt with a cropped, tight cheetah t-shirt. The t-shirt is a spandex material and a totally impulsive purchase I'd picked up in a thrift store back home. I actually never found a place to wear it, so I am excited Frank put these two pieces together for me.

I throw my long brown hair up high on my head into a cute topknot that looks effortless, but chic. I jazz up my makeup a bit thicker than I normally would, drawing out my eyeliner into a bit of a cat-eye look. I throw on a long gold-pendant necklace and make my way downstairs.

Frank must be impressed because he doesn't scream at me to run upstairs and start over. "You look decidedly fuckable, my dear."

"Oh?" I ask, cocking my head to the side.

"*I* wouldn't touch you with a ten-foot pole, and believe me, I've got one under here," he says, gesturing toward his crotch. "But if I were a betting man, I'd bet you'll draw some attention tonight."

"Aw, Frank, that's the sweetest thing you've ever said to me!" I answer, smiling gaily at him. "You look rather fetching yourself!"

"Thanks, my dear," he says, adjusting his skinny black tie over his denim button-down. Thankfully, he'd swapped the denim jeans for a pair of skin-tight red slacks. It's still nothing I've ever seen back home, but I can definitely see some style going on in there.

"If I had a dick," I pause, wondering how he'll react, "…I'd stick it in you."

"Oh, for fuck's sake. You and Leslie are definitely friends. Two bitches in a bloody pod. Let's fucking go."

CHAPTER SEVEN

As we walk into Shay, the music is roaring. I'm surprised to hear several American pop songs playing loudly over the grand room. The British music scene is pretty awesome, but it's nice to hear songs from home that I'm familiar with.

We walk around for what feels like a good twenty minutes before finally finding Leslie. She has a table on the upper level that surrounds the packed dance floor. She already has three mixed drinks sitting in front of her as she turns to me with eager and excited eyes, obviously appraising my outfit.

"FIN! Who knew you had it in you?" she stares at me with mock appreciation.

I self-consciously cover the exposed four inches of belly above the high waist of my skirt, and frown at her. "Oh, come on. You're not the only one who can have cute clothes, you know!"

"I know! But you're already a good foot taller than me, the least you could do is throw me a bone and let me win the clothing contest," she laughs, incredulously.

Leslie looks gorgeous. She's sporting a trendy little black dress with pointy shoulders and triangular cutouts on the sides. She's painted her pout a deep matte-red and her bob is fluffed with extra body.

"You made that, didn't you?" I ask, touching the shoulder point on one side.

"Yep!" she replies, proudly.

"You are too fabulous," I say, grabbing her hand and twirling her so I can inspect the back—or should I say, *no back*. Three silver chains drape across an open back and dangle sexily toward her bottom. I give her ass a good smack and she squeals in delight.

"What about me, Lezzie?" Frank asks, looking rather forlorn.

"Frank, you know I love your wacky style. You look cool, as always," she says, kissing him on both cheeks, "Now, let's drink!" she announces loudly, handing us our beverages.

Since the music is so loud, we do a lot of drinking and people-watching, but not much talking. I'm glad for that though; my thoughts seem to be getting darker and darker the more vodka tonics I'm served. I never have done well with hard liquor, but Leslie bought the first round and it seems easier to stick with what we have.

Frank takes over and starts buying all the drinks.

I yell over to him, "Frank, let me buy the next round!"

He shakes his head at me, "Stuff your money, I got this. Just drink. I like you better pissed anyway."

A BROKEN US

I laugh and oblige him by sucking on the straw of my drink again.

"Who's ready to shake their tail-feathers?" Leslie hollers at us over the music.

Frank shoots up out of the table, grabs both of our hands, and begins pulling us through the crowd. He shouts to the people next to us to hold our table and offers to buy them a round in return, so they quickly spread themselves out over our table and look eager for our return.

As we rub up next to the crowds of people, I can see men's eyes on me and it feels so strange. I've been with Brody for five years and just being here feels like cheating. I silently chastise myself and remind my brain that I am single now and this is like early college days all over again. I loved flirting in college and was really good at it. I can be that way again. So instead of feeling uncomfortable, I let the vodka's liquid-courage help me shake my round ass directly into Frank's crotch. Leslie laughs as Frank gives me a look like he's about to be sick. I giggle and continue dancing. Eventually, Frank finds a couple of guys that seem to catch his eye and leaves Leslie and me to our own devices.

Without Frank's watchful eyes, Leslie begins pumping her hips behind a random frat-looking guy dancing near us. She looks hilarious in her little black dress dancing like she isn't dressed to the nines. She might as well be wearing sweatpants right now with the way she's acting. Just when the frat guy turns around to see what the heck is going on, she dashes away like she wasn't just doing obnoxious sexual gestures to his back. I love the fact that Leslie is never *too cool* to be a moron.

I join in on the fun and jump directly in front of a huge black guy who hasn't even been dancing. I grab my right ankle with my right hand, put my other hand behind my head, and begin pumping my leg back and forth. No easy feat in a long skirt, but I've watched my fair share of 80's music videos, so I know I look goooood. The man pulls his sunglasses down his nose and eyes me carefully. Thinking my move isn't impressive enough, I jump up and drop down into a classic robot. Yeeeeah, I own this dance. This will surely impress him. He crosses his arms and lets out a big puff of air with a nasty sneer on his face. *Yeah, it's time to get the hell outta here.* I rush away from him and grab Leslie's hand to haul her to the other side of the dance floor. That dude looks ticked!

We pass a shot-girl and I quickly buy four long test-tube shots from her and hand two to Leslie. We pop the foil tops off them and down them one after another. They are sickly sweet and a bit nasty but I don't care. I am in London. I am starting a new life. It is time to celebrate!

Leslie is suddenly grabbed by a cute little guy with dark-framed glasses and buzzed blonde hair. She looks up at him like she's going to pull away, but changes her mind and starts dancing provocatively with him. She seems to be enjoying herself so I decide to let loose on my own and really dance.

I love to dance. Like, seriously. I. Love. To. Dance. I'm pretty decent at it, too, but even if I wasn't, I wouldn't care; the feel of a loud thumping bass, coupled with the syncopated movement of my body and an increased heart rate is, like, an all-time high for me. Brody always said that back in college, he noticed my dance moves before he noticed my face. I remember he told me once after we officially met that he'd never seen a girl dance like it was an athletic sport rather than some tease to get guys to notice her.

And that's exactly the way I dance. I don't care if I get sweaty and hot. The music moves me. It makes me forget about my racing heart rate and the burning feeling in my lungs I only get the few times a year I think I can be a runner—and then remember I fucking hate running. Dancing is my cardio.

Those shots are really hitting me now. That's good, it's what I want. Tonight is my farewell to the old Finley. Tonight I'm going to dance and drink myself into a state of oblivion. I want to permanently erase all the crap I ran away from. I don't want to feel anything anymore. I am in London, England. I'm starting a new life. There's no turning back now.

I refuse to think of Brody and our last time together. I refuse to remember the way he makes me feel when he looks at me with those gorgeous navy-blue eyes. I refuse to remember the way his curly hair feels coarse, like a brillo pad, when I thread my fingers through it. Or the way he whispers *I love us*, against my ear to make me giggle because he knows I'm ticklish.

The lights I'm gazing up at in the ceiling begin to blur as my eyes fill with tears. Shocked, I look down and feel the tears run quickly down my face. *What the hell?* Where did these come from? This is supposed to be a night of forgetting, not remembering. I look over to Leslie and see her facing her dancing partner; they look pretty intense. I don't want to ruin her fun with my sudden burst of emotions, so I sneak over and whisper-yell in her ear that I'm going to the bathroom and I'll meet her back at our table later. She turns to look at me but I dash away before she is able to see the tears on my face.

The bathrooms are located down a flight of stairs in a lower-level bar area that's much quieter and more laid back. I can still hear the booming music above, but I can also hear the voices of the people talking around me.

I find a big, comfy armchair in a quiet corner of the bar and sink down into it before anyone else grabs it. I glance around to see if there's anybody within listening distance and decide I'm secluded enough. I tuck my legs underneath my butt and grab my phone out of my clutch, flipping to the last text I received from Brody.

Brody: Not that I give a fuck, but I hope you're alive and shit. I have no clue where you are or who you are staying with. Hope you're having a ball. I'm in hell.

Guilt courses through my veins as my conversation with Cadence replays in my head. *He looks so sad, Finley. So incredibly sad.*

I pull up his contact info on my phone so I can see his face. He smiles happily back at me; my heart aches for the simpler times we had together, before all the baby stuff.

Before I can process what I'm doing, I hit *Call* on my phone. I just need to hear his voice again.

"Hello?" Brody answers on the second ring.

"Heeeey," I drawl out, realizing I sound a bit drunk.

"Hey?" he grunts, "Huh."

"What?" I ask.

"You're actually calling me right now, like for real," he sounds pissed.

"Yeah, I am. I just wanted to see if you were okay. After…well….after yesterday," I reply, tentatively.

"Okay? Am I okay?" he seems to be ramping up for something big, "Well, considering I got wasted last night and showed up on your sister's doorstep, basically crying and belligerent, I would venture to guess, no. No, Fin, I'm not o-fucking-kay."

"I'm sorry," I offer.

"You're sorry? Ha! That's fucking great, Finley," he spits. "I show up at your sister's house that holds three tiny girls. Beautiful little girls…girls I've grown to love and cherish like they are my own. I mean…I'd walk through fire for those little girls, Finley! That's how in love with them I am. To think they could have come downstairs and seen me the way I was behaving, makes me physically ill. I was the second person to hold Maya when she was born, for Christ's sake!"

He coughs hard into the phone, trying to clear his throat, "I'm so fucked up over all this shit that George, who happens to be a good friend of mine, nearly pummeled me in the jaw for being violent and malicious toward his seven-month pregnant wife!"

I firmly squeeze my eyes together, willing away the tears that are rising inside them as the horrible scene plays out in my mind. "I'm sorry!" I croak out, not knowing what else to say to him.

"I don't know who the fuck I am anymore, Finley!" he roars and I cringe at the volume booming through the phone. "One second, I'm madly in love with this incredible, vivacious girl who has completely rocked my world and changed me for the better…like forever. Then the next minute, she's gone and I don't have a fucking clue why or where to!"

"I know. It's just better this way," I cry back into the phone.

"What's better? We were trying to have a baby together, Finley! A baby! That isn't shit I go into lightly. You were my world and you just fucking left!" His voice cracks on the last half of that statement and I hear him breathing heavily, trying to get ahold of his emotions.

I never should have called him. This is making things so much worse. "I can't be the girl you need me to be, Brody. I just can't. I…can't."

"What girl do I need you to be?" he shouts, into the phone. "You're my girl, Fin! Just you. It's always just been you! Jesus, it's like I don't even know you anymore!"

"That's the thing, Brody. You don't know me," I reply, angry that he just doesn't get it. He doesn't understand the pressure this whole situation puts on me. "You care more about *us* than you do about me! I don't get that anymore, Brody. I don't want to get it. I want different things than you do. There's no reason to pretend that *us* even matters anymore."

"You make no fucking sense. None. The Finley I knew, the Finley I fell head over heels for in college, was with me through and through. We wanted the same things together. She isn't this person. This person I'm talking to right now is a mean, spiteful…bitch."

His words hang there over the line with ominous reverberation for what feels like eternity.

"Speak, Finley…because I am truly giving up on you," he sighs, then sniffles into the phone.

I shake my head back and forth, willing my heart to come up with an answer to whatever this fucked up situation needs. *Anything.* I'm desperate to say anything to fix this—to fix this pain in Brody's voice. But I know I have to stop myself or it will make it harder in the end. I so badly wish it didn't have to end so terribly…so treacherously. Maybe there is no good way for this to end. I need to suck it up and truly say goodbye to Brody this time. There is no coming back from the agony in this conversation. He is broken and ruined—and it is my fault. My beautiful, warm, heartfelt, incredible man is gone and it is entirely my fault. My body's fault. My body broke *us*. This perfect *us* we made together and loved together. Two dumb college kids thinking they found something nobody else ever had—but we didn't. He won't want me when he knows the truth; it's better to save him from the truth, not to mention the guilt of staying with someone who can't give him the basic thing in life that makes a family.

"I guess this is goodbye, then," he states, coldly.

"Brody," I say, softly.

"Bye."

I jump up out of the chair and run into the bathroom, locking myself into a stall, bawling like I have never bawled before. I don't know if it's the booze or the jet-lag but this breakup feels so much worse than the last breakup. Brody really is gone. He really did give up on me. And in my warped, screwed up brain, it feels like *he's* the one leaving because I can't have babies, instead of the other way around.

After a good, long cry, I come out of the stall and reapply my makeup. Once I feel complete again, I make my way out the bathroom door.

"Hiya," a voice says, from behind me.

"Hi," I reply, continuing to walk away without looking at who's coming up behind me.

The voice jogs up past me and walks backward in front of me as I continue my pursuit down the hallway toward the steps back up to the club. "Hey, um, I just wanted to make sure you were okay. That looked pretty bad there."

I sneer back at him, "Eavesdrop much? Jesus!" I push him aside and begin climbing the stairs up to the noisy club. *His accent is freaking sexy as hell! But I can't care about that now.*

He follows up next to me, obviously not taking the hint that I'm unimpressed, "Okay, okay, I deserve that. But crying girls are like moths to a flame for me, I'm afraid. You see, I'm a bit of a fixer. I see a situation or problem and I have to fix it. Have to. So please, tell me how I can fix this situation for you properly so I can sleep tonight. I won't be able to sleep a wink without cheering you up a little," he finishes his speech at the top of the steps that open up onto the dance floor.

I take in his appearance and decide he doesn't look like a complete creeper. He has on a stylishly faded button-down dress shirt with dark denim jeans. His hair is blonde and a bit longer on the top and swept off to one side in a hipster-style cut. He has kind brown eyes that look like he is genuinely trying to be a nice guy.

As I gaze around the crowd, looking for my friends, my eyes land on my dancing partner from earlier, and a funny idea comes to mind.

"A fixer, huh?" I air-quote at him sarcastically as he rolls his eyes and halfway smiles. "Well, if you really want to cheer me up, you'll go and ask that lovely gentleman for a dance." I challenge, and point over to the fun boat who's still standing in the middle of the dance floor.

"What? You mean, that giant *Green-Mile* looking bloke being the life of the party?" he inquires.

"Yep," I nod, pursing my lips together to contain my smile.

"Yeah, alright! I don't give a toss, he's probably a big teddy bear underneath all that scary business." And off he goes.

Oh my God, he's really going to do it! I watch him weave in and out of the crowded dance floor, making his way over to the incredibly large black man. I try searching his face for any amount of discomfort, but if he's feeling it, he's definitely not showing it.

When he stands in front of the man, he's a good foot shorter, which is saying something because he doesn't seem like a shrimp to me. Suddenly, *Mr. Fix-it* starts hollering at the crowd and clears a small area on the dance floor. *What the hell is he doing?*

He reaches his hand out to the man in a gentleman-like manner with a slight bow, receiving an unceremonious scowl in return. Seemingly un-phased, he shrugs his shoulders, turns his back to him, drops down and starts doing…*the Worm?* Oh my God! The Worm! I laugh hysterically as the crowd goes wild around him. I'm incredibly torn between watching the spectacle on the floor or the jolly black giant up above. Just when I think this tough guy might actually crack a smile, he grabs his sunglasses out of his jacket pocket and puts them on, turning his back on the ridiculous scene in front of him.

This new sexy Brit obviously has a warped sense of humor like mine. He stands up, looks at the man we're all trying desperately hard to please, shakes his head, and begins sauntering his way back toward me with lots of pats on the back from the crowd.

"I did my best!" he shouts over the music, as he gently grasps my arm, allowing a few people to squeeze their way behind him.

His gentle touch ignites prickles down my arm. I look at him with my jaw dropped and say, "Worth it."

"Worth what?" he quips.

"That scene," I gesture toward the dance floor, "made coming to this city completely worth it."

"You're American, right?"

I nod.

"Well, I'd love to hear more about what brought you here," he says, still holding onto my arm.

I quickly shake my head and begin scanning the crowd for Leslie or Frank. I do not like the direction this interrogation is going, so I need to run.

"Okay, okay, bad idea. Don't tell me why you're here…don't say a thing about it, I don't give a toss. But at least let me buy you a drink. I did just do the bloody worm, after all!" he says, looking hopefully at me as I see Leslie and Frank sitting at our table.

I turn to him and decide the only way to forget about Brody is to keep myself distracted. This guy seems like he could help with that.

"See the two redheads at that table?"

"The guy that looks like *Carrot Top*?" he asks, completely serious.

My nostrils flare as I bite my lip to hold back the laughter that is screaming to be released. *Oh my God, I can't wait to dump that one on Frank later!* "That's the one. The one and only. Those are my friends. You can buy me a drink and meet me over there."

"Got it!" he shouts, already retreating toward the bar.

"Do you even care what I want to drink?"

"I've got it covered!" he replies, barely audible.

Taking a deep breath, I hurry over to our table because I need a moment to talk to Frank and Leslie before this *fixer guy* hunkers down with us.

CHAPTER EIGHT

"What the fuck, Finley?" Leslie screeches out at me after I tell her what I did. "Why did you call him?"

"I couldn't help it!" I reply, feebly, shouting over the loud music.

"You are a moron of epic proportions. Epic!" she states dramatically, flailing her hands above her head in case I can't hear her clearly.

I quickly glance around to see if *Mr. Fixer* is on his way over yet.

"You were the one who ended it with Brody. You!" she points at me with dramatic hand gestures. "This is all in your crazy, fucked up head. If you want to end it with him, then end it and be done. Calling him and being nice and normal is plain torture." She aggressively sucks the remainder of her V&T through the thin neon green straw.

Frank gets up from his chair and stands between Leslie and me, "Alright kittens, retract the claws. We're here to have a good time, remember?" he coos, forcefully enough to be heard. "Now, Fin-Bin, who was that lovely piece of eye candy you were chatting with back there? He looks delish!"

"Is that me you're talking about—or the Green Mile bloke?" the fixer inquires loudly from behind.

"Well, hellloooo," Frank purrs at him, his eyes roving him up and down.

"I'll take that as me. I'm Liam," he says, in his delicious British accent, holding his hand out to shake Leslie's, then Frank's.

"Liam," Frank mouths, to no one in particular with a dramatic flick of the tongue on the L.

"This seat taken?" Liam asks, sidling up to the stool next to me.

He sets four closed bottles of beer down on the table in front of us and shoots me a wink. "Hope you like beer, it's the only thing I could buy with sealed lids. Speaking of which, I truly hope you don't accept open drinks from random blokes you meet at a bar! You could be roofied, for Christ's sake!"

"Yeah! Roofied, for Christ's sake!" Leslie repeats as she eagerly snatches her aluminum beer bottle and twists the cap off for a drink.

I eye Liam speculatively as he opens one and hands it to me. He then hands one to Frank and grabs the last one for himself.

"So, I'm Liam. And you guys are…"

"Frank. Frank. Just, Frank," Frank looks beside himself. He's awkward and fidgety and trying unsuccessfully to twist the cap off the beer, while staring directly into Liam's eyes.

"Keep your panties on, Frank. This one looks like he's into brunettes, I'm afraid," Leslie says, elbowing Frank in the side. "I'm Leslie, the best friend."

"Hello Leslie, the best friend. And you are?" he asks, turning his chocolate eyes at me, glancing quickly at my mouth first, then back up to my aqua eyes.

"Finley."

"Finley," he grins like he knows a secret no one else knows. "Leslie is correct, Finley. I do like brunettes," he smiles brazenly at me.

I raise my eyebrows and turn back to Leslie, "Whew! Lucky me. He doesn't even have to know me before he decides he likes me!"

He squints his eyes in response to my sarcasm, clearly not impressed.

"I was worried for a second there, but nope, now I got it. My hair is brown—I win! I'm the perfect female specimen because I have shit-colored hair," I hoot obnoxiously, taking a swig of my beer.

Leslie drops her chin and glares at me. Visibly uncomfortable, Frank looks down at his beer.

Liam lets out a huff of air and a small bark of a laugh as he stands up and gently smooths his wayward blonde hair to the side.

"Leslie…Frank…it was nice to meet you guys." He turns to me, "Fin, I'm glad to see you're feeling better. Enjoy the rest of your evening." And with that, he makes his way away from our table and back toward the bar.

Frank is the first to break the uncomfortable silence, "Christ, Finny. That was downright bitchy, even by my standards."

"Yeah," Leslie juts out her jaw, shaking her head at me. "Not cool, Finley."

What's wrong with me? Sure, I'm sarcastic and like to joke

around, but even I don't know what the hell that was all about. Without thinking, I jump out of my chair and press my way through the crowd toward Liam's blonde hair that stands out above the heads of people.

"Uh...Liam!" I shout, trying to get him to slow down so I can get through the swarm of people.

He looks back with a confused frown on his face as I finally catch up to him.

"I'm not a bitch," I say, in a normal voice.

Liam gives me a puzzled look, turning his ear towards me.

"I said..." I yell, "I'M. NOT. A. BITCH!"

He stares at me speculatively, dancing his eyes down to my mouth again. *Damn, why does he have to do that? It does serious things to my belly.*

"Prove it!" he shouts back at me.

Hesitating, I try to decide if he's worth the effort. I figure I need to do this for myself as much as I need to do it for him.

A railing that surrounds the dance floor is to the left of where we are standing. Three metal beams parallel each other horizontally with a good two feet between each.

I smile and hold my index finger up to him, encouraging him to watch me. I walk over to the bars and climb up the first two beams, throwing my leg over the top beam to straddle, and balance my feet on the second beam with my long red skirt bunching up on top of the bar. I look over to him as he gazes at me, expectantly.

I take a deep breath, cup my hands around my mouth, and shout as loud as humanly possible, "I'M NOT A BITCH. I'M JUST

HAVING A REALLY BAD FUCKING YEAR!"

"Oh stuff it, would ya!"

"Get a life, loser!"

"I'll shag ya!"

"Shut the fuck up!"

I glance around trying to place the voices of all the people heckling me, then look over to Liam. He's smiling and nodding his head approvingly.

As I crawl my way back down the tall barrier, I feel large hands grab me by my waist and guide me down to ground.

"No need to bloody shout!" Liam yells in my ear, pulling back and laughing softly at me. "Want to get some fresh air?"

"Sure," I reply. He leads me by the small of my back out the front door to where the doorman is holding back a line of people waiting to get in. We get stamps on our hands so we can return without having to get back in line, and Liam ushers me down the side of the brick building a small distance away from the people.

My head is readjusting to the deafening silence outside compared to the booming bass inside. I drag my hand down the side of the brick wall and look over to Liam with a smile on my face. He smiles back at me and it feels like we're having a complete conversation without saying a word.

"So," Liam starts, "A bad fucking year, eh?"

"You could say that."

"I've had some of those," he replies, leaning next to me alongside the brick wall and crossing his arms over his chest. "So, what are you going to do about it?"

"That's the million-dollar question," I say, turning around, picking at the brick with my fingernails.

"Have you seen much of London yet?" he asks, turning and mirroring my movements.

"Not much...some of the neighborhood I'm staying in, I guess, but that's it so far. I haven't been here long."

"What are you doing tomorrow, then?" he leans one shoulder against the brick and crossing his arms again like he's posing for a Senior Picture.

I can sense where this is going and my heart races with anxiety. This guy is cute, enormously cute. He's got an unbelievably sexy accent and seems nice and normal. But I can't even consider dating anyone yet or spending any significant amount of time with someone that is so obviously interested in me.

"I still need to do a lot of unpacking. My suitcases...and in here," I say, pointing to my head.

"Ahh, that's probably a heavy load," he replies, touching my head and lightly brushing his fingertips in my hair.

I close my eyes and relish in the touch for just a second.

"I should hope it's a heavy load, otherwise one could call me a ditz," I retort back with a small grin.

"That is one thing I can definitely tell you are not," he says, standing upright off the brick wall. He glances back toward the club. "Well then, perhaps I can give you my number on the off chance you finish unpacking early and want to buy more things to unpack."

"That would probably be okay," I reply, tentatively.

"And in case you forget that you want to purchase more items to unpack someday, maybe I can get your phone number, too. For purely logistical purposes, of course," he declares, dropping his chin and raising his eyebrows shamelessly.

When I look a little skeptical, he quickly adds, "It really is the least you could do after treating me so rudely this evening. And on my birthday, of all days."

My eyes turn wide, "It's your birthday?" I ask, shocked.

"'Fraid so," he sucks a big gulp of air between his teeth and rocks back and forth on his feet. "So, unless I get this gorgeous, passionate, and funny *brunette's* number tonight," he smiles, cheekily, "I may have birthdays ruined for me for the remainder of time and space."

I frown as I consider his ballsy joke. It takes guts to throw the brunette thing back in my face so soon, but it's exactly something I would do, so I can't help but smile a little. Not to mention *gorgeous* and *passionate* are ringing in my ears on repeat in his sexy British tone. I shake my head and concede, "You're good," I reach over and grab his phone out of his hands, "I'm giving you my freaking number just because that speech was *that* good. Bravo, Romeo. Bravo."

He smiles proudly at me. *He looks so adorably pleased with himself right now.*

After assuring me he understands I'm not ready to hang out any time soon, we part ways and I return to my table of redheads. Leslie appears to be deep in thought. I eye her speculatively but she shakes her head, so I let it go. I'm still feeling slightly gloomy about the whole Brody situation, but I know Leslie is right. I made this decision. I need to stick to it.

CHAPTER NINE

My first two weeks in London have gone by pretty quickly. I actually feel like I am finally getting into a groove with the city and my new roomies, though I don't see Julie and Mitch very often. They stow away in their bedroom most of the time, and when I do run into them, they seem to make excuses to leave again. I try not to take it personally, especially since Frank says he never speaks to them either.

Leslie and I slip back into our old routine of late night conversations and cackling fits over the most ridiculous impressions. We love imitating comedy actors from TV and voicing great movie quotes. Sometimes we laugh for no reason at all. As kids, we used to hang our heads off the side of the bed and force ourselves to laugh until the laughing became real. I don't know if it was the blood rushing to our heads that caused our fits of giggles, or just the ridiculousness that we were re-enacting stupid crap we did as grade-schoolers now that we are 25 years old, but that is right when Frank walks in on us. I'm sure the image of us both hanging our heads off the side of the bed looks insane to him as he tries to act all mature and superior, but only five minutes later, he dives in between us and joins in the fun.

We go out a few nights a week, too. Mostly to the pub around the corner, which is quickly becoming my favorite place in London. Frank and Leslie are sure to show me all their other favorite spots in the city, as well. They appease me and do the whole tourist double-decker bus tour with me. Frank keeps hiding his face, afraid someone might recognize him every time we are on busy corners, but I can tell he is enjoying the historical tidbits the announcer says into the microphone. Julie and Mitch even join us one night for some Indian food in West London. Mitch doesn't say much the whole time, but Julie is very chatty and friendly. I genuinely like her. I discover that Indian food is as popular in London as Mexican food is in the Midwest.

Val sends me two copy-writing assignments for a new indie author they are doing marketing and public relations for. When I'm not sightseeing with Leslie or Frank, I stow away in my circular room. I enjoy the noise of the skate park across the road as I type press releases and various synopsis options for the first novel I have to read.

I am really starting to love my circular little cave of a room. It lets in a lot of bright, natural light, allowing the old wooden floorboards to shine. I still don't have a desk or chair, so I do all my writing on the mattress that still sits in the middle of the room on the floor. I've sorted and arranged all my clothes to sit in folded piles inside the suitcases on one wall. I really should consider buying a dresser, but the idea of asking skinny little Frank to help me carry it up three flights of stairs seems like too much work. Leslie is probably stronger than Frank, come to think of it. She did grow up on a farm, but I can't ask her. She's been working a lot of hours designing an extra bag that Nikon wanted added to the line last minute.

I haven't heard from Brody and I know I can't call him, even though I desperately want to. All I hear echoing in my head is the pain in his voice when he told me he was giving up on me. I hate that we left it so badly. I've talked to Cadence a few times through Skype and she informed me she hadn't had any more drunken visits from him. I feel like she's holding something back from me. I keep pestering her to let it out, but she refuses.

I fear the worst, that Brody has met someone and moved on. I know I have no right to care because we're broken up, but I can't help myself. *I have to know.* I decide to reactivate my *Facebook* account. Val's assignment can wait. Life has been brutal without *Facebook* for two whole weeks.

I immediately pull up Brody's profile and a sick feeling washes over me as I see his relationship status changed to *Single*. Why the hell does that surprise me? I left him, for goodness sake. Of course he should be single. I click on his profile picture that used to be a photo of the two of us. Now it's just a photo of him at some outdoor festival. I can't tell where he is and it pains me to realize I don't know everything he's doing anymore. I scroll through the rest of his profile pictures, assuming I'll see all the old ones of us, but they are nowhere to be found. I broaden my photo search, desperate to find a picture of the two of us. He couldn't have totally erased me from his life could he? There is not one damn picture of me anywhere on his profile.

What I do find are multiple, very recent photos of Brody with a girl I know extremely well.

Olivia. My blood begins to boil.

Olivia is a *friend* from my early college days. I use the word friend loosely here because we don't speak anymore. She lived on the same floor as me in the dorms, but was two years ahead of Brody and I.

Olivia and I became fast friends because she had this sweet, good-natured way about her that everybody seemed to love. She was also really cool because she was older and had more connections and friends at the university. Therefore, she knew where all the great parties were. Everyone wanted to be friends with Olivia.

We hung out a lot in the beginning. She got my obnoxious sense of humor and we had some really fun times in our dorm rooms. We even went on spring break together.

Then there was *Jake*. Jake was a basketball player living in the same apartment complex we all lived in senior year. He was tall with really dark hair and one of those classically beautiful faces that made you look at him and want to say, *seriously?* I was smitten. We became close over the summer before our final year and then had a class together first semester. We were hanging out all the time since his apartment was straight across the parking lot from mine. Seriously, we did everything together. We went to parties together, ate lunch with each other everyday, watched movies, and went to the gym to shoot hoops. Jake would call me every night to talk me to sleep because he knew I had trouble falling asleep.

My roommate thought Jake and I would end up married and have a bunch of babies together. I always laughed at her, but secretly hoped she was right. Even Jake's teammates made comments. All my girlfriends knew I had it *bad* for Jake—it was so obvious. But for whatever reason, we never hooked up.

The beginning of senior year is when everything changed. We were all out at the bar, dancing and having a great time celebrating the start of our last year of college. Jake and I were dancing together, as we always did. He was a great dance partner and I loved having him with me so random guys wouldn't try to grind on me. Olivia was there with all of our friends, and everyone was having a blast. In the craziness of leaving to go back to the apartment complex for the after party, I got separated from Jake and Olivia. On a drunken high, I bounded into Jake's apartment ready to continue partying and found

Olivia. In bed. With Jake. My *friend*, *Olivia*. It was the most embarrassing thing I have ever experienced. I quickly dashed out of the room and sobbed into my girlfriends' arms as they consoled my drunken, dramatic, sorry ass.

My friends were outraged Olivia would cross such an obvious line with a friend. They banded together and we all completely stopped hanging out with her. Jake acted like he had no clue what was even going on, but I knew he knew better because we were never the same after that. We barely spoke in class and only saw each other at parties. We never hung out privately like we used to. *It was hell.*

Then I met Brody, and Jake was completely and utterly eclipsed from then on. I couldn't believe I ever pined for a guy like Jake when Brody was right in front of me the whole time. Seeing me with someone else must have bothered Jake because he repeatedly tried to get me to talk to him. It was definitely an area of friction for Brody and me.

Needless to say, seeing Olivia's arms draped over both of Brody's shoulders in a slew of pictures on *Facebook*, makes me physically pulse with anger.

I slam my laptop shut and snatch my phone up off the floor.

"Hello?"

"Are you fucking kidding me, Cadence?" I squeal, hardly able to utter the words because I am so revved up.

"Who is this?" she sings, cheerily in to the phone.

"You know exactly who this is! How the hell could you not tell me?" I boom into the phone.

"Tell you what, sister?" Cadence sings to me again, in an incredibly annoying placating tone.

"You know what! Olivia! *O-fricken-livia Gabriel.* Is he seriously seeing her, Cade?" I can't stop the shaking in my hands.

"I don't know why the heck you even care, Finley," she bites back. "Seriously, get your shit straight. You dumped him. You got it in your head he won't want you if you're barren and now you've pushed him into the arms of someone who will probably give him six precious little babies," she peals into my ear.

I feel my chest rising up into my chin, "That is a low blow, Cadence," I pause, my voice cracking, "even for you."

She sighs heavily, "Well, I'm not sorry! You know how I feel about this whole ridiculous situation you have going on here. You are getting what you asked for."

"I didn't ask for this!" I scream, unable to check my emotions, "I didn't ask for him to run into the arms of the one chick I've hated for over five years!"

"You asked for it when you refused to give him a chance to know the truth, Finley. Now you have to learn to live with it. Learn to live with the idea of him snuggling up to Olivia Gabriel. I see her when I go into the city, you know, and she looks good, Finley. She hasn't aged a bit!" Cadence cheerily adds the last line with melodramatic flare.

I hang up. *God, my sister can be a real bitch sometimes! This is bullshit, complete and utter bullshit.* I stand up from my mattress and throw my phone down against it as hard as I can. I toss my hair over one shoulder and take a big lap around the tiny room.

When that doesn't seem to help, I run back to my bed and quickly inspect my phone, fearing I may have damaged it. *It's fine, thank God. But shit, the drama of that toss felt good, damn it.* I tuck my phone into the back pocket of my Skinny Jeans and pull the sleeves of my long sleeve navy t-shirt down to stick my thumbs through the thumbholes.

Needing something to take the edge off, I pound down the stairs and head straight into the kitchen cabinet above the fridge where Frank keeps all the liquor. A bottle of tequila looks pretty good. I barely touch the stuff anymore because Leslie and I had once mixed it with root beer when we were teenagers and drank so much we got sick.

I rummage for a shot glass and can't find one, so I grab a coffee mug instead. I pour an inch or two of the golden liquid and throw back the cup. *Oh, crap!*

"That was way more than a shot! *Way* more than a shot!" I screech out loud, jumping up and down with my face pinched.

A strange squeal comes through my throat as I force myself to swallow. I place my hands wide on the counter and drop my head down low, gagging. *Oof! Why the hell did I grab tequila?*

I scream as loud as I can in frustration.

"Crap day?"

I jump when I see Mitch sitting in the breakfast nook by the window, sipping tea out of a mug.

I wipe my mouth with the back of my hand, "You could say that."

"That tequila is crap. Seriously, I think it might actually be poison," he gets up out of the booth and squats down by the stove, rummaging through the drawer below the oven.

"Try this," he says, handing me a bottle of clear liquid with a foreign label on it.

I eye it, cautiously.

"Trust me," he states, dumping the contents of his tea out and pouring a bit into his mug and mine.

"Salud," he says, clinking mugs with mine.

"Salud," I reply back, gently tipping the liquor back at the same time as him. "Wow! Tastes like lemons!" I say, and lick my lips appreciatively.

He nods his head with a smirk. "Finish it off if you like. But watch yourself, that's a lot stronger than the shit you get in America," he adds, walking out of the kitchen.

"Thanks, Mitch," I reply, feebly.

"Cheers."

He makes his way up the creaky stairs, leaving me to my own devices.

I take my coffee mug, fill it up with the clear foreign liquor, and head across the street to watch the skateboarders and have a good sulk.

After about an hour of watching the action, and giggling every time one of the guys gets seriously hurt, I reach into my back pocket and grab my phone. My fingers have a mind of their own and before I know it, I push *Call*.

"Hiya."

"Hiya," I repeat.

"Is it really you?"

"It's really me."

"You finally finished unpacking?"

"Pretty much," I breathe out. "Do you like skateboarding?"

"Love it. Do it all the time," he answers.

"Seriously?" I ask, giggling nervously.

"No, I wouldn't know the first fucking thing. I'm an uncoordinated sod-all bastard who'd probably end up disabled for the rest of my life if I ever tried."

I laugh. It feels good to laugh. "Do you like watching skateboarding?"

"Never tried that either. Sounds scary."

"I can protect you."

"Where are you?"

CHAPTER TEN

Within thirty minutes, Liam comes walking around the corner. He's looking delicious in a trendy cowl neck cotton grey shirt and jeans. His blonde hair looks softer than last time and it's draped loosely to one side. He has a slight blonde five o'clock shadow that makes me want to cuddle up in bed with him all day.

"Hiya you," he says as he approaches.

"Hiya you, back," I reply, shooting him awkward finger guns and clicking my cheeks twice. I love how the English say *Hiya* instead of just *Hi*.

He laughs and sidles up next to me on the metal bleacher, peering into my coffee mug tucked tightly between my hands.

"What ya got there?"

My eyes turn wide and the edges of my mouth turn down. "A little something I like to call *Lemon Daydreamer's Delight*," I click my cheeks two more times. *Okay, I have to stop clicking my damn cheeks.*

I reach over to the other side of me and pull out another mug I ran in to get before he arrived.

"I have one for you!" I sing out, merrily.

"Well, alright then! Now it's a party!" he exclaims.

I carefully pour the clear liquid into his mug, trying my hardest not to spill. Before I hand it over, I eye him speculatively, "Aren't you worried I roofied—*hiccup*—roofied it?"

"Did you roofie it?" he asks, dropping his chin and eyeing me carefully.

"If I did, I sure as hell wouldn't tell you! How could I rape you and sell you into human-trafficking if you don't drink this sweet, sweet, sweeeeet nectar?" I reply, sing-songing the last bit.

"I'll take my chances," he says, grabbing the extra mug from my hands and taking a sip. He nods approvingly and looks out at the skateboarders.

"Don't you have a job you should be at or something?" I ask, breaking the awkward silence.

"Eh, working is for the birds," he says, sarcastically.

"Seriously, what do you do?" I ask him again, tucking my hair behind both of my ears, eyeing him curiously.

He turns to me and does *that thing* again. That mouth glance thing. *God, I hate that.* Okay, I freaking love it, but I hate what it does to my insides.

"Honestly," he begins, "I'm the operations controller for a medical supply company. It's pretty dull. A glorified inventory taker, but the pay is decent."

"And don't you have work to work at today?" I frown at my phrasing choice.

"Yes," he replies, fidgeting in his seat.

"So, how is it possible for you to drop what you were doing to come here and watch skateboarders with me?"

He shrugs his shoulders and continues watching the skaters, avoiding my question.

I stare at him until he looks at me. I raise my eyebrows, "Well?"

"I blew off work to come here," he replies. "It's not a big deal, I was almost done for the day. They won't even know I'm gone."

I look at him and drop my jaw, nodding my head as I take another drink of my *Lemon Dreaming Sunshine*, or is it *Delight Dreaming*? What did I decide to call it? Shit! A fabulous liquid deserves a fabulous name. I wonder what Mitch calls it? He's a scary dude, but how can he be so mean and scary and then give me such a liquid deliciousness dream? Yes, *dream* must have been one of the words in my name for the booze.

"What are you thinking about?" Liam interrupts my thoughts.

"Oh, you know, really important, profound thoughts," I reply, sipping more of my drink as he sips his.

"What made you decide to call?" he asks.

"I just thought I needed to stop unpacking already. Everybody else seems to be done unpacking. Why shouldn't I?"

"Good point. I fully agree. Anytime you need to stop unpacking, you feel very free to call me," he smiles into his mug before taking another sip. "So, what is it that you do that allows you to drink Lemon Daydreamer's Delight in the middle of the day while watching skateboarder's impale themselves on poles?"

Lemon Daydreamer's Delight! God, that's a great name for this drink! Why didn't I think of that?

"I am currently on a leave of absence from my job back in the States, but I'm still doing some freelance for my company while I'm here, so I have some income coming in."

"What kind of freelance?" he inquires.

"Writing stuff mostly, for advertising and marketing-type things. It's fun. I get to meet different people and work on different projects all the time, but I just want to get out and discover a different world, ye know?" I stand on the bleacher our feet were resting on and stretch.

"You know you're still in the same world, don't you?" he pushes out his lips, playfully.

Ignoring his snide remark, I reply, "I like it here so far. Way, way, waaaay better than back home."

"I like it here, too," Liam says, looking at me as I hop off the bleacher and sit on the lower level. I twirl myself around and face him. His eyes lock onto my mouth.

"You have to stop doing that!" I exclaim, looking away from him.

"Doing what?" he asks, smiling thoughtfully.

"That thing you do with your eyes, where you look at my mouth like you're trying to decide if you should kiss me or not," I state, brazenly. Good Lord, I'm not holding anything back this afternoon.

Thank-you-very-much, Lemon Dreamy Delish.

"I wasn't even aware I was doing it," he says as he sets his mug down next to him and uses his arms to scoot himself down to my level.

Facing backwards while he is facing forwards, our mouths are dangerously close together. His eyes continue to dance between my eyes and my mouth.

"It does serious things to my under-carriage," I breathe onto his face.

He laughs, hard. "Did you just say *under-carriage*? Oh my word! That's a first. That's a true and definite first," he continues laughing hard and I look away, not the least bit embarrassed. *Lemon Days' Drink* makes me buoyant, apparently.

He composes himself as I continue to watch him thoughtfully. "Well," he says, "So far, I just love hearing what comes out of your mouth, I guess." He looks down and smirks. "It always seems to surprise me," he finishes, tucking a piece of my brown hair behind my ear.

It tickles and I reflexively turn my face into his hand. He takes the opportunity to stroke the backs of his fingers down my cheek and over my lips. His eyes are locked on my mouth as my lips part slightly and his face grows serious.

Before I can break my trance with this beautiful Brit's face, he kisses me. Softly at first, then he tilts his head and *really* kisses me. As he's kissing me, I just keep picturing his eyes looking at my mouth. I love it. It makes me feel desired. His hands slide from my face down my shoulders and he grasps my arms on either side. I feel the tickling of his whiskers on my mouth and smile slightly around his kiss in response.

When he presses his tongue into my mouth, I taste the lemon drink and shiver at the delicious aroma. Before I lose my head completely, I push my hands against his chest and pull back. His eyes flutter open and waver between my eyes and my mouth. We continue touching each other as our breathing slows.

"That's definitely packing more in when I just finally got unpacked," I say, looking down at my hands, still on his firm chest.

"Maybe you won't have to unpack again?" he questions, gently rubbing my arms with his warm hands.

"I don't know what's packed and what's not packed anymore," I reply, pulling away from him and turning around to look back at the skaters for distraction.

"Have dinner with me," he says, in a rush, looking at me earnestly while I continue to look away.

"I don't know."

"Sure you do. You fancy me, I fancy you. What's not to know?" he questions.

"It's so much more complicated than that."

"It's not, though. It's incredibly simple. Dinner, drinks? Anything."

That kiss was good. It was damn good. It wasn't Brody, but it sure made me feel like a woman again. And speaking of Brody and women, he was off doing God knows what with *Bitchy Bitcherson Old Balls Olivia*. Why am I feeling so damn guilty about considering Liam?

"Do you know what a, um, *tarts and vicars* party is?" I ask him.

He smiles sweetly at me and leans back on the bleachers with his arms draped out wide. "I've heard of the theme, yes."

"What is it? Frank won't tell me and made me promise not to look it up online! He said he's taking care of my costume and all I have to do is show up!"

Liam laughs softly and says, "Far be it for me to reveal Frank's surprise."

"I'm so mad at myself for not knowing! I've read tons of British Chick-Lit novels and I've never come across it!"

"Did you never read *Bridget Jones' Diary*?" he asks.

A light turns on as the memory comes flooding back into my brain.

"Oh God," I groan, and Liam laughs softly. I drop my head and cover my eyes.

"When is this party?" he asks.

"Day after tomorrow," I reply, scowling at the realization that Frank is going to make me look like a huge skank or an ugly priest.

He nods.

"You could come if you want," I offer him. "I almost regret bringing it up to you now because Lord knows what Frank is going to dress me in…but screw it, I don't care. You can come if it sounds like something you want to do."

He nods his head thoughtfully with the side of his mouth turned up. I know I'm not offering him a date like he wants, but this is the best I can do for now. A social setting seems much safer than an official date. I know Brody is off being a disgusting puke and hanging out with *Oldie Olivia*, but jeez. I went from trying to have a baby with someone to dating again. I need to tread lightly.

"Should I be a tart or a vicar?" he asks.

"How the hell should I know? I just figured out what this whole damn theme is," I reply, sullenly. "Frank is going to make me look like a fool," I pout.

Liam tips my chin up, "Impossible. Cheer up now, I think the party sounds fun. What time?"

"Frank said no proper London party starts before 11, so I guess anytime after that."

"I'll be there." He stands up to leave and starts to walk away, then stops, turns around and comes back. He bends down quickly and presses his lips to mine, leaning me back onto the bleacher. Once the shock wears off and my lips relax, he widens his kiss, shooting flutters up and down my entire body.

He pulls away, but before standing up straight, he whispers in my ear, "I hope your under-carriage remembers that until the party, Finley."

What have I got myself in to?

CHAPTER ELEVEN

Brody kneels beside my mattress and gently strokes my cheek to rouse me awake. I purr with pleasure at the familiar feeling of his hands on my face.

"Finley," he breathes on my face, "I've missed you so incredibly much." He groans as he leans in, whispering in my ear, "You have no idea how much I dream about you just like this." He keeps his cheek next to mine as he slowly pulls the lavender bed sheet down my body.

I follow his eyes as he peruses my body and am surprised to see I'm completely naked. I don't even remember going to bed last night.

"Finley," Brody sighs my name like I'm his most cherished possession.

"Brody?" I question, still trying to figure out how he is even here right now, "What are you doing here?"

He ignores my question and begins dropping small, incredibly light kisses on the mounds of my breasts. A memorable stirring begins in my groin as my mind and body decide which it wants first—answers or pleasure.

He takes my nipple into his mouth and sucks—hard. Pleasure wins. Oh yes, pleasure definitely wins.

I let out a small gasp at the sudden pressure around my nipple as he drags his teeth gently over the hard nub. "Brody!" I cry, torn between loving what he is doing, and being terrified of the pain.

"Finley," he replies, "Don't worry, I would never hurt you." He looks at my face so lovingly, I could cry. I see tiny flickers of light shimmering in his dark blue eyes from the security light streaming in through my lace curtains.

He leans down and kisses me, deeply. He presses his tongue so far into my mouth that I can't even kiss back. It feels like he is doing with his tongue what he wants to do with other parts of his body, and it is *hot*.

My hips twist to the side and rise off the mattress to press into him as he remains kneeling. He shoves his hands behind my back and continues attacking me with his mouth as his arms engulf me in a bear hug. It feels like he can't get close enough to me.

I slide my leg down to the floor in an attempt to wrap myself around him. He gets the memo and pulls back slightly to allow my legs to open to him. Spread out directly in front of him, I'm feeling entirely exposed while he is still fully clothed. It feels odd, so I grab the bottom of his shirt and pull it over his head.

His chest looks so good. So incredibly yummy, just the way I remember it. His creamy skin glows in the darkness and his chest is covered in short curly hair. I stroke the hair and move my fingers downward, to the path that grows from his navel to below his jeans; I relish in the memories of that familiar trail.

He hugs me again, kissing me fiercely. The skin on skin contact makes me instantly aroused. He keeps flipping his head from side to side, alternating his kissing angles like he can't get enough of me. His lips travel down my jaw to my shoulder. He gently bites down on my shoulder and I gasp in pleasure-filled pain. Then he sucks that spot, hard. He is marking me and I don't even care. It feels so incredibly hot.

His right hand moves from behind my back and strokes along my side. I flinch as he hits a well-known ticklish spot; he looks at me, smiling. Brody loves how ticklish I am on my sides.

His fingers find my wet center and begin working their magic.

I moan loudly in pure delight at the building pleasure inside my body. Brody groans back in response and continues filling me with his fingers.

"Brody!" I cry, breathing quicker as his fingers become more relentless. "Brody! I can't...I don't understand! What's going on?"

"Shhhhhh baby," he hushes me as he pulls his fingers out and reaches for the button on his pants.

He stands quickly and kicks himself out of his jeans. I help him pull them down and lie back, still distraught from being so incredibly close to release, and confused as to why he is here in London—in my bedroom—in the middle of the night.

Brody climbs on top of me, fashioning himself between my legs. In one strong swoop, he enters me and we both keen loudly with pleasure.

"Brody! I've missed you so much," I say, tears filling my eyes as he finds a good rhythm. I run my fingernails up and down his back as he works tirelessly for both of us.

"I've missed you, too," he replies, cupping my breasts with his large hands, "But I can't stay long."

"Why?" I moan out, getting closer and closer to climax.

"Olivia is due soon."

My hands drop as the crushing name echoes in the room.

"What did you just say?" I ask, clearly confused because there was no way in hell Brody just said Olivia's name while he is rocking inside of me.

He looks at me and cocks his head to the side, "I said, Olivia is due soon. With the baby."

I quickly push him off of me and scramble to the very edge of the mattress, pulling my legs up to my chest and squeezing.

"What the *fuck*, Brody?" I ask, trying to calm my libido enough to be angry.

"I thought this was what you wanted?" he replies, looking confused.

I push my hair out of my face and scream, "She's having your baby? That is most definitely *not* what I wanted, Brody!"

Brody sits back on his haunches and scratches his short curly hair, "She's having *our* baby, Finley. You know this. Why are you acting so strange?"

What the hell is going on? What kind of sick joke is this?

"This doesn't make any sense!" I scream, rubbing my hair like a mad woman.

"Maybe she's still making up her mind, mate," Liam announces, in his cool British dialect.

I swerve my head over to where his voice came from and see him standing there, fully dressed, arms crossed and leaning one shoulder on the frame of the door.

"Liam! How the hell did you get in here?" I ask, completely confused.

"Chill, Fin, it's *us*!" Brody replies, as if that answer would tell me everything.

Liam saunters over to the mattress and squats down beside it. "Yeah, it's *us*." He smiles, knowingly. "How's your under-carriage feeling, Finley?"

***

I awaken to the loud *crack* of a skateboard hitting concrete outside my window, and several teenage boys' voices whooping in response.

I blink my eyes quickly, looking around the room, trying to figure out what just happened. Bright daylight fills the entire room and I glance at the clock to see that it's noon already. I peek under the covers to see that I *am* naked. *Holy shit! Why am I naked?* I throw my legs to the side of the mattress and sit up quickly, my head screaming in protest at the change in angle. Oh God, my head. My head!

I can feel myself still aroused. I move slightly, to see if I can tell if I really had sex or not. Everything feels the same—I think. I rub my shoulder where I can still feel Brody's teeth, but there is no mark from him biting and sucking.

"Oh my God, it was just a dream," I say to myself as I take a huge gulp of air and sigh with relief. My eyes suddenly fill with tears and I let out a huge sob. *God, what the fuck is wrong with me?* That was the most fucked up dream ever. I pull the sheet tightly around my chest and stand up, unsure why all these tears are coming out.

I wrench my bedroom door open and dash over to the tiny bathroom. Just seeing the toilet, I begin gagging. I drop down to my knees and throw up the contents of my stomach, crying pathetically between heaves. I hate throwing up. I cry every time I throw up, and since I was already crying before I started puking, now I am really losing it.

"Morning, moron!" Leslie sings from the bathroom doorway.

I look at her from the corner of my eye and see she is dressed in a pair of red shorts and a black button-down blouse, buttoned all the way to the top with a triangle-shaped spikey necklace.

I dry heave two more times and breathe heavily, waiting for my stomach to calm down. "Screw you, Lez," I spit out between gulps of air.

"Believe me, I'd love to screw myself, I'm happy with what I see in the mirror every day. But I'm not sure you're feeling the same self-love these days," she says, checking herself out in the mirror. "You seem to be in the middle of a quarter-life crisis or something. I'm too good of a friend to just leave you hanging, Fin!"

I fall backward onto my butt, roughly hitting my back on the wall behind me. I use one hand to tighten the purple sheet around my chest and the other to wipe my runny nose and tears. I turn to Leslie; she looks so clean and put together, it depresses me further. What the hell is wrong with me right now? My chin begins to tremble.

"Jeez, Fin," Leslie says, sitting against the wall beside me. "What's with the tears?" she asks, concern all over her green eyes.

"I don't know," I croak. "I just had the most horrible dream, I'm hung over, I just puked, and I have no clue what the hell I'm doing anymore. I just—I don't know!" I cry, curling my legs up to my chest and burying my face in my arms.

Leslie's small arm wraps tightly around my back and she leans her head against my shoulder. "You always cry when you puke, Fin-Bin. It's fine. It's no big deal. You're probably still drunk. And contrary to popular belief, alcohol is actually a depressant, so you're not going to feel happier by drinking it, ye know."

I sniff loudly, "I know, but there's more to it than the alcohol and the puking. I just had a dream about Brody. It was a good dream...amazing even. But then it all went so fucked up and... dark." My voice rises to a squeak and I sob heavily into my arms.

"Are you sure being here is what you really want, Finley?" she asks, turning her head to face me, and resting her chin on my shoulder. "I mean, I want you here forever. I love having you here. But is this what's best for you and Brody?"

"Yes," I answer. "I can't change things now. It's too late, Lez. Brody's seeing Olivia now, anyway."

"Olivia?" Leslie questions.

"College Olivia, the one you called old. Remember?"

"Ick! *Oldie Oli*? Gross! Why would he be with her? She looked wrinkly back in college, she's got to look like a grandmother by now!" Leslie replies with disgust smeared across her face.

Leslie and I didn't attend the same university but visited each other as frequently as we could. When she met Olivia for the first time, Leslie asked me how old she was because she thought Olivia looked like an *alternative student* in her thirties. I can always count on Lez to tell it like it is.

I smirk slightly at her bashing of a woman I truly hate.

"There's pictures of them all over *Facebook*," I offer meekly.

"I thought you deactivated your *Facebook* account, Fin!"

"I reactivated it," I reply, shrugging my shoulders.

"Well there's your first mistake," she sighs dramatically. "What's really going on, Finley? Talk to me. This isn't you. You used to tell me everything. Even the cracks, remember?"

I smile to myself. Leslie and I used to say that to each other in high school when we were going through whatever sophomoric drama was happening at the time. "Empty out your brain, even the cracks." It is so nice having someone know all my deepest, darkest secrets. Brody used to be that person for me. I told him everything. And now I'm keeping the worst kind of secret I can from him.

"You know how when I was a kid, I used to love babies so much? I always snuggled up with your little brother; he just had the sweetest wittle gushy face..." I begin.

She lifts her head from my shoulder and looks at me cheerily, "Yeah, I remember. Of course I remember. Mom used to be afraid that you'd baby-snatch him."

I smile, "I can't get over the idea that my body won't ever give me something like that. It won't do what it's supposed to do and I can't change it! I can't fix it! Women are supposed to reproduce, make babies, be domestic, and live *happily ever after*. It's the next step for most people. It's for sure always been the next step for me. It *kills* me that I can't do it. I feel...I feel...ashamed!" I cry. I know I look and sound terrible right now but I don't care. This is Leslie; she can handle my ugly cry.

"There are other options, Finley," she offers.

"Not for Brody and me, Lez. It's Brody. *It's Brody!*" I groan, holding onto my chest, not knowing how to release the ache thumping inside of it. "It's all I've ever wanted, Leslie. A family. A forever. And when I found Brody, I thought the hard part of my life was over. I thought I'd been found! He was so incredible. *Is* so incredible. To think of delivering this news to him—this earth shattering, heart breaking, world-ending news—and watch him fall out of love with me," I bawl, "It's too much, Leslie. It's too much." I shake my head, my chin trembling wildly.

"I don't think you're giving him enough credit, Fin," she says, lying her head back down on my shoulder.

"If he looks at me differently after he knows, I won't be able to handle it, Leslie. I won't be able to forget. I don't think I can come back from something like that. And I refuse to beg him to stay with me. Refuse," I say, sniffing loudly. "I'm in survival mode right now."

"I think *you* are all Brody needs. And he is all *you* need. And I think you are fooling yourself to think you can't make a happy life together, just the two of you."

I look at her, feeling my chest rise as her words blanket me with a shred of hope. But that hope needs to shut the hell up right now. Hope is too painful right now.

"You guys have something really special. Unique. To think you can find anything remotely close to that with Liam, or any other guy that crosses your path for that matter, is a fool's errand, Fin-Bin. A fool's errand."

I watch her stand up off the bathroom floor and stretch. "You look terrible, by the way," she says, smoothing down her auburn bob in the bathroom mirror.

"Why am I naked?" I ask.

"Ha!" she laughs loudly, "You really don't remember?" she looks at me, her eyes wide and wild.

"I have no recollection. If I had to guess, I would say Brody found out where I was, flew over the ocean and seduced me in the middle of the night."

Her jaw drops. "You had a sex dream?" she questions.

I nod.

"You brazen little minx! I want details!" she squeals, while jumping and clapping like a child on Christmas morning.

I shake my head slowly, "No. No freaking way. It was way too strange to relive."

"Oh, come on! I'm not getting any action over here, I need to live vicariously through you. Even if it's just in your pretty little messed up head."

I look up at her and smile, figuring the least I can do is throw her a bone after the pep talk she just gave me.

"I'll tell you one thing and that's it. You have to swear on your life that you won't ask me for any more details," I bargain.

Her eyes turn wide, "Yes! Tell me, tell me, tell me!" she pants like a dog.

"I mean it, Lez. No more details," I chide as I stretch out my cramped legs in front of me.

"I got it, I got it!" she kneels down on the floor beside me.

I take a deep breath and say, "Brody wasn't the only one in my dream last night."

She tilts her head in thought.

"One word...*Liam*."

Her expression goes blank as she sinks further back on her feet tucked under her butt. She looks straight up to the ceiling and falls directly on top of me.

"Ow!" I cry, laughing. "Get off of me, you fat ass!"

"I can't. I've just died of a fascination stroke. I fascinated so fast and so hard about those two dreamboats that I came in my panties and died happy."

I shove her off of my lap and she flops onto her back, eyes closed. Suddenly she sits back up, "Seriously, you've given my vibrator material for the next year."

"TMI!" I shout.

"TMI?" she questions, "What about the cracks?"

Oh God, the cracks.

"Fine, fine. Thanks for sharing, Lez. Happy to help," I struggle to get up off the floor without stepping on my sheet.

"Seriously though, why am I naked?" I ask her one last time.

"You said—and I quote, *I want to feel the breeze of the house-air on my skin as I walk up three flights of stairs. I've never done that before. Bucket list!* Unquote." Leslie looks at me with a straight poker face.

"I didn't!" I scream, jostling the ache in my head.

"I'm afraid you did, my dear. You are so freaking lucky Julie and Mitch weren't here."

"What about Frank?"

She laughs hard and then tries to compose herself, "You *might* have been passing by his floor just as he was exiting his room with a magazine. He took one look at you, screamed like a girl, and ran back into his room. He hasn't been out since!" she laughs, obnoxiously kicking her feet and hands on the ground.

Poor, poor Frank and Beans.

CHAPTER TWELVE

After sleeping it off for another hour, I feel tons better. It has been a while since I've been hung over so bad I threw up the next day. I hated it then and I hate it now. Couple being hung over with the internal monologue constantly screaming in my head, and you have a recipe for upchuck.

However, I can't stop myself from popping on *Facebook* one more time to confirm the images I saw of Brody and Olivia yesterday. The date stamp is clear. The pictures are from a couple nights ago and it looks like they were at a bar or party of some sort. Together. Brody barely knew Olivia back in college. I wonder where the hell he bumped into her after I left. She sure as hell wasn't his type, but then again, I know Brody is a different guy since I left him.

It feels like a personal attack; he's always known about my distaste for Olivia. I explained the situation to him in the early days of our relationship. I watered down the parts about my crush on Jake. Brody and Jake had a history of conflict from our senior year because Jake tried to kiss me at a party shortly after Brody and I started dating. I wouldn't call Brody possessive, but Jake was a sensitive subject I always treaded lightly around. Brody hated the idea that I had unrequited love with anyone. He couldn't believe any guy wouldn't want me. Jake and I were always just friends, though. I did my best to assure Brody that I only had eyes for him after we met, but, when it came to me and my past with other guys, it was definitely a subject I avoided as much as possible.

I wouldn't call myself promiscuous, by any stretch of the imagination, but I was experienced. In high school, I had about four semi-serious boyfriends, and I ended up having sex with all of them. I was a young, wild teenager and extremely curious about sex. So when I had my first official boyfriend at sixteen years old, it was only a matter of time before I willingly gave him my v-card.

Connor Nelson. He wasn't anything special in the looks department but he was a senior, two years older than me. That gave him a definite *cool* factor. He was also one of the best players on the varsity football team, so even if he wasn't super attractive, all the girls wanted him. I felt like the queen bee when he singled me out from all the sophomores. We had a good relationship but had no fireworks or passion between us. It lasted until just before his senior graduation. Surprising everyone, I broke it off because I didn't want to be tied down to a long-distance relationship when he went to college in the fall.

My other three relationships only lasted about six-to-nine months each. One being just a summer fling, and the other two I ended before they became too serious. My sexual curiosity had been stirred with Connor; so having sex seemed like a normal progression of events in any relationship.

In college, I experienced my first one-night stand. It wasn't something I was proud of, but I was a freshman enjoying my newfound freedoms, *a bit too much*, and a football player caught my eye. Sure enough, he promised to call and never did. I hated running into him on campus because I felt like such a fool for sleeping with him the first night I met him. I told Cadence about it and she chastised me for weeks. Nobody needed to yell at me though, I knew I was an idiot and felt horrible about myself afterward. Thankfully, I was smart enough to use a condom. Back then I was terrified of getting pregnant; little did I know, it wasn't even in the realm of possibilities. Still, football players have nasty reputations, so I'm glad I wasn't a complete moron.

After that, my girlfriends called me the make-out bandit. I made out and got hot and heavy with quite a few guys after parties and stuff, but I never went all the way with them. That college football player scared me off from opening up like that, and the alternatives were just as fun. If I did find a halfway decent guy, he never seemed to hold my interest for very long; I would end things before they got serious. At the time, I seemed to care more about hanging out with my friends and going to parties than finding a boyfriend.

That was, until I met Brody. When I met Brody, all bets were off. I had never really found a guy I could be completely comfortable and at ease with. That's what made Brody a breath of fresh air to me. He was hot, funny, kind, and interesting. He was the total package for me. I noticed him for the first time when I was dancing at a bar. I had heard his name around campus before but never spoke to him. After the whole Jake thing fizzled out, I found myself trying to figure out what parties Brody was going to and who his friends were. I couldn't believe we had been going to the same college for three whole years and our paths never crossed.

After we started getting serious, he admitted he'd seen me around campus before, and had always regretted not talking to me.

He rectified that situation when he saw me two months into our senior year, walking in the parking lot of our apartment complex. I can't help but smile when I picture him standing there in a pair of jersey shorts and no shoes with a half-empty bag of trash. He later told me he only grabbed the trash as an excuse to come out and talk to me. It seriously felt like fate when it dawned on us we'd been living in the same apartment complex, just two buildings apart.

After that, Brody and I got super hot and heavy, but we were good about not being one of those couples that fall off the face of the earth when they fall in love. We both had really solid groups of friends and wanted our senior year to be the best it could be, so we tried hard to separate ourselves occasionally and be with our own friends. However, we managed to combine our groups of friends together a lot so we could have the best of both worlds.

I sighed at the thought of simpler times when our only worries were upsetting our friends for hanging out too much.

After showering, shaving, and dressing in a pair of denim Daisy Dukes and a hoodie, I begin to feel like myself again. I trot down the steps, preparing for a good session of groveling to Frank for flashing him last night.

I repeatedly thump on his door for a good five minutes, begging him to come out.

"Come on, Frank. I promise I have clothes on now. I'm not naked and I'm really sorry, okay?" I whine at his door.

"Seriously, Frank. I've been banging out here for almost ten minutes now."

I hear a muffled laugh from inside his room. Was he laughing at me?

"Frank, I'll *bang* for a whole hour if I need to," I reproach.

More muffled giggles.

"Frank, I can *bang looooong* and *hard* all day if I need to. I'll keep hitting this *wood*, that's how *firmly* I am committed to this friendship. I'll *come* to you anytime, day or night."

I know I'm making sexual innuendos in a desperate shot to get Frank to warm up to me, but I am in damage-control mode and have to make amends with my poor, apparently scarred for life, Frank and Beans.

Suddenly, Frank creaks open the door and looks at me with a naughty smirk on his face.

"Said the actress to the bishop," he titters in response to my clearly understood word emphasis.

I have no clue what that phrase means, but I surmise it means something similar to the American version of *that's what she said*. I've grown accustomed to asking Frank what a lot of his interesting British phrases mean.

Frank is dressed in loose flannel pants and a white knit sweater, his hair an orange rumpled mess, as usual. He looks a bit pale and mopey, obviously milking his disposition for all it's worth.

"You don't play fair, Finley. You know dick jokes are my kryptonite," he adds, idly scratching at the doorframe.

I smile at him, "Frank, I'm sorry. I was drunk. I was stupid. I didn't mean to waltz around your house naked last night. And I sure as heck didn't mean to scare you into hibernation."

"I've never seen a girl's wobbly bits before, Finley! It was quite shocking," he states deadpan, but I see a sliver of a smirk on his lips.

I smile and grab his arm to lead him out of his bedroom, "Just consider it a test that you passed with flying colors."

He brightens at that, "Not that I needed a test to know my preference but I was always crap at school, so it's nice to know I aced something!"

"Leslie is downstairs preparing for tomorrow night's party. There's going to be a lot of scantily clad girls floating around here then too you know. So really, now you're just better primed," I coo.

"They better not be butt-naked and showing all their slits like you last night. I'm not sure my heart can take much more of that," he says, scratching his head thoughtfully.

As we make our way down the steps, I hear Leslie and Mitch arguing.

"Bridget Jones did *not* invent the tarts and vicars party theme! You're a bloody moron!" Mitch crows at Leslie from the living room as she works feverishly at the dining room table putting decorations together.

"I'm not saying she *invented* it, I'm just saying she is what made it famous!" Leslie replies snappily.

"That's such an American thing to assume," Mitch scoffs.

Leslie's eyes turn to me as I come down the last step, "You look quite a bit better than earlier!"

After the *Epic Bathroom Floor Pukefest of 2014*, I was ready for some fresh air. Despite the brisk fall London weather, I figured my hoodie would keep me warm enough to run around town and pick up necessary party supplies. I feel good in the shorts and I want to be proud of my appearance, the way Leslie was of hers earlier. I even applied some mascara to bring a bit of my confidence back.

I nod a *thanks* to Leslie and look over to Mitch, whose scowl lightens as he looks at me. He gives me a small half smile, like he's deduced I didn't listen to his advice about taking it easy on his liquor.

"What are you making?" I inquire, noticing the bits of construction paper speckled all over the dining room table.

"Crosses!" Leslie declares proudly.

Frank sashays over and begins helping, "Heaven help us. These are shit. Glad to see you're holding the fort down in my hour of need, Lezbo! We best get cracking or we'll never make this place presentable in time."

Leslie scowls at him and mumbles, "More like eight hours of need. You've been moping all damn day since Finley flashed you last night. I've been down here doing all the work for *our* party! You really can be a dramatic queen sometimes Frank."

Frank shoots me a wink as he draws his hand back and cracks Leslie on the butt. She screeches and punches him on the shoulder.

"Ouch, Lez! You hit like a bloody footballer!" he cries. I laugh and saddle up to the table to dig in and help.

In two hours, we have linked together hundreds of crosses and draped them across the entire dining room ceiling. They remind me of the links we used to make for our Christmas tree as kids. I laugh happily, listening to Frank and Leslie bicker like an old married couple over the various links of chains they intend to hang from the living room ceiling. Leslie borrowed them from one of her factory retailer's supply closets, and was yelling at Frank to *not put tape on them or they would get all sticky and she'd get into trouble.* Then he told her *he would show her sticky*, and that was when I snuck out quietly.

CHAPTER THIRTEEN

I pull my phone out of my pocket as I scamper across the busy street to the skate park to sit on the bleachers. I shudder at the cold temperature of the metal bleacher on my bare legs. I pull up my mom's phone number and click *Send* without thinking what time it is back home.

"Uh, hello?" my mom answers, sleepily.

"Crap! Sorry Mom! Is it nighttime there? I didn't even think!" I silently reprimand myself.

"It's fine, honey. I'm fine. I'm glad you called," she replies.

I picture her getting up out of bed and shaking my dad to put me on speaker.

"Don't put Dad on speakerphone, Mom," I interject, while eyeing three boys sitting at the top of a ramp, blatantly smoking something that was most definitely not a cigarette.

"Why, honey? I'm sure he'd love to talk to you."

"I know, but I just want to talk to you right now. I'll call back at a better time to talk to dad, okay?" I reason, hoping she hadn't already nudged him. He is a heavy sleeper, so even if she had, he probably still didn't wake up.

"Spill it," my mom surmises.

I let out a heavy sigh at my mother's intuition. She can always tell when something is eating at me. When I was younger, I spent so many nights in the kitchen, sitting at the bar top watching her bake. She loved to bake; she told me I opened up to her the most about my problems when she was baking.

I picture her now, pulling something out of the oven. My mother is a tall, slender woman with curves. I definitely received her figure. If you saw us from behind, you wouldn't know who's who. She has slightly darker brown hair, but she's been dying it for a few years now; I don't really remember her natural color. She has large round aqua blue eyes just like mine, but hers are bigger, more prominent on her face. We share the typical soft, curved, Midwestern facial features. Slightly rounded nose, face, and chin.

Cadence looks more like my dad. He has brown hair too but with smaller, less striking facial features. Cadence looks just like him, aside from her dirty-blonde hair she accentuates with highlights.

"Is it about Brody?" my mom asks, growing restless at my delay in response.

My mom has known that Brody and I were trying to have a baby, but she doesn't know I found out it's next to impossible, or that I came to London to run away from my problems; I only told Cadence that part. Before I left, I told my mom Brody and I have grown apart and I need a fresh start somewhere else.

Thankfully, she loves Leslie; she seems almost envious of my courage to move overseas and move in with her. Her supportive response was a huge reason I had the guts to book the trip.

"Well, no. Kind of—I don't know," I stammer. "I've met another guy. Liam. He seems really great, Mom. Really nice, and cute, and funny, and has a good job."

"But..." she speculates.

"But, it just feels, so...so..."

"Strange?" she questions.

"Yeah, strange. Different. I mean, one minute I'm doing this huge thing with a guy. You know, trying to have a baby. Trying to be just like Cadence. And the next minute, I'm in a foreign country, flirting like I'm in college again."

"That would be a strange feeling," she offers. "Are you doubting your decision to move?"

"No! No. No." I assess. "I love it here, Mom. Leslie and Frank are great and Mitch and Julie are even warming to me, I think. The city is amazing, there's life all around me I've never even dreamed about, but..."

"It's not home?" she asks. "Or...it's not Brody?"

Ugh! She just freaking read my mind without me even knowing that's what my mind was thinking. How does she do that?

"That's the million dollar question, I'm afraid."

"Well, there's only one way to figure it out," she offers.

"How?" I ask.

"Give this Liam guy a chance. A real chance. If you can't get over the fact that he's not Brody, then you'll have your answer."

"Spell it out for me, mom. I'm freaking blank here." *And hung over.*

"If Liam sweeps you off your feet and you feel nothing but excitement and passion with him, you'll know you're probably just homesick. But, if you give Liam a good chance, and really try with him, and something still feels off…well, then, that's a Brody problem."

I nod my head, thankful for sage advice I can wrap my brain around. *Give Liam a chance, and if it's fireworks, I made the right choice. If it's not, I have much bigger fish to fry.*

"But Mom, what if…what if it's a Brody problem and it's too late because Brody has moved on? Or what if it doesn't even matter because nothing has changed and all the previous issues I had before are still there?" I ask her, hesitantly.

"Well, that's a pretty cryptic *what if*. I think if I knew the whole story, it would help. But either way, you've got yourself a Finley Problem, babe. And you've been getting yourself out of Finley Problems for twenty-five years now, I'm sure you can do it again."

I smile after we hang up, wishing I could have my mom here so I could watch her bake and she could talk me through my feelings some more. But she is right. I've been following my own rules for quite some time now and I've managed to get myself a great job, great friends, and now a great experience as a result.

I can figure this out.

CHAPTER FOURTEEN

Our house has been legitimately buffed, polished, vacuumed, and sanitized within an inch of its life. Leslie and Frank really outdid themselves, lining three long rows of red tea-light candles down the beautiful dining-room table, with five tall, red tapered candles in the middle. It has a very catholic candlelight vigil feel to it, which partners well with the vicar party.

I asked Frank why there were five tapered candles and he got really awkward and said there was one for each five of us roommates. He really can be sweet when he isn't being horribly obnoxious. The red construction paper cutout cross-links hang from the ceiling and cast a thick red glow to everything as it masks the dimmed overhead lighting. Frank and Leslie had to redo the crosses on the ceiling three times before they felt safe enough to not be considered a fire hazard. Just in case, they set a fire extinguisher in a basket in the corner. For being the token *religious room*, it has a very sexy feel to it.

The living room chains look amazing and shiny, hanging and clinking in short bunches from the ceiling. The overhead fan is on, so there's a constant motion to the chains as Julie lines a square design of black votive candles on the large refurbished barn-wood coffee table. She finishes forming a perfect rectangle just as Mitch turns up the music dock on the fireplace mantle. He bobs his head slightly to the beat, examining the dance-lighting machine currently spinning around the room. This house definitely knows how to throw a party. I don't recognize the song but Julie does because she quickly dashes away from her project and begins dancing with Mitch.

The music is booming and I can feel the party atmosphere bubbling from everyone in anticipation of our guests. I'm excited to meet more of Frank, Julie, Mitch, and Leslie's friends; the only other person I've met in London so far, is Liam. I am worried Liam might attach himself to my hip all night and look at this party as a date, so I texted him earlier and told him to bring some friends if he felt like it. He texted back a weird reply of *Okay?* with a question mark. I wasn't sure what it meant so I just ignored it and hoped it was a typo.

Frank suddenly bellows down the stairs, "Finley, my pet! It's time for your big transformation!"

I look over to Julie and Mitch with a *heaven help me* look and Julie smiles brightly at me; even Mitch looks slightly amused.

I make my way up the creaky wooden staircase, dragging my feet slightly as the nerves regarding what Frank has in mind for me to wear settles over top of me.

I enter his open door and see a few items draped over his large cheetah bedspread.

"Finley! Why do you look like you're about to be put down like an old dog?" he questions, buzzing around his room, grabbing more supplies.

"I'm scared, Frank." I have to admit, "I feel like you're still mad at me about the naked staircase climb and this is how you're going to get me back."

He looks at me and scratches his wooly orange hair, "I will admit, the thought had crossed my mind to dress you up like a frumpy, dumpy old vicar and keep all your nasty wobbly-bits completely concealed so no one could see them."

I perk up at that thought.

"But I thought better of it. Despite being *scarred for life* with the image of you naked forever being burned into my head, I did discover one thing," he offers.

I look at him questioningly.

"You are covering up way too much of yourself in all those nasty university hoodies. Seriously! Look at your legs right now! You have got killer legs, my pet."

I beam back at him with this wonderful change of conversation.

"We're going to accentuate those long legs and make you the life of the party tonight. You won't steal the spotlight from me...*that* I'm sure of. My costume is one no one will miss." He smiles a bit devilishly.

"Let's sexify you, Fin-Fin."

After what feels like hours but in fact is only forty-five minutes, I am tarted-up to the nines. Frank had gone consignment shopping and found a ridiculously tight lace dress. At first glance, I thought it was completely see-through and freaked out on him. But then he showed me that there was a nude layer underneath and that I was a fool to think he wanted to see those parts again.

On an average-height person, this dress would be short. On me, it was completely scandalous. I begged him to let me wear some tights underneath and he told me he already had something in mind for my legs. And boy did he. Sheer, black thigh-highs. They do not go up to the bottom of the skirt, so I have a good three inches of bare thigh showing between the hem of my skirt and the top of the stockings.

After rummaging through my shoes for a while, he selects my black suede wedge pumps. They have a rounded toe and are actually really comfortable. But they make me enormously tall. I am always leery of wearing them because they are one of my tallest heels and tend to make me feel like an Amazon woman around people of normal height.

As I inspect myself in the mirror, I realize this dress really is quite pretty. It's strapless, with a sweetheart neckline. The hem is scalloped with the black lace overlay and the nude color underneath gives it definite wow factor. If it had been knee length instead of hitting just below my butt, I would wear this to a wedding for sure.

The thigh-highs, provocative heels, dramatic eyelashes and red matte lipstick are what really give me a high-end hooker look. My long brown hair lays long and loose down my back. Frank runs the straightener through it a few times to give it a sexy, sleek look. No jewelry necessary, this dress and my makeup give it enough pizazz all its own.

Leslie bounds into Frank's room as I finish inspecting my look in the mirror.

"Holy crap, Fin-Bin! You look *hot!* You're the most expensive looking hooker I've ever seen!" she says, her eyes wide.

"Where did you find that top, Leslie? It's so cool!" I reply, unable to accept her compliment because I'm too busy admiring the splendor of her outfit.

She looks like a hooker from the Twenties, a vintage tart through and through. She has on a skintight pleather skirt with a loose-fitting white blousy-tank. The tank has some shabby looking lace along the edges, which reminds me of what women wore in the old west as under garments. It's the type of top you'd see on the cover of a Western romance novel, but she has on a red lacy bra peeking out at the bust. She even manages to do pinup curls with her pixie bangs. She looks stunning.

"I rented it from a costume shop, actually. The skirt is mine! Leave it to me to have hooker-gear hanging in the closet," she laughs.

"Where's Frank?" she asks.

"He said he was just going to change into his costume. I think he's in the bathroom."

Suddenly, I hear a throat clear from behind Leslie. I look around her and see Frank standing in the doorway dressed as...*The Pope*...enormous headpiece and all.

Leslie and I pause for a beat to take in his full ensemble. We then look at each other and burst out laughing, uncontrollably. Frank stares at us solemnly, waiting for us to gain control of ourselves.

"Are you quite done?" he asks, with a grave expression on his face.

Leslie and I continue cackling, in response to not only his outfit, but the serious tone he is taking with us.

"I should hope you could show me a bit more respect. I am a man of the cloth now," he says, walking over to the full-length mirror inside his closet door as he adjusts his hat.

Frank has on a long white robe with a short, hooded cape wrapped around his shoulders. Hanging around his neck is a large gold cross, and on his ring finger is a large golden ring. His hat is what makes the ensemble look truly remarkable. I'm not Catholic, so I'm not sure what it's called, but I know I've seen the Pope wear it in photos before. It's shaped like a spade you'd see on a deck of cards and sits nearly two feet high.

"I don't even want to know where you found such an outfit, but it's the bomb dot-com. Bravo, my dear friend. Bravo," I say, giving Frank a quick round of applause.

Frank tucks some orange strands back up into his hat and looks at us solemnly, "Tonight...we drink."

CHAPTER FIFTEEN

It is nearly eleven o'clock before we are dressed and ready for our guests to arrive. Frank, Leslie, and I clamor downstairs and find Julie and Mitch in the kitchen, making punch at the counter with three of their friends from out of town.

"Guys! You look fantastic!" Julie announces, brightly.

She's wearing a bright purple one-shoulder mini dress with zebra print around the edges. She couples it with fishnet stockings and knee-high boots. Mitch, looking perky as ever, is wearing a black fitted t-shirt, jeans, and a white priest-collar around his neck.

After introductions and appreciative conversation over everyone's costumes are complete, Julie announces proudly, "Who wants party punch?"

We all gather around the kitchen counter as she dishes bright red punch into black plastic cups and tosses a lemon slice on top.

Frank awkwardly scrambles up onto the countertop and sits with his cup held out.

"A toast, my dear popettes. A toast...ahem." He waits for us to quiet down.

"Here's to you, here's to me. The best of friends we'll always be. If ever we should disagree, then fuck you, and here's to me!" He laughs heartily and takes a big swig of his punch; his humongous hat nearly falls off as he tips his head back.

We all laugh and tisk in response, then take a drink anyway. The punch is sweet but I can taste the dull burn of booze after I swallow.

"Oooo, wait! I heard one a few weeks ago," Leslie interrupts, "Oh crap, how did it go? Here's to living...no wait, I got it, I got it. Here's to the girl with the little red shoes, she loves her nookie and loves her booze, she's lost her cherry, but that's no sin—she still has the box the cherry came in! Ahhhh!"

We all laugh and take another drink.

"You do one, Finley. Go!" Leslie says loudly over everyone's chatter.

"Okay, um...this one is kind of boring. For every wound, a balm. For every sorrow, a cheer. For every storm, a calm. And for every thirst, a beer! Er...punch!"

Everyone cheers appreciatively and drinks.

"I've got one," Mitch says quietly and we all turn our surprised eyes to him.

He looks quickly to Julie and begins, "Here's to the wound that never heals, the more you rub it...the better it feels. All the soap this side of hell, won't wash away that fishy smell."

Mitch finishes and takes a quick drink. We all stare wide-eyed and deathly silent at Julie as we wait for the definite rapture coming Mitch's way.

"Wait, what?" she says, cocking her head seriously. "I don't get it."

We all burst into laughter. Frank falls down sideways on the counter holding his drink awkwardly and gripping his ribs. I've never seen him laugh so hard, so I laugh harder in response. Leslie is squatted down trying to get a hold of herself, and tears form in my eyes at the sight of everyone laughing at Julie's confused reaction. I look at her one more time and another fit of laughter comes over me.

"Uh, hello?" a voice calls over top of our laughter.

We all turn our heads and see Liam and three other guys walking in beside him.

"We knocked, but no one answered," he offers, apologetically.

Liam looks good. *Damn good.* How is it possible he made a vicar costume look sexy? My eyes travel slowly from his feet to his head. He's wearing black jeans with chunky black boots, a sexy black belt with a very masculine silver buckle, and a black fitted V-neck t-shirt with a white collar, just like Mitch's. And over top of that he has a very sharp looking black leather jacket on. He looks masculine, he looks strong...*he looks sexy.* Damn it, anyway.

I can already feel the buzz of the red punch in my head as I walk over to greet him. He eyes my dress affectionately and then his gaze locks onto my mouth.

"Wow," he says.

I smile back at him shyly, looking to his friends for introductions, hoping to get the attention away from me.

He doesn't seem to notice my silent request as he continues staring at my matte red lips. I decide to take charge of the situation and offer my hand, "Hi, I'm Finley."

"James," his friend to the right of him says, taking my hand. He's really short, a good five inches shorter than me and has brown shaggy hair with dark olive skin. If I had to guess, I'd say he was of Italian descent.

"I'm Ethan," says this beautiful, tall, chocolate-skinned guy standing on the other side of Liam. "Nice to meet you. Thanks for inviting us," he says, as he leans in to brush his lips against my cheek.

I'm slightly taken aback by this intimate gesture and then Liam's hand clamps down on Ethan's shoulder and he pulls him back.

"Don't make me regret inviting you," Liam says in a very firm tone.

Ethan smiles playfully back at me and holds his hands up in surrender.

"Just being friendly," he quips, with a quick raise of his eyebrows.

"Go be friendly by the punch bowl," Liam barks, and with that, Ethan and James make their way over to the group crowding in the kitchen.

"This is Theo," he says, moving aside and allowing Theo to come forward and shake my hand.

Theo has buzzed blonde hair and looks really familiar for some odd reason. He looks over my shoulders and I turn to see him checking out Leslie. Without giving me a second look, he moves us aside and walks straight to Leslie. She turns when he grabs her arm and has a shocked look on her face. Theo looks pissed. I watch them curiously, wondering how they know each other.

"Finley," Liam whispers into my ear from behind. I feel his hands grasp my waist ever so lightly and I turn to face him.

His gaze dances from my eyes to my lips and he looks…hungry. That's the only word I can use to describe this look he has. *Hungry.* My belly flips at his perusal and I begin to feel uncomfortable with our close proximity.

He smiles as if he's reading my mind, then leans in to kiss my cheek, "You look way too beautiful to be a tart."

I smile back at him, "Thanks. I'm an expensive tart," I wink, playfully. "Can I get you a drink? There's punch, or tons of beer in the fridge. What's your poison? Frank has a huge stash of liquor too, if you like."

He backs away, seemingly accepting my silent request for lightness.

"Tell me the truth," he reasons. "Did you tell me to bring friends to prevent us from talking too much?"

I look at him and furrow my brow, "Talking definitely wasn't what I was worried about."

He smirks and diverts his eyes from my mouth, "Your legs look incredible."

I half-smile at him, "You look pretty good yourself, for a nasty old vicar."

He laughs, "Beer would be great, cheers."

I head over to the fridge and feel Liam's presence following me. He has all of my senses on high alert. I eavesdrop on Leslie and Theo's conversation and what I hear makes me stop and check on her.

"…why you just left…" Theo stops as I put my arm around Leslie's shoulders.

"Hey!" I offer brightly, trying to lighten the mood. "You guys know each other?" I ask, as I take a gulp of my punch.

Theo turns and nods at me with a deep scowl to his brow and Leslie looks at me like she's about to burst. She gives me a nod to follow her to the other room and I look back at her, confused.

As we move to leave, Theo grabs Leslie's arm and gives her an intense look like he's not going to let her go. Leslie eyeballs him for a very intense moment and Liam places a hand on Theo's chest.

"Let the ladies chat, Theo," Liam says, pushing him back. "C'mon mate, there's beer in the fridge."

Leslie and I totter in our heels through the dining room and into the living room where the music is much louder. I look at her like I can't hear her and she hurriedly grabs my arm and leads me down the short hallway into the small bathroom.

She shuts the door quickly. It's much quieter but we're standing toe to toe in the tight quarters. It only has a toilet and a small old-fashioned basin. I hate using this bathroom because my long legs hit the sink's hardware when I sit down. The master suite and attached bathroom are just down the hall but I've still never seen that room. I usually just walk up the three flights of stairs to use my own private bathroom that offers a lot more leg space.

"Holy crap, holy crap, holy crap!" Leslie stammers, her eyes wide as she pulls the white strap of her loose tank top back on top of her shoulder.

"What is it, Leslie? Spill it! Who is that guy?" I question.

"You remember that night at Shay when you met Liam?" she asks.

"Yeah, duh. Of course I do."

"Well, do you remember the guy I danced with? The cute one with the dark-framed glasses on?" she asks, nodding her head at me encouragingly.

"Shit! That's him?" I ask, shocked. London is a huge city, there's no way the one random guy she dances with on the dance floor happens to be Liam's friend.

"Yes! Holy balls, this is so weird!" She rubs her hands over her cheeks and inspects herself in the mirror to make sure she didn't mess up her makeup.

I pull a small eyelash off her eye and ask, "Why does he seem so grumpy?"

"He's pissed! Like royally pissed," she screeches at me like I should know.

"What the heck for?" I ask still clueless.

She looks uncomfortable and I furrow my brow at her reaction.

"What, Leslie? What did you do?" I ask, grabbing her arms so she faces me and stops looking away.

"Oh God, oh God, oh God! I can't tell you! I can't!" she shakes her head at me, looking away as her cheeks blush a bright crimson.

"The cracks!" I scream at her, growing frustrated with her demeanor.

She drops her head low and sits down onto the toilet lid.

"Ugh, okay. God, this is so embarrassing," she begins. "So that night at Shay. You and I were dancing, remember? Acting like fools."

I nod in agreement.

"And we took those shots, two in a row, you know? We were

feeling good. *Really* good." She pauses and adjusts her red lace bra up a bit, "Well, it's been a while for me since I've been with a guy. Like too long, Fin-Bin. Scary long. There's probably cobwebs down there for God's sake. And apparently, my coocha has a mind of her own because…"

She pauses again with a horrified look on her face, "I can't, Finley. I can't!" she cries.

"Leslie, if you make me say cracks one more time…" I threaten.

"Ohmygod. Okay, okay, okay. I came on his fucking leg!" she blurts out.

"What?" I question, assuming I heard her wrong.

"I was horny, Finley. H-o-r-n-y. Those shots and the vodka tonics, the music, the lights, I don't know…it like…kick-started my cooch or something because she was wanting to do more than just dance," she says, pointing down toward her crotch.

"Did you have sex with him?" I question as realization sets in.

"No! Jesus!" she barks, pissed off.

"Then what did you do, Leslie?"

"Argh! We were dancing really hot and heavy. You were doing your own thing. I don't know. Theo can move, what can I say? We were dancing and his leg was in between my leg, you know," she says, standing up and demonstrating by placing her leg between mine. "I guess it was the friction of his jeans or something. My panties were really thin that night and…holy crap…your face right now. I can't finish if you keep looking at me with that face!"

"This is my face! My face is my face! I can't help my face! Finish! I'm dying here!" I screech.

With a big gust of air, she spews out the rest.

"We were dancing so hot and horny and apparently the friction of jeans and the fact I haven't seen a man's penis in over a year made me come on the damn dance floor amongst a crowd of people. I had an orgasm in public, Finley! I came on a stranger's leg like a horny dog that can't help but hump. I'm a freaking humping pervert of epic proportions and I've shamed myself into celibacy. I've probably lost you as a friend; if Frank ever finds out, it'll be all over the damn Internet. I won't hear the end of this. My life is officially over," she says, sullenly. "I'll never look at a leg the same way ever again."

A silence creeps over the bathroom as her confession marinates in my brain. I purse my lips together, trying to contain my smile. When she looks up at me with sad, puppy-dog eyes, my mind instantly connects the puppy eyes with her humping dog reference from earlier and I spit everywhere as my lips part in a hearty laugh.

I laugh so hard and so loud, the noise radiates off the tiny bathroom walls and is nearly deafening. Leslie's sad face turns to a glare as I wipe tears from my eyes.

"Holy crap, Leslie! I can't believe you didn't tell me."

"Really?" she retorts, not impressed. "Really. You're surprised I didn't tell you about the most mortifying thing that's ever happened to me? Shocking. Truly and utterly shocking." She states in a flat monotone. She is getting pissed, so I attempt to pull myself together.

"So, what's his problem? Why is he all mad and caveman-like right now?" I question.

"He's apparently pissed I ran off and never said anything to him. I asked him what the hell he wanted me to say…*Thank you*?"

Another burst of laughter erupts from me and Leslie shakes her head, trying to conceal her own smile.

"He seems interested in me but I don't know if I can get past the horror of what I did. I can't believe he thinks I'm anything but a perv! I can't believe he's even here. Afterward, I told him I had to go to the bathroom and he made me promise I would come back. I literally crawled on my hands and knees at the club to ensure he wouldn't see me heading back to our table. I was freaking mortified! Now he's here, making me relive the whole sorry event."

"Well, give him a chance. If he doesn't think you're a freak, maybe he's a really nice guy?" I offer.

"Or maybe he's a freak like me. Two peas in a damn pod. Good Lord." Leslie smoothes her auburn hair down and gently touches her gelled curls.

"Lets get back out there. We can't avoid him all night," I say, ushering her out the door.

"Just keep your legs where I can see them. I can't be trusted!" she says, and I burst out laughing again. *God I loved this girl, even if she is a freak.*

CHAPTER SIXTEEN

An idea comes to mind as we join everyone back in the kitchen. Leslie is in dire need of some cheering up. Just looking at her in her ridiculous tart getup and sulky face is enough to make me laugh. She is definitely in need of a distraction from her embarrassing dance-gasm with Theo. Not to mention, Theo is continually throwing daggers at Leslie.

My eyes search the room for Liam, who is visiting in a small circle with his friend James, Mitch, Julie, and a few other new faces that must have arrived while Leslie and I were having our bathroom heart to heart. *Must not laugh at Leslie. Must not laugh at Leslie.*

"Alright, everybody!" I announce from the dining room doorway. No one stops talking to listen to me, so to get their attention I pound my foot on the floor. *Nothing.* I chug the rest of my red sweet punch, set the cup on the dining room table, and drag a chair into the kitchen entry. I motion for Ethan because he's the nearest guy. He saunters over, a bit too smugly. I ignore it and press my hand on top of his shoulder to hoist myself on top of the dining room chair.

"HEY!" I shout loudly this time with a giggle afterward.

Leslie dashes over from her conversation with Frank and stands below me with a big smile on her face, eagerly awaiting my announcement.

"I have a little surprise for Leslie!" I reveal, while catching Liam's eyes traveling up my legs and to my face. He doesn't look very happy.

Ignoring him, I continue, "We're going to play a game. A game Leslie and I used to rule in our formidable years." I pause for dramatic effect, "It's Tippy-Cup Tiiiiime!" I announce proudly, smiling down at Leslie.

She jumps up and down, eagerly clapping her hands as the straps of her white tank top fall off and reveal more of her lacy red bra. Theo rushes over from the kitchen to pull her straps up protectively, then attempts to pull the front of the tank up to cover the bra entirely. Unfortunately for him, her tank top isn't long enough for that, so he gives up and scowls at her broodingly. *Leslie is going to have her hands full with that one.*

Leslie brushes him away and shouts up at me, "I can nearly see your kooo-ca, you saucy minx!"

My eyes turn wide and my hand immediately goes down to pull the hem of my lace dress down. It's incredibly tight and doesn't budge an inch. I feel warmth traveling up the back of my calf and turn to see Ethan's hand caressing it.

I reach out to swat his hand away and see Liam in front of me. He places his hands on my waist and lifts me down off the chair in one swift motion.

"I'm telling you, Ethan," Liam glares at him, accusingly.

"Relax, mate! We're all here to have a good time, get a little wild. Right love?" Ethan winks over at me.

Before Liam can reply, I say, "Hands-free fun is fun too!"

"No such thing," Ethan drawls out.

"If you're so in love with your hands, use them on yourself," I say. Leslie falls into a fit of giggles beside me.

Ethan doesn't look amused and Liam looks like he's about to hulk out on Ethan any second.

"Aw, Fin! Look at these callouses!" Leslie says, grabbing Ethan's large hand. "His unit is probably bruised and bloodied from overuse of his hands! Poor buddy, you haven't had any in a long time have you? No wonder he was touching your leg, Finny! He probably mistook it for that whopper of a dick he's packing!" She giggles again and makes a jerking motion with her hand.

I explode into laughter and watch her nudge Ethan with her hip in a playful manner. Ethan's hard glare doesn't last long before he smiles back at her. She obviously stroked his ego just enough to not anger him. Plus, Leslie has the best laugh. It's infectious, so when she laughs hard like that it's impossible to stay mad at her.

She grabs Ethan's arm and leads him into the dining room to join James and the others.

"Was the chair-announcement really necessary?" Liam murmurs into my ear.

"Just trying to get people to notice me," I reply.

He looks down at my mouth and says, "It's impossible to *not* notice you."

I look back at him and squint my eyes. I don't know if it's the strong punch or if I'm just feeling extra brazen as a tart, but I decide to say exactly what's on my mind.

"If I didn't know any better, I'd say you're behaving how a jealous boyfriend behaves. Last I checked, I was single." I feel a pang of guilt saying that out loud. I think it's the first time I've said the word *single* since college.

Liam gives me a hard look and I nearly regret my words. But it's true, he's acting too domineering given that this is only the third time we've hung out. Frank rushes past us into the dining room with an arm full of beers and clean plastic cups, "Fucking straight! I'm going to whip you Americans. You'll regret ever teaching me how to play this insidious game!"

Liam glances over to Frank and sighs, tilting his head thoughtfully at me.

"Did I say or do something to upset you?" he asks.

I consider his question. He really didn't do anything bad. But just the way he's looking at me and shielding me from Ethan feels way too familiar. It feels like…Brody. A twinge of pain hits me as I remember how protective Brody was in the early days of our relationship. There were several college parties that ended in me dragging Brody out by his arm before he started a fight with someone who got too fresh with me. The whole Jake fiasco turned Brody into a bit of a caveman. It took months of convincing and placating to get him to relax and trust me more.

"I'm just not used to other people protecting me I guess," I offer him. It's a cryptic reply and I can tell he knows it, but he chooses not to press it further and moves away from me into the dining room.

I do my best to ignore Liam's watchful stare as I sidle up over to Leslie. We decide to separate ourselves and be team captains. Frank appears to be the only one who knows how to play Tippy Cup, so we explain the rules. There are two teams that stand across from each other on either side of the table. You fill your cup with a small amount of beer, usually no more than a swallow or two. When the game starts, the first two people of each team chug their beer, set their cup down on the edge of the table and tip it with their fingers until it lands on the topside of the cup. As soon as you successfully tip and land your cup, the next person on your team goes. First team to finish wins and you start the whole process over again.

Leslie picks Liam as her teammate first. I'm thankful for that and decide to pick Mitch for my team. I feel like we have a bond ever since the lemon-drink day, and he seems eager to play…well, as eager as Mitch ever could be. I also get Ethan, Theo, and one of Leslie's coworkers from Nikon. There's an even sixteen of us to play, which is good because no one has to sit out a round. Thank goodness Frank's dining room table is large, though it's so beautiful and I feel bad for a second about the amount of beer that's about to get dumped on it. Frank doesn't seem to mind though, he's just sulking because he was picked last for my team.

"It's like bloody primary school all over again," he looks down sadly.

"We just saved the best for last, Frank," I coo into his ear.

"I bloody well hated primary school. I never quite fit in, you know?"

He looks at me with a surprised look on his face and it's all I can do to conceal my smirk. He's asking me this question so seriously while wearing a two-foot tall Pope hat.

"How about you be our team leader and go first?" I suggest, which seems to perk him up some. We move all the chairs away from the table. Leslie and Frank are at the heads of their sides of the table, then it's me across from Liam, Mitch across James, Ethan is facing off against Julie, then Theo is up against one of Frank's friends he knows from school. Then Leslie's two other work friends are facing off against each other. Rounding out the last two pairs are Julie and Mitch's three friends, whom I haven't been introduced to yet, against another one of Frank's friends. I haven't been formally introduced to everyone but that doesn't matter. Tippy Cup always helps make fast friends.

Liam shoots me a wink as a peace offering, and I smirk back at him. He smirks back and raises his eyebrows quickly at me. I shake my head at him and give him an *all business* look to indicate we need to focus on the game, not each other. He licks his lips thoughtfully as he eyeballs mine. *Damn him.*

"Alright! Everybody know the rules?" Leslie yells loud enough to be heard all the way down the table.

Suddenly, Mitch and Ethan switch places and Ethan's arm brushes up against mine as he readies himself to face off against James. I look over and see Julie mouthing off to Mitch that she's going to beat him. Liam eyes Ethan cautiously.

"Ready. Set. Tip!" I shout. Frank and Leslie are off. Frank's hat immediately drops off the back of his head as he tips his drink back, revealing sweaty orange hair. *God, Frank is funny even when he's not saying anything.*

"Stuff it!" he shouts, as he readies his now empty cup to be tipped. He misses and looks over to Leslie who can't seem to get hers to land right either. *Shameful, Leslie. Just shameful.* She must be out of practice.

Frank nails his landing and I snatch my drink up and gulp the entire contents down in one swoop. I calmly place my cup on the table and peg the landing on the first try. Ethan whoops loudly and takes his turn. I look over to Liam and see that he's struggling. A lot. I smile as his expression turns serious while he tries to concentrate. Leslie is coaching him from the side but he just can't seem to figure it out. Finally, he lands his cup and I look over to see that Ethan and Mitch have already successfully tipped their cups and Theo is up. He fumbles a few times and then gets it, and our final teammate, Leslie's coworker, begins chugging her drink.

Julie seems to be struggling on the other side of the table and I can't help but laugh fondly at her. Her slanted eyes are squinting so hard in concentration; Mitch seems to be enjoying Julie's struggles as well. I glance back to see Liam's eyes locked on me. My smile drops; his look is intense and it sends flutters down my belly.

Suddenly, cheering erupts from my side of the table and Ethan swerves around and high fives me. Frank sings *We Are the Champions* while I laugh so hard at Julie who's still trying to land her cup.

"I don't know what I'm doing wrong!" she cries. Mitch heads over to give her some pointers.

"Okay then! Now Liam and Finley will start it off and Frank and I will finish," Leslie announces.

Everyone goes back to their places and readies their cups with beer.

I lock eyes with Liam.

"Ready. Set. Tip!" I shout, and Liam's and my death stare breaks when we both tip our cups back into our mouths. *God, he looks hot drinking his beer.*

I land mine on the first tip again and Liam gets his on the

second. James struggles for a bit but then Julie is up. She cheers loudly as she lands hers on the first tip. Theo struggles for much too long, and Leslie's team wins.

We all play nicely for another few rounds and it becomes obvious everyone is feeling the effects of all the beer chugging. We decide to do one more round and then call it quits for awhile.

It's down to the end and Ethan and James are the last ones to tip. They both fumble over and over, adding suspense to who will win the final round. When Ethan finally lands his cup, our side bursts into cheers and Ethan turns and scoops me up into a big hug. He lifts me from the ground and I feel my dress sliding up dangerously close to my butt.

Liam appears next to us, grabs my arm and pulls me out of Ethan's embrace. His look is conflicted as he pulls me over off into the living room.

"You need to be careful with Ethan," he says, his voice deep and authoritative.

"Careful of what?" my words slur slightly as they come out and I smile back at Ethan, feeling good.

Liam pulls at the white collar around his neck, "He's my mate but he's a complete wanker."

I look at Liam thoughtfully, my eyes slightly drooping, "I don't need protecting, Liam. I'm not worth it." I slur the last bit.

He looks from my eyes to my mouth like he's torn with what to say next.

"Why would you ever say that?" he asks, looking at me seriously.

Why does he look so serious? Doesn't he know I just want to have fun? How can he be so serious after drinking so much?

I pat his shoulder reassuringly, "It's the truth, Liam. Get out while you can."

I turn to the dining room and shout, "Let's dance!"

Everyone cheers and breaks away from the table. Some go into the kitchen for more drinks and others head into the living room toward the music dock to pick out more suitable dancing music.

Liam grabs my arm roughly, "Seriously! What the hell, Finley?" he asks, looking for answers. Answers I don't have. Answers I don't want to give him because it's hard enough saying it in my head, let alone out loud.

"Is there a problem here, mate?" Frank interjects, eyeing Liam seriously.

Liam pushes his hand through his hair.

"Course not, Frank. I'm just trying to understand Finley a bit better," he says.

Frank looks to me, then to Liam.

"I think Finley just wants to have a bit of fun tonight. So let's do that, shall we? C'mon lad, you can dance with me!"

Frank leads Liam into the living room and Leslie comes up behind me with two cups of punch and hands one over to me.

"Come on! I need you to dance with me and keep me away from Theo!" I laugh, and let her drag me into the living room.

CHAPTER SEVENTEEN

Leslie drags me to the middle of the dance floor and I lose myself in the music for awhile, willing my brain to not think about the vague comment I'd made to Liam. I don't know why the hell I even said it. *Damn Tippy Cup, it really sneaks up on you.*

A few songs later, I feel a pair of hands slide around my hips and cinch me up close. I turn my head, grateful to see Liam, and not Ethan. I'm done with the drama. My mom told me to give Liam a chance and all I've been doing is pissing him off and testing him. Let's cut the crap and see where this goes.

I turn around and curl my hands up behind his neck and move with his body. He leans his lips into my neck, kisses me softly, and blows air down my neck and chest. I squirm with the feverish feeling his lips are causing on me.

We continue dancing for a few more songs. Liam ditches his jacket and vicar collar; he looks incredibly handsome in his black shirt and jeans. I rub my hands along his chest and belly. His body feels different than Brody's. Firmer, more rigid. Brody was physically fit but he wasn't quite as sculpted as Liam.

Liam moves his lips up to my ear and whispers, "I want to see your room."

I smile at him, "Okay, *Captain Obvious*."

His chest rumbles as he laughs.

"I just want to see if you're all unpacked."

I nod and look over to Leslie who is dancing awkwardly with Frank and attempting to stay as far away from Theo as possible. Theo is sitting on the arm of the couch, drinking and brooding by himself. Ethan and James have latched onto Leslie's coworkers and Mitch and Julie are full-on making out on the dance floor.

I motion to Leslie that I'm taking Liam upstairs and she eyes me cautiously. I nod that I'll be okay and am grateful we can have a silent conversation around a room full of people.

I lead Liam up the wooden staircase and feel his finger brush the hem of my skirt as we stop on the second floor landing. I swerve around and eye him cautiously.

"Looks like it's you I should be watching out for, not Ethan," I say, haughtily.

He shakes his head side to side, "This dress," he says, placing a hand on my side and slowly moving it down to my thigh. "It's way too short."

"Too short for who?" I ask.

"For your father's approval, I guess. I don't know. It's just been hard to watch you walk around in this all evening with everyone's eyes on you. I should give you a proper talking to," he says, laughing cheekily as he presses me against the wall.

"A talking to, huh?" I reply. What a lame reply, I can't think of anything better though when he's looking at me this way.

He looks down at my lips for a few seconds, then up to my eyes as he leans in and kisses me. My hands are splayed against the wall beside me as his tongue enters my mouth. He strokes his hands down my arms and laces them with my fingers.

This kiss feels a little different than the last one. It's a good kiss—a steamy kiss. I can tell he's using the same technique as he did in the skate park, but for whatever reason, all I'm thinking about is Brody kissing Olivia.

I tilt my head and kiss him back harder, desperately willing away thoughts of Brody and Olivia. Liam takes my response positively and presses his body up against mine, his hands roving upward to the sides of my breasts. He feels so good. He feels so strong. But most of all, he feels so different.

I break the kiss quickly and look away, trying to get a grip on my emotions.

Liam turns my face toward him.

"Did I do something wrong?"

I compose myself and shake my head.

"Of course not!" I say, a bit too brightly.

"I feel like you're somewhere else," he says, softly, looking down at my chest, but staying close to me.

"Let's move this upstairs," I reply without addressing his concern.

He looks sad, but follows me up the next flight anyway. When we come into my room, I walk over to the window to look outside, trying to get as close to a breath of fresh air as I can. Liam walks around my room, inspecting the very few possessions I brought. As I look at it from his perspective, it's kind of pathetic, really.

On one wall are my clothes and shoes. On the other wall is my laptop and a few books. Then, near the door where a mirror sits are my makeup and toiletry items.

"Where's all your stuff?" he asks.

"This is it," I reply.

"No photos of your family…your friends?"

"I guess not."

"It looks to me like you're not planning to stay," he says.

I consider this thought and realize it does appear that way. But that's most definitely not the case.

I sigh, "I don't know what I'm planning anymore."

I kick my shoes off and make my way over to my tiny twin mattress. I grab the blanket and cover my legs because this dress was most definitely not made for sitting.

Liam finishes his perusal of my room and comes over and sits down beside me.

"What was with that comment downstairs?" he asks.

"What comment?"

"When you said you aren't worth it."

He looks genuinely concerned and I feel terrible about myself for even bringing it up.

"You don't want to know all the crap in my life," I reply.

He reaches over and rubs my hand, playing with my fingers.

"If it involves you, I want to know."

He looks me in the eye and my eyes start to well with tears. A feeling creeps over me I've never felt before. *Shame.* I feel incredibly shameful right now. I'm ashamed of the way I'm lying to Liam. I'm ashamed of how he's looking at me like I'm something special and I know I'm not. I'm ashamed of this huge lie I'm living. Just over a month ago, my life was consumed with baby making. How does someone go from trying to have a baby with the love of their life, to getting drunk at parties and making out with guys in stairwells?

I pull my hands away from his and look down to fumble with the purple comforter on my lap. Tears slip from my eyes and fall down onto the blanket.

Liam clears his throat, "Finley. I'm a fixer. Remember?"

He grabs my hands and I look back up to him.

"I fancy you, Finley. I fancy you a lot. You're outspoken and funny and smart. I can see this incredibly quiet depth in your eyes that you're not showing to anyone and I am wracking my brain trying to figure out why."

We both look down at our entwined hands.

"The fact that you're knockout gorgeous is like fuel to an open fire."

I laugh self-deprecatingly and exhale a large sigh.

"But I get a strong feeling you're not finished unpacking."

I look up at him and his eyes drop fleetingly to my mouth. Damn it, why can't I just do this? Why can't I just dive in with Liam and forget about Brody, and babies, and life?

"I really want to be done," I speak, finally. "Everyone else seems to be all unpacked." I offer him this tidbit because I don't know what else to say right now.

"Does the other person who has supposedly unpacked know how you feel?" he asks.

I shake my head no.

He leans closely into me, forcing me to look him straight in the eyes.

"There is no man on the planet that would willingly unpack you, Finley. If he has, then he's either an idiot, or he's operating under false assumptions."

He lets out a frustrated growl. "Judging by your comments downstairs, my guess is, this bloke doesn't know all the facts and you are lying to yourself about something big."

I look at him and wonder if he's figured out what we're even talking about.

With that, he jumps up out of the bed and stretches.

"I'm being way too kind right now. If we stay here much longer I'll convince you I'm the only man on the planet that deserves you."

I look up at him and smile.

"If there's a proper bloke out there that's captured your heart, he's a lucky bugger; I think you're intelligent enough to know who's best for you."

He reaches his hand out to help me to my feet.

"Let's go back downstairs where there's booze and other things to look at besides your gorgeous red lips," he smiles adorably at me and kisses my cheek.

I half smile at him.

"I can't make you any promises, Finley. It seems like space is what you need right now, but I'm only human."

I look back at him, slightly perplexed.

"Just because we're mates doesn't mean I won't flirt."

I shake my head at him.

"And kiss you," he adds. "Maybe consider us…friendly friends." He tweaks his eyebrows at me and leads me by my hand out of my bedroom.

CHAPTER EIGHTEEN

Liam and I spend the rest of the night dancing and flirting shamelessly. It's fun and feels a lot more carefree and less intense than the feelings earlier in the night. I appreciate that about him because my mind is on overload and I can't handle any more thoughts right now. He even seems to back off the possessive attitude toward Ethan, and Ethan takes full advantage of it as he twirls me on the dance floor.

When I walk Liam to the door and step outside to see him off, I'm surprised when he grabs me and pulls me into the little patio area.

He presses me up against the ivy-covered side of the house and whispers into my ear, "Don't expect me to run off because you have baggage, Finley. My head wants to be a good friend but my heart has other ideas." When he captures my mouth with his lips, instant zingers shoot from my head all the way down to my feet.

Just when I press into him wanting more, he breaks the kiss and steps back with an incredibly sexy and naughty smile.

"Dream about me," he says, and walks away.

I'm left shaking my head at his tease when Frank comes bounding out of the house.

"Finley!" he shouts.

I compose myself and step out from the patio area.

"Yes, Frank and Beans?"

"Ah, Fin-Bin. My pet. We're having a roommate dance off on the coffee table. Join us you sexy leggy brunette, you!"

He grabs my hand and hauls me inside and I laugh at his exuberance.

***

Waking up the next day, I stir restlessly in bed thinking about Liam and Brody. What a mess I've put myself smack dab in the middle of. Here is Liam, right in front of me, all sexy, British, and perfect, but I can't stop aching for Brody and the comfort of a man who gets me so perfectly. I've decided to close the door on the idea of Brody and me together because I can't give him everything he deserves, so why am I struggling to dive in with Liam?

Regardless, I really need to stop moping around about boys and start being productive again. I have a stack of press releases Val is waiting on, and my deadline is fast approaching.

I stretch and check the time, shaking my head to see it's already noon. My internal clock is so screwed up here. I used to consider myself a morning person back in the states, but here I can't ever seem to get an early start on the day.

I head into the bathroom to shower. Thankfully, I'm not feeling too hung over. Once Liam and I went back downstairs last night, I quit drinking and chose to just dance my ass off. It felt good. It was probably the most exercise I've had since moving out here.

I look at myself in the mirror and am grateful Leslie helped me take off all my makeup before bed. It was a thick pain in the ass, but we had fun and laughed through the process anyway. My dress is in a rumpled heap on the floor and I make a mental note to ask Frank if I can keep it. I don't know if I'll ever wear it again because it's way too short, but it's also too beautiful to just toss aside.

I take a scalding hot shower, chastising myself as thoughts of Liam and Brody keep creeping in my head. I know I need to do something about my predicament, but good Lord, can my brain just shut up long enough for me to take a shower? I dress in my comfy yoga pants and another college hoodie and head downstairs to get some coffee so I can get a few hours of work done.

Julie is sitting in the kitchen nook as I come walking by.

"Damn, we should have cleaned up last night while we were drunk," I say, taking in the disaster of cups, sticky liquid, snacks, and beer cans all over. It looks so much worse in the light of day.

"Frank has a cleaning crew coming in an hour. Don't worry about it," she says with a rasp in her voice. Julie looks hung over.

"Where does Frank get all his money?" I ask, surprised I've never wondered this before. He's always buying drinks and food for the house and never accepts my offers of compensation.

"His parents are loaded. He's practically a socialite, except he doesn't hang out with anybody popular so the paps don't give a toss about him. He says he prefers to hang with peasants like us," she lifts her mug to me and takes another sip, her head resting on her propped hand.

That makes sense why Frank has never told me what he does for a living. I've asked him a couple times now and both times he always just replies with, "A little of this. A little of that." One time he said sexual favors but I knew him well enough by then to know he was joking. I get the sense Frank doesn't have all of us as roommates because he needs to. I'm sure his parents cover all of the expenses of the house. It's probably even paid off. So we're definitely not around for the extra cash. I smile as I think back to the five tapered red candles he set out last night on the dining room table for all of us.

"What are you up to today?" I ask Julie once I've made two coffees.

"Work. I feel knackered so I'm positively dreading it."

I nod kindly, thankful I'm not a waitress like Julie. That would be a hard job to do with a hangover. I make my way past her and back out into the foyer.

"Hey," she calls before I hit the steps.

"Nobody ever explained Mitch's toast to me last night. I'm gutted because I still don't get it."

I laugh back at her and head up the stairs leaving her to continue pondering.

I stop on the second floor and knock softly on Leslie's bedroom door.

"Come in!" she replies, brightly.

"Hey," I say, walking in and curling up on her antique-style daybed. She's at her large black desk that has two huge computer screens on top. She appears to be working on some type of design. Whatever she has up on the screen, I can't make any sense of.

"What are you working on?" I ask.

"A freaking strap. It's a strap and I can't get it how I want it. Hey! Is that for me?" she asks, eyeing my second cup of coffee.

I nod and smile, reaching over to hand it to her.

"Finny, you know me so well," she says, looking down and seeing her extremely light coffee. Leslie basically drinks milk with a splash of coffee. I don't understand why she even bothers. I've always preferred mine black because that's how my dad drank his and I figured if he could do it, so could I.

"How are you feeling?" she asks.

"Pretty good. Not hung over at all. I'm glad we quit drinking early last night."

"Me too," she says, taking a sip.

"So, whatever happened with Theo?"

"What do you mean, 'what happened with Theo?'"

"Did you do anything with him?" I ask, blowing on my steamy cup of coffee.

"No! God! I can't even believe I had to be in the same room as him all night last night!" she replies, adjusting her denim vest that she fashionably paired with a humongous pair of sweatpants and a white t-shirt.

"Did he try to talk to you again?"

"Yes, but I told him to get lost. One time, he was waiting for me when I came out of the bathroom!"

"What'd he say?"

"He got all up in my face and said I had some nerve for leaving him stranded on the dance floor after what we shared. God! I'm turning red just thinking about it!"

I laugh as her cheeks turn crimson, matching her auburn hair.

"He said he searched for me for hours!" she starts giggling.

"You're terrible! Why are you laughing at the poor guy?"

"Because I saw him coming by our table once and I ducked and pretended to be messing with my shoe until the coast was clear!" she laughs hard, spinning in her desk chair.

I laugh with her all the while shaking my head and silently chastising her.

"I don't know why you're so embarrassed. You never get embarrassed. It's so unlike you."

She shakes her head like she's having a thought but then appears to think better of it and smiles brightly at me again.

"How are you feeling about everything else?" she asks, eyeing me curiously.

I take a tentative sip of my coffee, mindful not to drink too much and completely scald my tongue.

"I feel like I need to have a conversation," I say, getting really serious.

She nods her head, equally serious, "A conversation."

"A conversation," I reply.

"A conversation with...," she waits for me to fill in the blank.

"Brody," I say, exhaling heavily.

"Woah," she replies, "I'm shocked. After seeing you with Liam last night, I thought Brody might be fading into the background."

I nod my head, "Well, we just...we didn't end things well the last time we spoke and I don't know. I guess I think I need better closure than that." I cringe on that word. Closure. I hate that word. It sounds like a word that belongs in a self-help book, but I'll be damned if that isn't what I need right now.

"Ick. Closure. Sounds terrible," Leslie replies.

"Thanks for the encouragement, Lez," I say back, flatly.

She takes a drink from her mug, "Are you sure your closure doesn't have more to do with Ol' Saggy Tits Oli' than it does Brody?"

"Fair question," I reply. "I'd be lying if I said I wasn't curious how the hell those two found each other and what goes through his mind when he's with her. But overall, the real reason is to hear his voice again. I need to hear it without all that hate and anger."

Leslie gets up from her desk chair and crawls onto the daybed and sits with her legs crossed facing me.

"You need to tell him everything then, Finley," she says, seriously.

I shake my head, "No way. Absolutely not. I can't. I won't."

"Then what are you going to say to him that's any different from the last time you spoke to him?" she asks.

"I don't know. I guess I thought maybe I'd at least tell him where I'm living, what I'm doing. Maybe that will help him not be so angry with me anymore. It's a little piece of his puzzle that probably feels really incomplete. If he knows I'm here and I'm okay, then maybe we can both move on and I can quit caring about who he's sleeping with...ugh, nope. I'm lying. I will always being grossed out by the idea of him with Olivia. It will bother me forever."

Leslie's face screws up in disgust, "Yeah, she's a nasty granny."

I smile at her, fondly.

"I have to talk to him. I have to hear his voice."

"Well, good luck to you," she clinks her coffee mug with mine.

"I can hear your voices in there." Frank's voice muffles from the other side of Leslie's door.

"What the hell are you doing, Frank?" Leslie replies.

"I can hear your voices and it sounds like you're having a cuddle."

Leslie and I look at each other, biting our lips, desperately trying to contain our giggles.

"Why are you sitting outside my door eavesdropping like a creeper?" Leslie asks with a disgusted but happy look on her face.

Silence.

"Get in here Carrot Top!" I shout. Leslie bursts into laughter and Frank swings the door wide open.

"Carrot Top?" he replies, his jaw dropped. "Oh God, I think that's the worst thing you've ever said to me, Finley!"

"Get on this bed right now, Frank!" Leslie demands.

Frank hangs his head and makes his way over to the bed and squeezes tightly in between us.

"Seriously guys…do I look like Carrot Top?"

Leslie and I giggle and hug him affectionately.

CHAPTER NINETEEN

It takes a couple of days for me to muster up the courage to call Brody. I have a ton of work to get done for Val and I need the freelance money. I've been in London three weeks now and only have a week of paid vacation time left, so I'm taking all the work I can get to bank a little safety net for when the paychecks stop. I hesitate to look for another job because I haven't even begun to apply for an official work visa. Val has a ton of work for me though, and the freelance money is actually better than what I made as a salary worker under her.

I tell myself I'll deal with Brody when I finish my list of projects. Liam continues to text me several times a day. Nothing too serious, mostly it's just funny stuff he sees around town. He likes to insert his face into random things he comes across. Like today, he sent me a picture of himself looking confused; behind him was a man with an incredibly long mullet. It makes me smile and I appreciate his friendship. He keeps hinting at seeing me again but I tell him I'm busy with work, which is mostly true.

As I close my laptop, I decide to stop putting it off and call Brody already. I need to get this off my chest. I'll feel better afterward. I hope. I look out my rounded windows and see a slew of skateboarders all over the skate ramps. There must be some kind of event there today because this is a way bigger crowd than normal.

My fingers are trembling as I press Send on Brody's contact number. It rings five times and I begin to feel depressed that he's not going to pick up.

"Hello?" his deep voice answers.

"Hey, um, hi, uh, Brody," I bite my lip to stop myself from continuing on the same inane path. I take a deep breath and say, "How are you?" Real smooth, Finley.

"Um, I'm fine. How are you?" he asks, with an edge of caution in his voice.

"I'm doing well, I was just calling to see how things were going and everything."

"Are we doing that now?" he asks.

"I don't know. I thought we could but I guess that's up to you," I reply.

"So what, you think you can just call now and we'll chat like old friends?"

I sigh into the phone, "Alright, fine Brody. Don't let me beat around the bush or anything."

"Well what do you expect, Finley?"

Oh! Just the way he says my name brings back hundreds of

wonderful memories. Happy memories, intimate memories, carefree memories, emotional memories. How can I ask him to just say my name again over and over and over so I can bathe in the beauty of his voice and memories of simpler times?

I clear my throat, "I didn't like where we ended things last time we spoke. I feel…remorseful. I regret how I handled things."

"You think?" he barks, slightly.

"I feel like I need to be more honest with you and then maybe we can both get a bit more closure after we air everything out."

"Closure? That doesn't sound like the Finley I was in love with for over five years. The Finley I knew would have never used the word closure."

I roll my eyes even though I know he can't see me.

"I know its cliché, Brody. I'm just trying to be honest here," I say.

"Okay, then. Let's hear it."

"I'm in London," I say, quickly, before I lose my nerve.

"Like, England?" he asks.

"Yes."

"For what?" he questions.

That's a fair question.

"I'm living with Leslie. She lives in a house out here in South London. I'm doing freelance for Val while I'm here."

"How long are you staying there?" he asks.

"Indefinitely," I reply.

"What does that mean?" he asks.

"It means I have no plans to go back to Kansas or Missouri or anywhere near the Midwest again."

Silence falls between us.

"Brody?"

"Yeah, I'm here," he replies.

"I just felt like it was time I tell you where I was because I know that was a big reason why you were so angry with me when we broke up…all the secrecy about where I was going. I know that's why you went to see Cadence and George that night. You were angry; you had a right to be. At the time, I thought it was for the best, it would give us a cleaner break, but now I feel like I at least owe it to you to tell you where I'm at."

"A cleaner break," he repeats my words back to me. "And why are you telling me now, exactly?"

"I…" I stumble on what I want to say next, "I guess I just thought you'd want to know."

"I think you thought wrong, Finley," he says, with a definitive huff in his tone.

"I just thought…" I start, but he interrupts.

"You just thought you would call me and tell me you're living in London, another freaking country, thousands of miles away from me, and I would feel, what? Relief?" he asks.

"I guess I…" I don't get to finish.

"You thought I would feel relieved to hear you had to move to another continent to get away from me? You think that makes me feel like anything more than the piranha scum you can't get off the bottom of your shoe?"

"Brody! No."

"Do you think I'll feel closure knowing I am the reason you no longer live driving distance away from your family? Your nieces? Your friends?"

"It's not your fault, Brody. You're not the cause," I start, but I don't know how to finish.

"How is it possible you think you can call me and tell me you're in London, England and I'm just going to say thank you and end this phone call on a happy note?" he seethes.

I'm tired of him acting all wounded like he cares.

"I thought perhaps you were ready for some closure since it appears you've already moved on!" I snap at him.

"What do you mean, Finley?" he says his words slowly, with emphasis.

"Olivia, Brody!" I bark at him, "I saw the pictures of you and Olivia all over *Facebook*. You guys look great, playing happy family together."

"I thought you canceled your *Facebook* account, Finley," he replies, adding a long F at the beginning of my name.

"Screw you, Brody. Don't sit there acting all angry and wounded that I'm in London when you're with the one girl I hate from college. Olivia, Brody? Really? You couldn't find anyone else to climb on top of?" I ask, knowing I sound nasty right now but unable to help it.

"At least she's in my continent!" he booms, into the phone.

"Glad to see you've set your standards nice and high!" I reply, my voice getting louder at the end.

I look down and watch the skate ramps. A group is standing off to the side, laughing, appearing to be having a great time while I'm up here in my circular prison cell.

"My standards couldn't be any higher, Finley. You sort of ruined that for me," he says, sounding quieter and more reserved now.

I shake my head not knowing how to interpret that comment. Does he mean Olivia is better than me? So much for closure.

"Well, I wanted to tell you where I'm living and how I'm doing. Now I've told you, I would like to hear how you're doing, but I pretty much already know. Take care, Brody. Have a nice life with Olivia. I'm glad I met you." I hang up, squeezing my phone tightly in my hand in frustration.

I don't know why I added that last bit. Laying on the guilt, I suppose. It's hard to stay disconnected from him and not be jealous and possessive when I know I need to be. I'm the one who ended things. I remind myself of everything I can't give him but I'm seething at the idea that Olivia could be the one who does. Picturing her with a round, pregnant belly, and his hands on her—breaks me.

I collapse onto my bed and cry hard. Seriously, God! Why? Why can't I give Brody a baby? Why can't I be a woman like all other women and do this for him? I want to give him this! But I can't and it's killing me inside. Even the idea of Liam doesn't cheer me up because he's just another guy I'll have to reveal my barren secret to down the road. It's terrible, and it's heart-wrenching, and I can't fix it. This is my lot in life; I need to get the hell over it.

***

CHAPTER TWENTY

Val assigns me a new client who's actually from the UK, so she's really quite happy about my current location and the fact she can send me over to the client without sloughing it off to the sister company. She must be taking advantage of my current location because she's never had an international client before. I'm just happy she's still okay with me not coming back to the States and hasn't pressured me about returning. Not to mention, I'm extremely grateful for the distraction.

I dress sharply in the one formal business suit I packed and hop on the tube, London's version of a subway, for my meeting. Val wants me to meet them personally and get a feel for how their business operates and a hands-on feel of their product. The client is a family-run business that specializes in Christian inspired jewelry. *Faith's Miracle Jewelry* is the name of their jewelry line. They want Val's company to take over their marketing in the U.S. I'm to meet with the family and report back.

Frank and Leslie help me figure out what train I need to take because the business is located on the outskirts of London. I enjoy the beautiful country scenery on the thirty-minute train ride while adding more to the list of questions Val prepared for me.

When I get off the train in Esher, and make my way out toward the parking lot, I see a white-haired elderly man with a big thick gray mustache holding up a sign with my name on it. I smile brightly at him and offer my hand.

"Ah, Finley! Lovely to meet you lass, I'm Mr. Adamson. Right this way to the car," he greets, with a kind smile.

Adamson is the name of the family that runs the business. I'm surprised to see he didn't just send a driver rather than pick me up himself, but he doesn't seem the least bit put out. He directs me over to his vehicle and opens the passenger side door for me to get in.

"Mr. Adamson, thank you for picking me up, really," I say, trying to start conversation.

"Of course, dear. Of course! We're excited to have some American blood in our house," he replies, while navigating us out of the parking lot. "My wife has been polishing the jewelry-line all morning. It's been her dream to have the jewelry go international."

I'm surprised to hear she's polishing it herself and they don't have staff for that. Val indicated to me that this company started off small but are huge in England now. They are able to outsource all the manufacturing so they can focus solely on the sales side of the business.

"I'm really excited to see it, Sir," I say, smiling at him again. He seems so jolly with his big mustache and crinkly eyes. I hope Mrs. Adamson is this approachable.

We drive in comfortable silence through the hilly countryside of England and I make a note to ask Leslie and Frank if we can take a vacation to the country sometime because it's like a whole other world out here. Huge rolling hills of sheep and pastures, and little old cottages dropped sporadically throughout. It's simply beautiful.

"How long have you been in London, love?" Mr. Adamson asks while reaching into his suit-coat pocket, silently offering me a butterscotch candy.

"Almost a month," I reply, taking the candy, unwrapping it, and popping it into my mouth.

He nods his head appreciatively while popping one in his mouth, too.

"Do you miss home a lot?" he asks, tucking the treat into his cheek to make it easier to talk.

"Yes, parts," I answer. "But it's incredibly beautiful out here, I'm happy to be experiencing some new areas."

We pull up to a beautiful little brick house with several peaks. An older woman with long white hair is standing in front of the house waiting to greet us.

"Mrs. Adamson, I presume?" I ask as the woman rushes up to shake my hand and pulls me in and kisses me on both cheeks.

"Is it Finley, love?" she asks.

"Yes, that's me!" I reply.

Mr. Adamson comes around the car and they usher me up the sidewalk, pointing out the yard and all the landscaping they work on every year. Mrs. Adamson is most definitely just as friendly as Mr. Adamson. I sort of love that they don't ask me to call them by their first names. It might seem more formal this way, but it suits them. Watching them both talk animatedly about their yard is endearing, and I find myself smiling fondly at them.

A BROKEN US

When we walk into their house, they offer me some tea. I haven't quite jumped on the British tea craze yet, but I accept to be polite. Mr. Adamson heads to the kitchen to pour the tea and Mrs. Adamson leads me into the dining room. A short, round African woman is adjusting the jewelry splayed all over the table.

She looks up when we come in and walks over to introduce herself.

"Hi there, I'm Sheila Adamson. So nice to meet you," she shakes my hand and gives me two quick kisses just like Mrs. Adamson. "We're really excited to have you here."

I smile back at her and can't help but wonder how she's related because of the obvious difference in skin tones. She looks like the right age to be their daughter, so she could be adopted. Or maybe the Adamsons have a son, and this is his wife?

She gestures for me to sit down and I pull my binder out of my satchel and ready all my meeting points and supplies. I eye the jewelry thoughtfully.

Mr. Adamson comes in with four teas and we settle ourselves around the table. We make small talk for a while. They ask about my journey out to the country, how I like London, and where I'm from in the States. I can tell I'm going to get along really well with these clients. They all seem like very kind people; I'm so pleased to have something to take my mind off all my personal issues.

"I'd like to start," Mrs. Adamson says, pushing her white hair off of her shoulders and leaning her arms on the table. She's seated directly across from me and squints her large grey eyes at me.

"May I ask if you have any children, Finley? I know it's a personal question, but it would help me to know if you had any children before I tell you about our jewelry line we are very passionate about."

I'm taken aback by this question, but I remain composed and respect her no-nonsense approach.

"No, no children," I smile back at her.

"Okay then, that's okay. Here's the deal. This jewelry line was something I started forty years ago because I was hurting and needed an outlet for my pain. I'm going to get very deep with you for a moment, Finley. I hope that's okay."

"Please do," I offer.

"I had a miscarriage when I was thirty years old. I wasn't very far along in my pregnancy and miscarriages back then didn't appear to be that big of a deal. Everybody just swept them under the rug and didn't talk about them. But, as you may be able to tell by first impression, I'm a bit of a talker. I wanted to talk about the baby I lost. I wanted to memorialize the baby I lost. Grieve the baby I lost. Because that's what it was, Finley, a baby."

My face turns serious and I nod, listening to everything she's saying. I'm fighting an internal battle with myself not to tear up because it would be completely unprofessional, but I can feel my emotions bubbling inside of me.

"Nobody wanted to talk to me about it or even acknowledge that this little babe, who had changed my life so dramatically, even existed! But I wanted to remember, Finley. I wanted to remember my baby like he or she was alive. So I made myself a necklace."

She fumbles under her shirt and pulls out a very primitive looking piece of jewelry. It isn't anything special but it has an interesting quality to it. The chain is silver and looks newer than the piece hanging from it, which is a tarnished cross with thinly looped wires shaped into angel wings fastened behind it. It is beautiful and the way she rubs it shows me that she does that a lot. I look a little closer and engraved on the cross is the word *Faith*.

"Are you a Christian, Finley?" she asks.

"Yes," I reply.

"Good. This piece of jewelry around my neck says the word Faith. That was the name of our little babe and that's what brought us this beautiful little girl sitting next to you," she says, gesturing to Sheila.

I nod with a small smile over to Sheila and she smiles back, appearing to be very used to hearing this story. The adoration and love I see in Mr. and Mrs. Adamson's eyes makes my eyes well and I can't make them stop.

"Losing that wee babe broke me, Finley. I didn't think I would ever recover. Mr. Adamson here was the one who told me that if we couldn't make a baby ourselves, we'd adopt. Simple as that," she laughed and looked over to him.

"Sheila is our miracle, Finley. She was the driving force behind the start of *Faith's Miracle Jewelry*. We adopted her in Liberia at a time of deep despair. She was only five years old when she came to us. All I wanted to do was cuddle her and all she wanted to do was make jewelry!" She laughs heartily and reaches over to pat Sheila's hand.

I smile at the exchange and two small tears slip down my cheeks. I avoid wiping them for fear of calling attention to myself. Thankfully, Sheila lightens the mood with a loud sigh.

"Now that my mother has told you my life story," she laughs, "We'd love to show you all of our pieces, Finley," Sheila says, standing up and grabbing a piece that was on a necklace stand in the middle of the table.

I clear my throat at the sudden change in conversation but am thankful that Sheila must have picked up on my emotions and is trying to help me out a bit.

Sheila hands me a gorgeous, shiny, brand new, high-end version of what Mrs. Adamson has around her neck. It is stunning; a definite showstopper. All three of them interject while they explain all the detailing in the piece to me, where the products came from, how it was developed, and who designed it. I rapidly take notes. I can feel excitement bubbling for how beautiful the rest must be. They then take turns showing me all the other pieces, explaining the inspiration behind each one. The first piece is the only one related to angels. They call it their memorial piece. The rest are a bit more generic, something-for-every-type-of-Christian jewelry, but equally beautiful. They also have many pieces that aren't Christian inspired at all, just beautiful. I'm excited to see there is something for everyone on the table because it's essential for marketing successfully.

I feverishly finish my notes then begin snapping photos on my phone trying to capture the true essence of this line to report back to Val. Sheila knows the product backward and forward. I can tell she is just as passionate about the jewelry, if not more, than her parents. I am certain this will take off in America, and I am thrilled to be a part of a new and exciting international client for Val.

When we finish going through all the products and selling points for their jewelry, Mr. Adamson tells me that Sheila will be taking me back to the rail station. Mrs. Adamson hugs me goodbye and gives me a kiss on each cheek.

"I like you, Finley. There's something about you that really works here. You tell Val we want you to be our contact at the company. I love Val and I'll talk to her anytime, but I'd like you to be the one handling everything else," she says, looking straight into my eyes while holding onto my arms.

I beam back at her, "Well that's very sweet of you to say. I'll relay the message to Val but I'm not sure how everything will be handled. It's not really up to me."

"I'm sure we can work something out." She hugs me one more time and lets the embrace linger. It feels like she can tell I need it and I don't pull back. I take it and I love it. It feels motherly. It also just feels good to have someone who's so happy and content in their life hold me for a moment, almost like it will seep into me and ease away all my aches and pains.

After our final goodbyes, Sheila and I jump into the car and are back on the winding country roads. I'm smiling broadly out the window, unable to contain the inner light I feel after such a great meeting. The Adamsons made me feel lighter somehow.

"My parents are pretty amazing, aren't they?" Sheila asks, pulling my gaze from the scenery to her beautiful dark-skinned face.

"They are. And so are you. You guys are a remarkable family," I reply.

"I can't even imagine having a better life than I do now. It's where I belong," she says, looking at me with a small smile on her face.

I nod back at her; it seems like a rhetorical statement but I can't help my curiosity.

"What do you mean by that, exactly?" I ask.

She laughs softly, "I've heard that story about how *Faith's Miracle Jewelry* got started loads of times, my mum loves to tell it. But it always takes me back to my childhood before them. Since I was five years old when I was adopted, I do have a few memories of my life before them. They are fuzzy now that I'm nearly forty, but they're there."

I look over to her and try and decipher where she's going with this.

"I just know, deep down, this is where I was always meant to be, and I'm with who I was always supposed to be with. They are my parents. And that jewelry line is my baby…my everything. I'm incredibly passionate about it. I hope you could feel that," she says, looking at me seriously.

"I definitely felt it," I nod.

She smiles again, "Call it God's plan, fate, faith…whatever. But something definitely brought me to them and I'm thankful for that everyday."

I nod, mulling over what she's saying.

"And the jewelry is a great perk," she adds, laughing.

"Jewelry is a sweet perk!" I agree.

Sheila has a great laugh, it's infectious. When we both finish laughing, she says, "They don't do that with everyone you know."

"What's that?"

"I mean, they tell the story of *Faith's Miracle Jewelry*, but not quite like that. They really do like you, Finley."

I smile back at her; it's so easy to smile with this family.

"We're a small family business and we don't let outsiders in…ever. This is a big step for us to expand. Going international has always been my mum's dream. I'm glad we have someone like you to help us in the process. I know you'll always keep our best interests at heart."

"One-hundred percent," I reply, looking at her seriously so she sees my sincerity.

She smiles back at me and looks out at the road again.

When we arrive at the rail station, Sheila gives me a big hug and two kisses. Like mother, like daughter. It's amazing how different they look from each other, but are so incredibly alike. Instead of looking over notes and beginning to organize my proposal for Val, I simply stare out the window and enjoy the scenery on the ride back to London. I truly feel like the Adamsons gave me a glimpse into a world I needed to see. I smile to myself thinking about Sheila's *faith* comment.

The Adamsons look at their daughter, Sheila, as an amazing gift from God. I've never even met someone who was adopted before. I feel ashamed to admit that I am surprised with how deeply she feels for her parents. I always feared an adopted child would want to know who their real mother and father was at some age, but Sheila doesn't seem anything but perfectly content with her parents and *Faith's Miracle Jewelry.*

Sheila even inspired Mr. and Mrs. Adamson to build a business that helps people cope with loss and hang onto their faith when they may be floundering. I can't contain my giggle when I picture Mr. Adamson's face watching his two girls talk excitedly about their jewelry. What a good day. What an amazing family. I consider the idea that I never would have met them if I hadn't come to London.

CHAPTER TWENTY-ONE

After my meeting with the Adamsons, I'm jam-packed with work for the next few days. Val and I have to Skype a lot to work out a marketing strategy. Val seems to have an extra investment in their success, too. I suspect it's because of her history with struggling to conceive a child.

I tell her about the Adamsons wanting me to be their point person indefinitely and she brushes it off since she knows I'm coming back in the next couple months. I still don't have the nerve to tell her my plan, so I let it lie for now. She's more than willing to have me work with them exclusively while I'm still in London. I'm excited at the prospect of going back out to their house and working with them again.

Liam continues to text me and is getting a little disgruntled about my lack of response to hanging out with him. He told me he wasn't going to make it easy on me and he was right. When I finally finish my proposal and email it off to Val, I decide to throw Liam a bone and invite him over for movie night with the roommates. That should be safe enough.

As I'm picking out my clothes for what Frank calls family flick night, I'm torn between dressing for comfort and dressing for Liam. I choose somewhere in between and grab a soft pair of jeggings and a thin white tee. I slip on a bright pink bra, easily seen through the tee, and head downstairs. It's a little provocative, but fashionable looking and comfortable. I've worn this several times before so I don't feel like I'm calling too much attention to myself. Leslie would be the first one to call me out for trying too hard.

I come bounding down the stairs as Frank appears out of the dining room with a bowl of popcorn in hand.

He tosses a few kernels into his mouth and says, "Like your tits in that top."

I laugh and say, "I thought you hated my wobbly bits."

"I do...when they are naked. I can appreciate a good see-through top as long as you have undergarments on."

I finally take in what Frank is wearing and I burst out laughing.

"What the hell do you have on?"

"What the bloody hell is wrong with it?" he barks back at me.

He's standing in a solid red onesie pajama outfit with footies and everything.

I shake my head and watch him head into the living room and burst out laughing again when I read the back.

On the top it says: O.C.D. And then below that: Obsessive Cumming Disorder. He adds a little wiggle to his walk and I run into the kitchen to grab a pop, laughing.

I hear a knock on the front door and run to grab it, but Frank's already there greeting Liam in all his onesie glory.

As Liam comes in the door, Theo steps in right behind him. This should be interesting.

Frank leads them into the living room just as Leslie comes flouncing down the stairs singing loudly, "faaaamily fliiiick niiiiiight." She's attempting unsuccessfully to get really high on the last note and I shoot daggers at her to stop.

She's dressed head to toe in the same PJs as Frank, only hers are cheetah print. I rush over to her and grab her shoulders, roughly facing her toward the living room so I can look at her back before anyone else can. Please don't let them say Obsessive Cuming Disorder on the back. Please don't let them say Obsessive Cuming Disorder on the back! Thank fucking God, the back is blank.

Liam and Theo are looking into the foyer at us where I'm holding Leslie from behind and I feel Leslie's whole body tense as her eyes land on Theo.

She quickly turns in my arms and looks at me with wide eyes. I silently push her back toward the stairs and follow behind her as quickly as I can, but the bitch is fast. Apparently, Theo is faster and comes bounding past me, quickly following right behind Leslie into her bedroom.

"Theo!" I shout, but the door is slammed in my face.

"Liam! Frank!" I shout down the stairs and they both come running up the steps as I press my ear to the door to listen and make sure Leslie is okay.

"Is she okay in there with him?" I bark at Liam accusingly as

Julie and Mitch come out of their bedroom hand in hand.

"Yes! Of course she is!" Liam answers back confused.

"Well, it would have been nice if you would have told me you were bringing him, for God's sake! This is a great way to get uninvited from our house ever again, Liam!" I yell at him, pounding my finger into his chest. I can't help it. Theo just manhandled his way into Leslie's bedroom uninvited and I feel completely helpless right now.

"She's fine, Finley. Theo wouldn't hurt a fly. He's…," he pauses, looking nervous for a moment.

"What?" Frank and I both say in unison.

"He fucking loves her, I think!" Liam says, running his hand through his thick blonde hair on top of his head.

"Someone loves the Lezbo?" Frank says with his jaw slightly dropped.

"She's a lesbian?" Liam asks.

"No!" Frank and I both shout in unison again.

I press my ear up to the door and hear soft murmuring between Leslie and Theo.

"Leslie! Are you okay in there, hon?" I ask, knocking at the same time.

"Umm, uhh…yes!" she yells back through the door. "We'll be down in a minute!"

I breathe a sigh of relief and glare at Liam. Julie, Mitch, and Frank shrug their shoulders and head downstairs.

"I'm sorry!" Liam says, looking at me with puppy dog eyes. "I really didn't think he'd march in like he owns the place."

I shake my head and move past him to head downstairs. He grabs my hand and pulls me backwards into his chest.

"Hey," he breathes into my ear. "I haven't even had a chance to say hello to you yet."

"Hello," I reply lightly, enjoying the feel of his warm breath on my neck. He smells awesome, like a fresh laundry detergent.

I feel his lips gently kissing my shoulder and moving their way up my neck.

"Liam," I shake my head back and forth, feeling a shiver prickle all over my skin.

"Finley," he growls into my neck and nips at my ear.

Goosebumps crawl straight out from the spot he nips me and I break away from his grasp.

"Friends, remember?" I say, holding my hands up defensively toward him.

He scrunches his lips to the side, "I don't like the sound of that."

"I know, I'm sorry, but it is what it is. Let's go downstairs. It's family flick night for goodness' sake."

I start to make my way down the steps and Liam rushes up behind me, throwing his arm around my shoulders playfully. He growls in my ear, nipping at it again. I giggle into his touch and my heart hits the floor as my eyes glance down to the foyer.

Dead in my tracks, I stop. Everything around me blurs as Liam continues his descent and looks up at me, grabbing my hand. When he takes in the frozen expression on my face, I hear him say my name, barely. I can barely hear him because blood is rushing in my head. I can feel my heart beat pulsing in my eyes as I begin to feel faint.

Brody is standing in the foyer with a small suitcase in hand. Brody. In. London. Liam drops my hand and turns to look at what I'm looking at. I hear Leslie and Theo come down the steps behind me. They stop beside me when they see me frozen in place. Leslie gasps as she sees Brody.

A steely expression smears over Brody's face and I see the muscle in his jaw tick rapidly. Even in his obvious anger, he looks incredible. His brown curly hair is longer than I've ever seen it and I love it. My hands twitch instinctively, imagining what it feels like between my fingers. He has a thin five o'clock shadow, likely from a long flight. Holy shit. Brody is in London.

"Finley?" Liam says my name again and I can hear him a little better this time. "You alright?" he says to me, coming up to stand just one step below me.

"Yeah Finley," Brody's voice cuts through the foyer loudly and authoritatively. "Are you alright?"

He smiles, meanly. I've never seen such a mean and nasty smile before. I get a nervous feeling at his tone. Liam turns his head and looks down at Brody and I can feel tension building in his shoulders.

My eyes fill with tears at the realization of Brody being here in London.

"What are you doing here?" I ask Brody, unable to move from the step I'm on.

"I wish I fucking knew," he spits out, shaking his head. He turns to walk out the door.

"Brody!" I cry out, but he doesn't turn around. He stomps out the door, slamming it closed behind him.

I rush down the stairs but Liam grabs my hand.

"Let me go, Liam!" I cry urgently.

"I just want to make sure you're okay, Finley," Liam says with desperation in his eyes.

"I'll be fine. I'll be okay. Just let me go."

He releases me and I ignore Leslie calling my name behind me. All I care about right now is Brody and getting to him before he leaves. Seeing Brody again awakens all the old feelings that have always been there for him. I don't care about being barren or not having an us baby. I care about Brody. As I sprint through the foyer, images of Brody and I flash through my brain. Images of happiness, laughter, lightness, us.

"Brody!" I screech as I burst out the front door, my voice cracking with emotion.

I run down the outside steps and see Brody crossing the street toward the skate park.

"Brody!" I shout his name again and see him tense and stop on the corner right by a set of bleachers.

Traffic is zooming down the road; I begin to run into the street but stop quickly as a car honks.

"Finley! Be careful!" Brody shouts out.

Oh my God, his voice, Brody's voice. It sounds like Brody again. Loving. Protecting. Us. I need to get to him. I need to touch him. I dance on my feet, waiting for a clearing in traffic, glancing at him as he watches me. My eyes fill with tears as it pains me to be so near him and not be able to touch him.

His steely expression softens as he watches me. Finally, there's a gap in the traffic and I sprint across the road as fast as humanly possible. Without slowing down, I run directly into his arms, smashing into his soft familiar chest.

His arms instinctively wrap around me and hold me off the ground.

"Brody," I cry his name this time, relishing in this moment of him being here in London and having my arms around him again. I slide my face along his rough cheek so I'm face to face with him. I blink quickly, making sure he's actually here right now. Without waiting for permission I connect our lips and kiss him with all the ferocity I can muster.

I kiss him and open my heart up, hoping he can feel and understand just how much I've missed him and how wrong I've been for breaking us. His grip around my back tightens and his long arms nearly wrap around me twice as he squeezes me as close to him as he can.

I release my hands from behind his neck and bring them to squeeze his cheeks while reverently rubbing my thumb over the stubble. Brody is kissing me back. He's kissing me back hard. Nobody kisses like Brody. Nobody. How could I ever think I wanted to kiss another man ever again? He brings his hand up to my face and runs all four fingers from my forehead down to my jaw. When that doesn't satisfy him enough, he breaks the kiss and I gasp for breath, flashing my eyes desperately from each of his eyes, unsure which one I want to look at more. I'm desperate for his lips to be on mine. He ignores my silent plea, sets me down and runs his fingers from either side of my forehead to my neck letting his thumbs drag over my lips. My eyes close as he familiarizes himself with my face.

"Is this really you, Finley?" Brody croaks, his voice thick with emotion.

"Yes, Brody. I'm so sorry. I'm so…" I begin to cry and he kisses me, swallowing up my pain. I kiss him back and throw all my pain into my kiss. I don't allow myself to think of the future or what I'm going to tell him or what we're going to do. I just kiss him like I've never kissed him before.

I break the kiss this time and reach out to thread my hands with his. His hands feel warm, soft and dry. Firm and comforting like always. I release them and place his hands back on my face kissing both his palms first.

"God, Finley," Brody groans, leaning his forehead against mine, softly stroking my cheeks with his thumbs. I thread my fingers through his thick curly hair and pull gently.

"I wasn't sure I'd ever get you like this again," he whispers, his voice cracking as we breathe each other in.

"I'm here, Brody. I'm so sorry. I've missed you so much," I cry, trying to catch my breath.

I press my lips to his once more for a softer kiss this time. More comforting. More soothing.

"Will you come inside?" I ask, pulling only a centimeter away from his mouth. I'm nervous what his answer will be because I'm unsure how he's feeling about everything right now.

He pulls back from my face further and looks at the house. I see that jaw muscle tick again.

"Who is that guy, Finley?" he asks, looking down at me heatedly.

I see the pain and anger in his eyes and my heart breaks when I realize I'm hurting him again. As if I haven't hurt him enough already.

"He's just a friend," I reply, stroking his cheeks.

He looks at me and shakes his head, obviously unconvinced.

"Okay, he wants more," I rush out. "We kissed. That's it, Brody! That's it!" I screech out as Brody turns away from me, sharply putting a hand on his hip and stomping his foot into the pavement.

"It happened over a week ago. I told him I wasn't ready after that and he knows about you, Brody. He knows he's just a friend now, I promise." I rub his back silently, begging for him to turn back to me and be the Brody I love. My Brody.

"I'll fucking kill him, Finley," he growls, through clenched teeth. "God!" he shouts as he roughly rakes his hand through his hair, stomping his foot again.

"Brody, please…pleeease," I beg. "I'm so sorry babe. It's me you're mad at, not him. I was lost, Brody. I was missing you. He's just a nice guy. A friend. I was trying to forget you but I can't, Brody. I can't forget you. Never. You're it for me, you're all I want forever, Brody. I want to fix this! I want to fix us! I love us!" I'm crying loudly now, my voice echoing slightly off the skate ramps.

Brody finally turns to me and I see his face soften as he takes in my emotional state.

I bring my hands up to his face and drag them down to his chest. His familiar, wonderful chest. He lets out a huff of air and takes my hand.

"Finley," he whispers into my palm, kissing it roughly.

"Please, please come in, Brody," I beg once more.

He gives me one long, earth shattering look and then leans down to pick up his suitcase. Once the traffic clears, he protectively guides me across with his hand on my lower back, dragging his suitcase with his other hand.

We enter the house and I take Brody straight up to my bedroom. I assure him I'm going to go see if Liam left and if he hasn't, then I'll tell him to leave. Brody doesn't look happy, but he also doesn't object. He tells me he's going to take a shower. I'm grateful he won't be sitting here stewing while I talk to Liam.

I rush downstairs, my nerves jumping all over the place. My hands are shaking. I glance into the living room and see Leslie, Theo, Mitch, and Julie in there, but no Frank or Liam. I turn around and head through the dining room into the kitchen and see Frank talking seriously with Liam.

Liam looks up to me and gives me a sad look. My heart breaks at his expression. Why do I keep hurting these great guys?

Frank puts his hand on Liam's shoulder and hops off the counter and walks over to me. He pecks me silently on the cheek and leaves the kitchen.

"Finley," Liam says sadly.

"Liam," I say, pulling out a barstool and sitting at the counter across from him.

"Are you okay?" he asks.

My chest contracts at the fact that he's worried about me right now instead of being angry with me like he should be. I nod my head and he places his two hands on the edge of the counter and drops his head down.

"You told me," he starts. "You told me you weren't done unpacking. And I bloody well ignored you." He throws himself back off the counter and turns away from me and looks at the fridge.

"I'm so sorry, Liam," I say. "This isn't fair to you."

"Why do you say that, Finley?" he asks, swerving around and looking intently into my eyes.

"Because you're amazing!" Tears well in my eyes. "You're amazing, Liam. You're wonderful, you're…"

"Not him," he interrupts. Just hearing him say the word *him* makes me cringe.

"I'm sorry, Liam. You don't deserve this." I sniff loudly. "He's it for me. He always was. I've been lying to myself all this time."

He shakes his head again.

"I hope he knows it, Finley," he says, leaning across the counter and looking deeply into my eyes. He's willing me to see just how much he really cares for me. "And I hope you're honest with him about whatever crap you have floating around in that beautiful head of yours."

I look down at my hands on the counter and nod.

"I guess this is goodbye, Finley," he says, standing up tall and walking around the counter toward me. I hop down off the stool and he opens his arms to me for a hug. I lean in and breathe in his clean scent.

"Goodbye Liam," I whisper into his ear.

"Bye Fin," he whispers and drops a small peck into my hair.

CHAPTER TWENTY-TWO

Leslie is sitting on the steps in the foyer waiting for me to come out of the kitchen. Liam walks behind me and out the front door without looking back. She motions for me to follow her upstairs and I gratefully escape into her room with her.

"I swear I didn't tell Brody where we live, Finley!" she bursts out as soon as the door closes.

"I'm not worried," I reply.

"It had to be Cadence."

"I don't care," I say again.

"Are you okay?" she asks, clearly noticing my emotional state.

"I can't believe he's here Leslie," I sigh.

"I know! What are you going to do?" she asks.

"I have to tell him everything," I say. She nods sympathetically. "But I can't do it tonight."

"I don't think you have anything to worry about Fin," she says, and I smile back at her.

"How did Liam take it?" she asks, with concern furrowed in her brows.

"Eh, not horrible," I shrug. "Not great either, but I never made him any promises, so it is what it is and he gets it."

"Yeah," she says.

"Still sucks though, he deserves better."

She nods silently.

"What's going on with Theo?" I ask.

She shakes her head silently at me.

I shake my head back mirroring her expression.

She gets up and opens the door to her bedroom, clearly not ready for this conversation. I'm grateful for that because I have Brody to get back up to. She half smiles and pulls me down for a hug. I embrace her short frame and savor the moment, willing myself to find the strength to go.

I hear the shower running when I hit the third floor. I hesitate outside of the door for a moment, wondering what I should do. If this were us back in the States, I'd barge in and take whatever I wanted from Brody. But there's an uneasiness here. Brody feels awkward and angry and I'm not sure how to approach him after the whole Liam thing.

I rub my lips with my fingertips remembering the incredible passionate kiss we shared outside and I shake my head forcefully.

This is us. Brody came here to get me back and seeing him has made all of my previous worries and issues a distant memory. I need him right now.

I open the door and steam comes rushing out. I quietly undress and toss my clothes in a heap on the floor next to his. I draw back the curtain and Brody is standing under the shower spray with his hands on the tiled shower wall and his head hanging low. He looks so sad, so defeated. I hate it.

He hears the rustle of the shower curtain and turns. His eyes rove down my body and return to my eyes and a second of excitement ignites within them. I step into the tub and he turns to face me completely, his dark blue eyes locked on mine.

We stand before each other for a moment, having a serious but silent conversation. His eyes are boring into me with intensity, pain, passion, and desire. Mine are boring back into his with remorse, need, and want.

I reach out and drag my hand down his chest. He grabs my hand and holds it against his heart. I can feel it pounding rapidly beneath my palm.

"I've missed you so much, Brody," I say, softly.

"Finley." His deep voice echoes in the small bathroom.

Losing all control now, I fall into him and take his mouth with mine. He grips his hands tightly beneath my behind and hoists me up onto his hips. He turns and presses my back against the tile side of the shower. I cry out at the cold wall but he swallows my cries with his mouth.

"Tell me again, Finley," he says, roughly.

"What?" I ask, distracted by the intense feeling of his hips pressing against my center.

"Tell me how much you've missed me. Tell me how much you want me."

I move my hips against him, desperate for him to feel how much I've missed him.

"I've missed you, Brody. I want you so much right now," I say, breathing loudly. "I've wanted you the whole time I've been gone."

My hands run down his back to his butt and I feel him clench his buttocks in response. Our kiss is fast and fierce as we frantically attempt to make up for lost time.

"More," he growls against my lips.

"I've dreamt about you, Brody. I've dreamt about you coming here and making love to me. You're all I want," I moan out.

He stops moving against me and looks directly into my eyes.

"Brody!" I cry as he enters me in one quick strike.

He continues staring straight into my eyes as he begins rocking hard inside of me. I relish in the comfortable feeling of being with him again. It's slightly painful because of the length of time it's been since I've had intercourse. Brody and I never went more than a few days without having sex. We were penurious for each other and felt an intense passion and connection during intercourse.

"Are you okay?" Brody says, pulling his head back and looking into my light blue eyes.

I wiggle my hips against him, willing myself to adjust to his size quickly.

"Yes, yes…don't stop!" I say, kissing him hard and thrusting my tongue deep into his mouth.

He moves one of his hands up from my butt and strokes it up my hip to my rib and then cups my breast tightly. Our lips plop loudly as he pulls away from my mouth and dips his head down to take my nipple into his mouth.

Just watching him suck on my breast brings me to a peak and I cry out loudly as I near a tipping point.

"Yes!" I cry, dropping my head down onto his shoulder and biting while trying to gain control of myself.

Brody kisses up my chest and to my neck and then sucks my ear lobe into his mouth. His hand releases my breast and moves up into the nape of my neck. He pulls my hair lightly, but firmly, the way he knows I've always liked.

As he takes control of my head with my hair he rocks into me hard and fast and I come apart looking directly into his eyes. A few more thrusts and he's following me. He stills inside of me. I know not to worry about using a condom. That unspoken knowledge of the fact that getting pregnant is impossible weighs heavily in my heart. I kiss him hard, willing myself to forget and not fall down that rabbit hole.

"God, Finley," he says, pulling back and looking at me. "Tell me you're with me forever babe. I can't...I cannot lose you again," he says, his eyes brimming with tears.

His emotion shocks me and my jaw drops.

"Yes, Brody! Yes!" I reply, cupping his face in my hands and dropping soft kisses all over his cheeks, lips, nose, and eyes.

He sighs hard and kisses me passionately on the lips again.

"I'm with you forever, Brody. I love you. I love..." I pause, wanting to use our special phrasing but unsure if it still holds as much value since I left him once already. "I love us."

He nods his head at me and I can't help but think how young and scared he looks. Why did I do this to us? Why did I not trust him with this deep, dark piece of me? I can't give him a child. I know this. Why did I think he wouldn't want me despite it? I know I need to tell him everything, but right now I just want to reconnect and get us back on firm ground before I drop another bomb on our very fragile relationship.

Brody sets me back down onto my feet, grabs my sponge hanging from the faucet and fills it with my body wash. He proceeds to scrub my body gently, using his bare hands to rub the soap in and familiarize himself with my body. I take the sponge from him and do the same to him, taking extra time on his back and dropping kisses all over his body in the process.

When we're both clean, he shuts the water off, grabs the towel he laid out for himself and dries my hair off with it. He wraps the towel around my shoulders, rubbing my arms soothingly. He then hops out to grab another towel and quickly wipes himself down.

I stand in the tub and watch him. I can't believe my Brody is here and we're together again. I thought I'd lost him forever, yet here he is drying off his yummy naked body right in front of me. He finishes and ties the towel around his waist. Without hesitation, he scoops me up into his arms and carries me across the hallway into my bedroom.

I see him hesitate slightly at the tiny mattress on the floor before he sets me down onto the bed and covers me up with the purple sheet and comforter. He flips off the light, ditches his towel, and tucks in right behind me, pulling my towel out too.

After a few moments of silence, he breathes softly into my ear, "I love us, Finley." He tucks my wet hair behind my ear and kisses my neck softly.

"I love us too, Brody," I reply, turning in his arms to face him. The skin-to-skin contact reminds me of the last time we were together. I wrap my arms around him and kiss him again.

Before I know it, we're making love again. But it's slower and softer this time. I've reassured him enough for now, we are just making up for lost time. I sigh into his neck and look up to the ceiling, praying that we can make it through all this. I can only hope the power of my heart and my love for him is enough to keep him. I hope his dreams can change and shape with me. Regardless, a huge weight is lifted from my heart by having Brody here with me again and I squeeze my eyes shut tightly and focus on that. We're back together again. We're us again.

CHAPTER TWENTY-THREE

The sun is streaming in brightly through the lace curtains. I feel hot and butterflies flutter in my belly at the recollection that Brody is here—on my tiny twin mattress—with me. His large arm is wrapped tightly around my waist and I gently stroke the fuzzy dark hair on his forearm. God, I can't believe I ever thought I could leave him so easily. *This is Brody.*

I slowly and carefully turn in his arms and he lets out a big sigh in his sleep. I'm inches away from his face, marveling in his beauty. He looks so content right now. His shaggy curly hair is perfectly rumpled from sleep, his milky skin looks beautiful in the morning sunlight and I notice the familiar freckle that sits right below his right eye. I can't help myself from reaching over and kissing it lightly.

He stirs and excitement rushes through me as I'm giddy for him to wake up and talk or *not talk* to me. Flutters rush all over my body as my mouth develops a mind of its own and kisses his freckle again, then slowly makes its way down his cheeks and neck. I drag my lips from spot to spot so I never have to break contact from this amazing, gorgeous, sexy man of mine. I reach his chest and try to shimmy down further to kiss his belly but his arms suddenly grip me tightly.

"No fair," he moans, with his eyes still closed. "If you're going to be kissing me, I at least deserve to be awake for it."

His dark blue eyes flutter open and he grins sleepily at me.

"Otherwise, how can I return the favor?" he says, pulling me back up and nuzzling my neck. When I feel a flick of his tongue against my skin, I can't take it anymore.

I press him flat onto his back and straddle him. I rake his chest with my hands and he shudders below me. He's fully ready for me and I smile, gently easing myself on top of him. His face grows serious with desire as I begin to move in slow, sensuous motions.

"God, Finley," he croaks out with his deep, raspy morning-voice. "You are so beautiful."

My heart soars at his words. For years Brody has made me feel like the most beautiful woman he's ever seen. There is nothing sexier than this man making me feel good about my body in the throes of passion.

His hands reach out and fondle my breasts gently and he sits himself up to press his head into my chest. I cry out when he nips at my breast.

"Brody!" I say, giggling.

He bands his arms around my waist and rolls me under him. He quickly grabs one of my legs and puts it up on his shoulder, which deepens him into me. I savor the full feeling of him and my eyes flutter back open to look into his eyes. His gorgeous, navy-blue eyes. My hands find their way into his coarse curls and I comb my fingers through them as he continues moving inside of me.

"I've missed us so much, Finley. I've missed *you* so much. I can't lose you again Finley, I can't," he says, his face turning serious as his eyes bore into mine.

"You won't, Brody," I say, lifting my head off the pillow. "I'm here with you, forever now, baby. I can't leave you ever again. You're everything to me. Everything."

I roll him to his back and take control again. I need him to know how serious and in control of my feelings I am, and taking over the sexual position feels like the best way to relay that message. For the next thirty minutes, that's exactly what I do. *Relay the message.*

When we finish, my limbs are tangled with his, the lavender-colored sheet covering just our essential parts. The purple comforter is a rumpled mess on the floor.

"I feel weird saying this, but do we need to be worrying about birth control right now, Finley?" his voice hangs in the room.

I immediately shake my head, "We're fine. There...there's nothing to worry about."

He sighs, "Well, I know it never happened for us before but that doesn't mean it won't happen now, Finley. We probably need to be more careful until we decide what we're going to do."

My heartbeat increases and I can feel it pounding in my chest. I'm not ready to tell Brody there truly is nothing to worry about. I will tell him soon, but I'm not wanting to pop this incredibly sexy bubble we have going right now. I wrack my brain to figure out what I can say in reply to his concerns.

"Um...we can pick up some condoms today if you want, but for now I'm sure we're safe. I know where I'm at in my cycle…we're fine," I say, sitting up with the sheet held tightly to my chest, feeling like the worst kind of liar.

I glance back at him and see a fleeting look of sadness, but he doesn't let it show for long before half-smiling back while gently scratching my back.

"For the record, you can wake me up like that anytime you want," he says, sitting up next to me and nipping my shoulder.

I giggle against him and check the time. It's nearly ten.

"Are you feeling jet-lagged? Or do you want to see the city today?" I ask.

"I feel like a million bucks right now," he says, stretching and laying back on the mattress with his hands behind his head.

He looks so happy right now, I can't help but grin right back at him.

"Well, it's Saturday and the farmers' market here is really cool. Wait 'til you see all the different stuff they have."

He grins back at me, "I'm not gonna lie, I'd be perfectly content to stay in this room all day long." He sits up onto one arm and raises his eyebrows at me. "Though, I wouldn't mind a bigger bed."

He gives me a hilarious unimpressed expression and I giggle and jump on him.

"You weren't complaining last night or this morning!" I say, pushing his shoulder down into the mattress as hard as I can. He barely budges.

"Promise me you'll stay completely naked every time we're on this mattress and I'll get over it, I suppose," he quips back at me.

"You *suppose*," I mimic back to him. "Come on, let's get dressed and go downstairs. I really want you to meet Frank. And I'm sure Leslie would love to actually say hi to you at some point." I say, standing up butt naked, acting like I'm not the least bit concerned about it.

His eyes rove over my body and he shakes his head before jumping up at the speed of light. He rams his shoulder into my stomach and stands up with my body draped over him. I squeal when he slaps my ass really hard.

"Ouch, Brody! Damn it!" I scream. "That hurt!" I cry out, with a big goofy smile on my face as he walks us toward the door.

"What do you expect, woman? You stand up in front of me like that and you don't expect some repercussions? I'm going to teach you a really good lesson in that shower again because there are a few areas I want to inspect a little closer," he says, giving me a quick tweak on my butt.

He opens the door and marches across the hallway toward the bathroom. I glance down the stairs giggling, and my eyes land on Frank walking by the lower stairwell with a bowl of cereal in his hands.

I clear my throat and attempt to stifle the laughter bubbling up inside me. *Don't look up, Frank. Don't look up!*

He looks up. *Aw frick, he looked up!* His eyes zero in on Brody's bare ass and my naked body draped over his shoulder. I burst out in a loud riotous laughter as Frank's spoon remains suspended in the air.

Brody turns to see what I'm laughing at and gives Frank a full-on frontal assault of his manhood. In epic slow motion, Frank's jaw drops and milky cereal dribbles off the edge of his bowl onto the floor.

My voice catches in my throat, unsure what to say.

"I, uhhhh, Brody! Turn around!" I screech. I can't even begin to handle the look on Frank's stunned face right now.

"Sorry…uh, yeah…um, sorry!" Brody yells down the steps and shuffles us into the bathroom and quickly closes the door.

I shake my head incredulously as he sets me down. Brody looks at me with a huge shit-eating grin. *He's proud of himself right now, the cheeky bastard.*

"Frank is never going to let me live this down, you big jerk!" I say, shoving him light-heartedly in the chest.

A sweet rumble of laugher shakes his shoulders as he captures my hand against his chest.

"Who is Frank?" Brody says, laughing at me.

"My roommate! I do not appreciate you showing him our *ass*ets like that. Damn!"

Brody pulls me into his arms and holds me with the happiest smile I've ever seen on him. "Frank didn't look like he minded one bit," he murmurs, while kissing up my neck to my ear.

"I mind!" I reply.

Brody leans down and consumes my mouth with his tongue.

I suddenly mind a lot less.

CHAPTER TWENTY-FOUR

Brody and I get cleaned up and make our way downstairs for some coffee. Leslie and Frank are sitting in the kitchen nook and I smile brightly at them, unwilling to acknowledge the peep show Frank saw only an hour ago.

"Morning!" I say, cheerily, pulling a not-so-confident-now Brody behind me into the kitchen.

"Gooooood Mooooorrrrnnnniiiiiing," Frank replies saucily, and Leslie spits out her cereal all over the table.

I look at Frank and squint my eyes.

"A very good morning indeed, isn't it, Brody?" Frank says, looking Brody up and down.

Brody's adorable face turns beet red as he shifts awkwardly.

"Brody," I say, in a warning tone while boring daggers at Frank. "This is Frank."

Frank's lanky body stands up and he saunters over to Brody. Frank is dressed in another original ensemble of zebra-striped pants and a thermal long-sleeved white shirt. Oh, bless my sweet Brody right now. He was so brazen and arrogant an hour ago but now he's gone shy on me.

"Very, very nice to meet you, Brody," Frank drawls out slowly, shaking Brody's hand much longer than necessary. "I've heard so much about you. And happy to *see* so much of you now, too. I love those jeans you're wearing."

Brody clears his throat and digs deep for some confidence again. He smiles back one of his signature panty-dropping smiles and replies, "Nice to meet you, Frank. Sorry about giving you an eye full earlier. I uh, was just feeling pretty happy to be here with Finley, I guess."

"No need to apologize, pet. By the looks of it, you were feeling *very*...what was the word you used? Oh, yes...*happy*." Frank smiles ear-to-ear and glances down toward Brody's crotch.

Brody clears his throat, "Hi, Les!" he says, releasing Frank's hand and making his way over to sit next to Leslie. He gives her a hearty hug. She smiles back, obviously enjoying the little show Frank and Brody are putting on for our enjoyment.

Frank looks at me, batting his eyes innocently. I glare back, keeping my eyes trained on him as I walk backwards into the kitchen for coffee.

"I'm going to take Brody over to the farmers' market if either of you want to come," I say, softening my death glare on Frank. "I thought I'd pick something up for dinner tonight so we can have a big family dinner if you guys are going to be around."

"Sounds great to me!" Leslie says. "But I have work to do today, so I'll just join you for the actual eating of the food, not the shopping and cooking…that sounds terrible. I'm the type who likes to eat the sausage, I don't need to see how it's made."

I give her an unimpressed look and then turn to Frank.

He lifts his eyebrows up at me trying to decipher what I want him to say.

He raises his chin up high and replies "I willllllllll *not* come…" he finishes, the word dropping his chin slowly to his chest, "…in *that* way…but I will eat?" he says with a question mark, like he doesn't know what I want him to say.

"Yes, Frank. You will eat." I smile at him. The saucy bugger is obviously not as offended at seeing Brody's naked bod as he was by seeing mine. "And we will all be fully clothed. In fact, let's make it a fancy family dinner and dress up a bit!"

This perks Frank right up. "You're lucky I love clothes, Fin-Bin. Otherwise, there's no way I'd agree to a dinner with that hunk-of-a-man in anything but his birthday suit."

Brody laughs hard and I crack a big smile, no longer able to continue my façade of being put out by this situation.

"Ha ha. Okay, Frank. You've seen Brody naked. Now piss-off about it already or we're going to force you to even the score."

Frank does a quick twirl and says, "Even away, love! And let me tell you," he pauses, and shoots a sly expression Brody's way. "The carpet *definitely* matches the drapes."

Leslie spits out another mouthful of cereal all over and Brody laughs, wiping some spray off his face. I shake my head and smile at my crazy roommates. I feel a sense of peace with myself now that Brody is here to experience all of this with me.

***

Brody and I eventually leave and spend the day alone at the farmers' market, sampling various foods and purchasing necessary supplies for supper. We do a lot of the same things Frank and I did on my first day here. It's fun. It's light and carefree and I'm excited to cook for Brody again. It was always something I loved doing in our relationship and he loved everything I made him, even though there were many *Pinterest*-fail recipes that definitely didn't turn out like their pictures.

It feels good to be hand in hand with Brody, walking the streets of London. It feels natural and normal. Brody and I were together for five years and never really took a vacation like this before, so this feels new and exciting to both of us. So much has changed since then. Not just with me, but Brody seems different, too. The same, but different. We forgot what it was like to just be together. To just be *us*. The world of baby-making feels like another life to me now.

It still amazes me that Brody and I managed to stay close and passionate during all our months of trying to get pregnant. There were so many times that we *had* to have sex because I might have been ovulating and the sex wasn't passionate, it wasn't fun. It was forced and it sucked. Thankfully, Brody was so incredibly good at making me feel beautiful and desirable that just when I didn't think I could do it again, he'd find some special way to make it feel spontaneous.

"You seem different," Brody says, as we stand in line to pay for the ears of corn we picked up.

"Do I?" I ask, not knowing how to respond.

He's standing behind me and grasps my hips, splaying one hand over my belly as we wait for the line to move forward. He's had his hands on me most of the day, unable to break away for more than a few minutes at a time.

"I feel like I'm home again," I reply, turning in his hands and facing him. His face looks pained for a fleeting second, so I stroke his hair encouragingly and kiss him lightly on the lips.

"You feel like you're home, in London?" he asks.

"I like it here a lot," I say, pulling out of his embrace and standing next to him with my head on his shoulder. "But having you here with me makes it really feel like home."

I quickly pay for our stuff and we make our way down the busy sidewalk, swerving around people and vendors.

"You told me you loved London because of how your books romanticized it, but you never seemed that serious about ever coming out here," he says, waffling his hand with mine and taking the bagged corn to carry it for me.

"It seemed like a pipedream back then. You and I were settled and had a plan. When things changed and Leslie was out here, it just seemed like the best place for me to go to. It was different enough. I needed different."

Brody slows our pace dramatically as we continue down the sidewalk that leads directly to Frank's house.

"I still don't even understand what changed. I didn't think what we had and where we were was so bad," he says, looking sadly at his shoes as we walk.

Choosing to ignore that statement, I say, "You seem different, too."

"In what way?" he looks up.

"Your hair is longer," I smile, ruffling my fingers in it. "You haven't had it cut since I left, have you?"

He gives me a small smile.

"Well, you see," he starts, and I'm relieved to hear lightness in his tone again. "I had this really hot chick that took care of all that stuff for me. When she left, a lot of stuff went to shit, I'm afraid."

I smile back sadly at him and he returns the same despondent look.

"I think I like it, actually," I offer.

We pass a small children's park and he pulls me down onto an open bench just inside a shaded grass area.

"What's going on with your job? Were they okay with you coming here?" I ask.

"Yeah, they were cool. I would have come sooner but I had to finish an estimate for a new visitor center building. Once that was done, they were fine with me leaving for a few days," he replies, putting his arm around me and tucking me in closely next to him.

His smile fades and he turns to look at me intensely.

"I still need to know why you left, Finley," he says. "I'm trying to go slowly here for you because I don't want to spook you and I don't want to lose you again. But you have to give me something, Fin."

I pull my legs up onto the bench and hug them, facing him.

"I wish I knew the reason too, sometimes," I begin. "Or at least had an easy and obvious answer. At the time it felt like the right thing to do. To say goodbye to you and leave. To start a new life. Our life together, it just…mostly, it just all became too much, too hard…too painful."

"Too painful to let me help you?" he asks, tucking a strand of hair behind my ear.

"I guess. I don't know," I say, dropping my feet down onto the ground and looking down, shamefully.

"In a million years, Finley, I would have never seen that coming. You leaving…I would have never guessed you'd just leave me like that."

His words cut me deeply. I feel a sickness roll over me for what I did to him and what I did to *us*. I turned something pure, and beautiful, and magical into ugliness. A broken ugliness. I shake my head, willing these painful thoughts away.

"We were trying to make a baby together, Fin. I mean, that's heavy stuff. I know you and I never wanted to get married, but was that part of it? Did you want me to ask you to marry me?" he asks, looking at me with wide blue eyes.

"No!" I reply. "No, Brody, it was never the marriage thing. I still don't care about that. I hate the idea of doing stuff because other people tell us it's right."

"That's what I thought, Finley, but when you left…I felt like I didn't know you anymore. I've been wracking my brain trying to figure out what would cause all of this. What would cause you to throw away everything we had?"

Tears form in my eyes at his completely honest and raw question. I look up from the ground and into his eyes. Without having the ability to stop myself, my hand goes to his cheek and strokes it softly.

"I love you so much, Brody. I'm horrified, seriously *horrified* that I've done this to us." I start crying and have to look away from his beautiful face because it hurts too much.

"Look at me, Finley," he says, but I don't look back at him. He grabs my cheeks in both of his hands and turns my wet eyes toward him.

"Don't ever hide your tears from me, baby. I need to see them. I need to know you're not hiding this whole world from me again. Not again. Not ever, ever again."

I swallow a huge lump in my throat as the guilt mounts to an all new level. I know now is the time for me to open up and tell him everything. I need to tell him what the doctor said. I need to tell him I'm scared to adopt because I'm scared it isn't what he wants. I'm scared once he knows the entire truth, he won't want me anymore.

It's the last fear that prevents me from coming clean and I reach over and hug him tightly, relishing the time I have with him right now. I have no idea if Brody will want me when he discovers the truth, but for right now, he's mine.

"I cannot believe you're here with me and wanting to love me still. I don't deserve it, Brody. I don't deserve any of it. But I will take it, babe. I will take it and cherish it and do my best to never ever hurt you again," I say, into his shoulder.

He pulls back and kisses me softly. His kiss is so soft and sweet, I cry through it. I can feel all his love and adoration for me and it's painful to accept, knowing what I know. I break the kiss, wipe my cheeks, and make an awkward noise with my throat to try and lighten the mood.

"Let's hurry back to the house. We have some time before we need to start cooking, and there's plenty I'd still like to show you in my bedroom."

He jumps up dramatically and starts sprinting down the street, leaving me sitting shell shocked on the bench. God, he is so funny. He's this tall, hot, incredible guy, yet he has no qualms about making the biggest ass out of himself at the drop of a hat. I love this man.

Just when I think he's not coming back for me, he spins around, sprints back to me, grabs my hand, and throws me up onto his shoulder like a rag doll.

With another slap on my butt, he says, "I'm so sorry, baby. I totally forgot you hate to run…and exercise…and well, do anything sporty."

I squeeze his sides and laugh happily as he jiggles me down the block and back to the house.

CHAPTER TWENTY-FIVE

I dig out the votive candles leftover from the Tarts and Vicars party, and arrange them in a cluster on the big dining room table. It's been a while since we've all had dinner together, so I figure we can attempt to do it up right.

Brody is a huge help with grilling the chicken. We're having barbeque chicken, sweet corn, and garlic mashed potatoes. A very Midwestern traditional meal. BBQ back in Kansas City is legendary. I know this won't come close to that, but it should still be pretty good.

Brody presses up behind me as I'm lighting the tea lights. He moves my hair away from my neck so he can kiss me and I melt under his touch.

"God, I've missed this," he murmurs into my neck.

"Missed what? My cooking?" I say, turning to kiss him on the lips.

"Just being normal with you. Doing regular things together," he squeezes my side and I flinch at the ticklish spot.

"Quit, Brody! I need to get the potatoes finished," I laugh, feeling giddy and light from his affection.

"Okay, I have to go get the chicken off the grill anyway. Damn! I can't wait to get you home so I have you all to myself again."

He gives me a loud-smacking kiss on my cheek and takes off for the patio area. What the hell is that supposed mean? He's expecting me to just go home with him after all this? I guess that would be an obvious assumption since we made up. Shit! I let the match burn too far down and fried the tip of my finger.

Damn it, that hurt. I suck on my finger as I ponder what the hell I'm going to do about Brody. I know I need Brody. I have to be with him, that's non-negotiable. But I guess I was just hoping we could start a whole new life together in London. Maybe none of this will even matter when he knows all there is to know? God, just when I was feeling so good, freakin' reality has to ruin everything.

"Problems?" Mitch's voice breaks through my inner monologue.

"I burned my finger. I'm fine," I say, a bit rudely.

"That's all?" he says, heading over to the cabinet and pulling out another foreign bottle of liquor. He holds it out to me and I nod my head, so he proceeds to pull two coffee mugs out of the cabinet and pours us both a shot.

"To complicated shit?" he says, raising his glass to me with a toast.

"To impossible problems," I reply, with my own toast, raising my glass back at him.

"To being cool enough to figure out unique solutions," he says, and then takes his shot.

I shoot mine back and hold the cinnamon-tasting liquor in my mouth, pondering what he said. Mitch seems to have this wonderfully quiet way of always helping me with my problems. Unique solutions. Unique solutions. Surely, Brody and I can come up with a unique solution.

"Brody, right?" Mitch says.

"Yeah," Brody replies, walking into the kitchen with a pan full of BBQ chicken.

"I'm Mitch. Do you like cinnamon?" Mitch asks, grabbing another coffee mug out of the cupboard.

"You bet," Brody responds, looking at me sweetly.

Brody and Mitch talk amicably over another shot and I finish up the food and set everything on the table. Julie comes in looking all cute in a little black dress and heels, so I give Brody a quick kiss and excuse myself to go up and change. I'd be lying if I don't admit to being excited to dress up for Brody.

I pop my head into Leslie's room and she's sitting on her bed, obviously deep in thought. She's wearing a sexy, black, one-piece jumpsuit with gold metallic trim around the sleeves and down the center.

"Hey! You look hot!" I say, and she waves me off like she doesn't want to hear it. "What's wrong, Les?" I say, sitting down next to her on her daybed.

"Boy problems, Finley," she groans, and lies down on her side. "I'm so confused."

"Well, I'm here. Let's talk."

"I don't think I'm quite ready to talk yet. I know, I know…the cracks. But you know how sometimes I just need to process for a bit? Well, now is one of those times. I promise, as soon as I'm ready, I'm coming to you, so don't get your panties in a wad, Mama Bear."

"Okay then."

"Besides, you have enough on your plate right now as it is."

I sigh, heavily. "You aren't kidding. Brody thinks I'm coming back to Kansas."

"Aren't you?" she asks.

"Do you think I should?" I ask, genuinely curious.

"Hell no! I'll keep you here forever if I can. But I guess I kind of assumed the same thing."

"I need more cinnamon," I groan.

"Like, the food? Or is this a metaphor?" she asks, deadpan.

"Mitch has yummy cinnamon liquor downstairs," I say.

"Yum! I want some!" She looks like a kid in a candy store.

Frank walks into Leslie's room and stops in his tracks in the doorway.

"For fuck's sake, Finley!" he says, angrily gesturing to my university hoodie and leggings. "You cannot be trusted to dress yourself anymore! I'm going to burn every last one of those nasty hoodies of yours. Get your arse upstairs…now!"

Leslie and I look at each other and giggle.

"I agree with Frank. You are hideous," she crows, shoving her hand in my face and making a puking gesture. "Get your ass upstairs before Frank has another one of his fits."

"Screw you. I love my hoodies," I say, getting up off the bed. "And Frank, if you burn even one of my hoodies, I will burn those hideous pajamas of yours."

He squeals like a girl, and dashes back out into the hall.

"What's he doing?" I ask, looking back at Leslie from the doorway.

She laughs heartily, "He's hiding them!"

***

"Finley, babe…you look so beautiful," Brody says, in front of everybody as I walk into the dining room.

I have to give Frank credit, this outfit rocks. I'm wearing white skinny, leather leggings and a sleeveless electric-blue top with an exposed silver zipper down the front that's opened scandalously low. I'm wearing my sky-high black wedges again and tons of silver bangles around my wrist and two long teardrop crystal earrings.

"Thanks," I say, awkwardly, not enjoying everyone's perusal of my outfit.

"How do you handle her strange obsession with hoodies, Brody?" Frank asks, coming up behind me in skinny black jeans, a white button down, and a black bow tie.

"I love her in everything," Brody says, smiling at me from across the table. My heart flutters like crazy and I look down, trying to hide the blush I feel creeping on my cheeks. Hopefully, the makeup Frank applied on me upstairs is covering it.

"Thanks for setting everything out, guys."

"Finley, my pet, this looks positively splendid!" Frank says, with more fervor than necessary.

"Yeah, thanks for cooking, Finley!" Julie quips brightly, sitting down by Mitch at the table.

"Oh, I got us some wine. I'll go grab it," I say, heading into the kitchen.

Brody follows behind me as I knew he would. I saw that look in his eye and I knew he'd have to touch me before we could eat. Before I even get around the corner, he's shoving up behind me and twirling me around to face him, walking me backwards into the counter. My butt hits the edge and he kisses me. Hard. Possessively. Demanding. Hot. Hot as hell. Holy shit, this kiss is hot.

"Babe, you look too good," he says, shaking his head, his lips raw and pink.

I smile and run my thumb over his lips to wipe off the pink gloss that's smeared all over his mouth.

"Stand down, soldier. There's plenty of time for that later," I say, winking at him.

I swivel in his grasp around my hips and grab two bottles of red wine. His hand creeps around to my chest and pulls my zipper down to my navel. He reaches inside and cups my breast. I stifle a moan as he kneads my breast with his hand. Oh my God, that feels so good.

"Brody," I say, embarrassed at the moan in my tone.

He pops a quick peck on my cheek and zips my zipper back up, a lot higher than it was originally. He whispers in my ear, "Mine." He grabs the two wine bottles and heads into the dining room.

I'm left there feeling tragically turned on and all alone. I'd like to be pissed and outraged at the possessive gesture of him zipping my zipper up so damn high, but damn, I'm too busy being way too turned on by it.

Everybody seems to be enjoying the Kansas-style meal Brody and I prepared. I feel my heart swell with pride at how great Brody is fitting in with all my roommates. Even Mitch seems to be getting pretty chummy with Brody, and Mitch doesn't get chummy with anybody.

"So, Brody, how long are you staying?" Julie asks.

"I leave day after tomorrow," he replies.

My heart drops as he says this. He's leaving already? He just got here.

"What's your plan, Finley?" Julie asks.

Damn it, Julie, can't you just leave this alone?

"I...um...we haven't completely worked all that out yet," I reply.

Brody looks at me, confused and bewildered. I shift in my seat as his expression turns from confused to angry.

"I, uh...think Brody and Finley still have a lot of catching up to do," Leslie says, trying to break the tension. Bless her.

Frank starts up a random conversation about Zoey, the bartender at the pub, and how he heard she had sex with a customer in the bathroom while working. That seems to distract us all for a while, but I can feel Brody's eyes boring into me, searching for answers. Answers I don't yet have.

CHAPTER TWENTY-SIX

"To the pub?" Frank asks.

"Yes!" Julie squeals.

Mitch and Leslie both nod in agreement.

"You up for it?" I ask Brody, as we finish loading the last few dishes in the dishwasher.

"If you want to, that's fine," he says, a bit sadly.

I shake my head, grab his hand, and walk him out of the kitchen and away from the roommates. When we're in the living room alone, I stand directly in front of him and put my hands on his cheeks so he looks at me.

"Brody, we have more talking to do. We do. But I'm trying to show you my world here right now. Can we just have one more night? One more night of carefree *us*? And then figure everything out after that?" I ask, kissing his lips chastely.

He half smiles back at me.

"Okay, I guess that could work," he replies.

I shove him back, slightly, "Lighten up, babe. You're about to get a glimpse of your first legitimate old English pub."

He laughs and pulls me into him for a great big bear hug.

***

"This is it?" Brody says, as we stroll into the pub twenty minutes later.

"This is iiiiiit!" Frank sings, spreading his arms out wide. "Zoey! A round of drinks for my mates!"

"Stuff it, Frank!" she shouts back at him.

"You stuff it, Wench!" he says, guiding us to our usual table. "She has a thing for me, the poor gal. What can I say? I'm irresistible."

I laugh as he wafts his tall orange fuzzy hair.

"Here's yours, Fin-Bin," he says, handing me a tall dark beer.

I smile back at him and watch Brody as Frank hands him the same thing. His eyes smile at me as he takes a long drink. He looks so great tonight in his grey pants and white button-down. I have to hold myself back from kissing the tiny chest hairs that poke out at the top of his two open buttons.

Our group looks a tad fashionable for the regulars around here, but no one seems to notice or care. There are still the standard old geezers bellied up to the bar, and the jukebox is playing some kind of Irish rock and a college-aged group is shooting pool in the far corner.

"Confession time!" Frank announces to the table on our second round of beers when everyone is starting to feel pretty happy and loose.

Frank drops his head down onto the table, and shoots it up quickly, "I saw Brody naked in the hallway today!"

Squeals erupt from Julie and Leslie.

"And he has the most magnificent bum...I've ever seen."

A cacophony of cackles continue and Brody just smiles, smugly, like he doesn't have a care in the world.

"I feel so much better getting that out, guys. I've been bursting with this for hours and I just can't keep it in anymore. I saw his bum...I saw his bum and I saw his man candy in full salute...God that feels good getting it out! You all must know how glorious it was!"

Brody lets out a hearty laugh and turns red and even Mitch appears amused. I smile looking amongst my friends and feeling grateful that Brody seems to be handling all this so effortlessly.

"Thanks for the high praise, Frank. What can I say?" he laughs again and raises his eyebrows at me in a flirty gesture.

"You can say whatever you want with an arse like that, mate. Feel very free to walk around naked in my house anytime," Frank sighs, taking a big drink of his beer.

"Or not!" I say, finally having enough of this banter. I walk over to Brody and sit on his lap. I grab his chin with my hand and turn it toward me.

"I think I'd prefer to keep your wobbly bits to myself if it's all the same to you." I finish, with a dramatic smacking kiss to his lips.

When I pull away from his lips, his eyes are crinkled at the edges with his beaming smile.

"That's the only way I want it, babe," he says, looking me in the eyes. His smile is so incredibly happy and content, I can't help but grin right back at him.

"Enough, already! You're making me sick over here!" Leslie says, with dramatic tone.

She gets a naughty look in her eyes that makes me nervous.

"If we're doing confessions, Brody, I have to know…have to know! What the fucking hell were you doing with Oldie Oli' on *Facebook*?" she says, my heart drops and my eyes turn wide.

Leslie registers my shocked expression and her jaw drops, "Have you guys not discussed this?" she asks.

I silently shake my head *no*, and tension creeps all over my body.

"Who's Oldie Oli'?" Brody asks.

I shake my head angrily at Leslie for opening her big mouth. I wanted to have this conversation alone with Brody to dig a bit deeper into the whole Olivia thing. If I'm being honest with myself, I still get the willies just thinking about him being with her. But I was taking everything slowly with him because of the whole Liam thing. I didn't feel like I had a right to accuse him of anything about Olivia. Not yet, anyway. I definitely didn't plan on having this conversation at a table full of my roommates.

"Olivia, from college. I don't know her last name," Leslie answers, despite my fierce look in her direction.

Brody starts laughing and I turn and glare at him.

"Funny, Brody?" I ask, cocking my head to the side.

"Yes, actually," he laughs some more.

What the hell is so funny about this?

"Explain, Brody!" I bark at him, unable to contain my jealousy anymore.

"I wasn't with Olivia. God, you guys call her Oldie Oli'? I totally get it. That's really funny." He wipes an imaginary tear from his cheek, then continues, "I happened to run into Olivia when I was out with Mark one night. She was with a bunch of people from our college graduate class, so we all hung out for a while."

"I'm failing to see the funny part of this story, Brody," I say, flatly.

"I made Mark take those photos with Olivia because I wanted to make you jealous. And it totally worked," he says, laughing again.

Still not feeling any relief, I say, "So wait, you guys weren't together?"

"No!" he says, with a little look of disgust on his face that pleases me greatly.

I look over at Leslie and tilt my head, "Did I just get played, Les?"

"I'd say you did, Fin-Bin! Like a fiddle." She's laughing with Brody now and I'm just sitting there stunned.

Brody tweaks my sides and I squirm in his arms, "Oh, come on, Finley. I'm here now, that's all that matters, right?"

He pulls my face down to his and kisses me.

"Barf!" Leslie cries out, "I'm going to go put something on that we can dance to so I don't have to watch you two go at it all night! Plus, this jumpsuit deserves a dance," she says, shimmying her butt over to the jukebox.

When *Meatloaf* breaks over the pub's speakers, I leap off Brody's lap and run over to Leslie, flailing wildly. My dad was a huge classic rock fan and Leslie and I grew really fond of it as a result of him booming it throughout our whole house growing up.

Julie joins Leslie and me on the dance floor and I'm laughing and having a ball, dancing and singing our hearts out. Brody watches me with the same happy, content smile that makes me melt from the inside out. *We can figure this out. We can make this work.*

When the guys join us on the dance floor, I know it's only a matter of time before we head back home. Brody's moves are so good that I'm afraid I'll have a Leslie-moment on his leg if I'm not careful.

CHAPTER TWENTY-SEVEN

Brody and I walk back to the house hand in hand. I can't believe I only have two more nights with him. My heart already aches at the idea of him leaving.

He's making it completely impossible for me to open the front door because he's standing directly in front of it, kissing me like his life depends on it. I reach around his hips and fumble the key into the door. "I'll race you to my room," I whisper into his ear. He whips the door open behind him and we both fall into the house. I kick off my wedges and start sprinting up the steps. He stops directly in front of me and I smack into his back and fall to the side, whacking my elbow on the railing.

"OW! Damn it!" I say, giggling and rubbing my elbow.

He stops and cages me in against the railing.

"Poor baby," he says, and bends over to kiss it. "And poor loser."

He runs up the steps again. I laugh and race up after him.

When I get to the third floor, he's breathing heavily against my bedroom door, but his smile has faded. The only way to describe his look right now is…desire.

I walk up to him, my chest rising and falling as I attempt to catch my breath.

His expression turns serious as he looks down at my shirt. He grabs the zipper and pulls it down slowly. The zipping sound is loud in the quiet hallway. When he spreads my shirt open, revealing my sheer teal bra, he smiles knowingly as my chest rises for very different reasons now.

He quickly claims my mouth with his soft lips and we shed all of our clothes, frantically pushing through the doorway and onto the mattress.

After working me up to a state of fervor with his magical fingers, he sits back for a moment on his knees and grabs a condom out of his wallet in his jeans pocket.

"I love you so much, Finley. I love *us* so much," he says, as he situates himself on top of me.

I didn't have the heart earlier to tell him not to bother buying them, and right now all I want is him inside of me. He rolls it on himself and enters me slowly and holds still inside of me. I lift my head off the pillow and he threads his fingers through my hair and grips a handful, tightly.

"Brody!" I cry, rocking my hips against him, begging for him to move inside of me.

He tilts his head and looks at me seriously, and then begins thrusting in and out of me at a slow, leisurely pace. I grab his hair roughly, desperate for more movement, desperate for a release. Desperate for everything.

He pulls me up by my waist as he sits back on his knees and lets me ride him. He gently lifts his butt up and down as I swivel against him. He groans loudly in response.

"Yeah, baby, just like that. Move just like that. I love how you do it just like that."

I work myself into a fervor watching his erotic facial expressions. Every once in a while he looks straight into my eyes with all the adoration in the world and it's enough to break my heart. I feel a tear slip down my cheek and I shake it away.

His brow furrows and he rubs his thumb over my damp face.

"Baby," he says.

"Stay with me, Brody," I cry out softly into the room.

"Of course, Finley. I'll always stay with you," he says, looking at me with a slight look of alarm.

"No, I mean it, Brody," I say, stopping my motion on top of him, "I need you to promise you'll stay with me," I swallow. "No matter what."

He's looking at me, concerned now.

"What is it, baby? Tell me," he says, pushing my long brown hair out of my face and dropping a soft kiss to my lips.

"I can't, Brody." I shake my head and two more tears slip their way down my cheeks. I hug him and bury my face into his shoulder to prevent him from looking at me.

"Why are you crying, Finley?" he says, obviously anxious now, while stroking my back.

I can't take his comfort. It's too much. Air rushes out of my mouth as I fight a sob back. My body starts to tremble in his arms.

"Please, Finley. Tell me. I can't handle this anymore," he says as he pulls me away from his shoulder with both hands on my cheeks. "What can't you do?"

"I can't have a baby," I cry, my voice cracking at the end. I close my eyes tight unable to find the strength to see his reaction.

"I don't understand, Finley," he says, shaking his head and dropping two more feather-light kisses on my face.

I muster up the strength to open my eyes and say my piece, "I met with a doctor, Brody. A fertility doctor. He told me…he told me to look into…adoption." Just saying that word out loud stings because it feels so final. "They did tests, Brody! Tons of shitty, horrifying tests. He told me my body can't have children and there was nothing they could do to help us. We'd be fighting a losing battle if we kept trying."

Brody's hands grip my arms and he moves me off of him, shaking his head, confusingly.

"You did all of this without me?" he asks, raking his hand through his curls and turning away from me.

I rush over and perch on my knees beside him, holding onto his arm.

"I couldn't tell you, Brody! I knew it was me, I could feel it in my bones…something was wrong with *my* body." I look at him, pleadingly, urging him to look back at me, to no avail.

"I was embarrassed! Ashamed, I don't know. I just knew I had to *know* the truth I was feeling in my heart."

He shakes his head, continuing to look at the floor.

"I can't believe you. Why are you only telling me this now?" he asks, with an eerie calm to his voice.

I let go of his arm and sit back on my butt, wrapping my arms around my legs. "Because you need to know why I left, Brody. This was why I left *us*. I can't do it. I can't give you a baby. I'm less of a woman. And right now," I say, looking up into his eyes, intensely, "Even right now, I'm terrified of that look on your face. You want out of this now, don't you? Now that you know the truth, you don't want me! That's why I left; I didn't want to wait around for you to just leave…leave me!" My voice is quaking.

"You," he sighs, deeply, closing his eyes. "You left because you thought I wouldn't want you if you couldn't give me a baby?"

I shrug my shoulders, "I know how important it is to you, Brody. Babies, a family, all of it. It was our dream. It was all we talked about. Our own little *us* baby. It's all I ever dreamed of with you and the fact that I can never give you that was too much for me to handle, Brody! It was too much, I was too hurt. I couldn't stomach…"

"You couldn't stomach what?" he barks.

My head snaps up to see his stony expression.

"I couldn't stomach the idea of you not wanting me anymore once you learned the truth! I couldn't stomach the idea of you looking at me the way you are now!" I say hurriedly.

He lets out a hard huff of air and stands up.

"What are you doing, Brody?" I ask.

He's shaking his head and I can see the anger vibrating off his body. He grabs his pants and puts his legs through the holes. He huffs again as he pulls the condom off and drops it on the floor.

"Brody! Speak!" I cry.

"If I speak right now, I'll fucking *ruin* you, Finley!" he roars at me, and I flinch at the volume of his voice in my small, quiet room.

"You promised, Brody! You said you'd stay with me! I begged you to stay with me!" I cry again, standing up and holding the sheet to my chest, feeling suddenly embarrassed of my body.

"That was before I knew you thought so little of me, that you'd think I'd fucking *leave* you if you couldn't give me a child. God, Finley! It's like you don't even know me!" he snaps, as he finishes buttoning his shirt and throws his clothes into his suitcase.

"What are you doing? Why are you packing?" I ask, my voice rising alarmingly high.

"I'm leaving, Finley."

"Your flight doesn't leave for two days!"

He marches across the hall into the bathroom and grabs his toothbrush and throws that in with everything.

"Seriously, Brody, where are you going?" I ask again.

He stops what he's doing and swerves around to face me, bending slightly so he's eye-level with me.

"I'd rather spend two days in the fucking airport than sleep under the same roof as you again," he says, his eyes glaring into mine. "I'm sure you understand since I'm basically a piece of shit in your eyes."

"No, Brody! I never said that! It wasn't you, it was me!" I cry.

"The *not you, it's me* speech, huh? That's great, Finley. That makes me feel so much better," he says, wheeling his suitcase out the door.

I scramble off the bed and rush over to the door as he pauses at the top of the staircase.

"Brody, I can't. I don't…I just…" I drop to my knees in the doorway at a loss for what to say or do to make him stay.

He looks back at me, "You've ruined us, Fin. *Us* doesn't even exist anymore. This is all on you."

He turns on his heel and stomps down the steps and out of the house. I consider throwing clothes on and running after him, but my heart is too busy shattering into a million pieces. I scream loudly and slam my bedroom door. My greatest fear should have never been that Brody would leave me because I couldn't give him a baby. It should have been that he would leave me because he found out that's how low I thought of him. This is completely my fault. I don't even know how to fix this anymore. He's right. I've broken us.

I crawl back onto my mattress and cry the ugliest cry I've ever cried.

***

CHAPTER TWENTY-EIGHT

"Finley, come on. You have to come out eventually." Leslie is shouting and banging on my door.

"Fin-Bin, love. I miss my leggy brunette. Please, come and say hello. You can even come out naked," Frank coos loudly through the door.

I can't move. I can't function. I can't do anything that requires any type of effort. My face feels tight from the massive amount of tears that dried on it last night. I pray hard it was all a bad dream but based on the fact that I'm still naked, I know better.

I grab my phone to see if Brody has replied to my hundreds of calls or texts. *Nothing.* My heart burns at the sight of my phone's background. A selfie we snapped on our walk yesterday: He's nipping at my cheek and I'm laughing. I look so happy. I have no clue who that girl is anymore.

"Finley, please, honey. I think you should talk to us," Leslie says.

I drop my phone down and look around the room. I see Brody's white t-shirt rumpled below the mattress. I sit up and pick it up off the floor. I can't even help myself, I take a big whiff of it and tears overcome me again. It smells like Brody. Clean and manly. Safe and protective. I pull it over my head and stand up to go look out the window.

"Seriously, Finley. You have to at least say something…anything, so I know you're alive in there," Leslie's voice says, in a definite tone.

After staring at the empty skate park for a few seconds and drying my tears, a coldness creeps over me. I trudge over to the door and pull it open, right in the middle of Frank's eighteenth knock in the last twenty minutes.

Frank looks more serious than I've ever seen him. He's wearing a huge knitted-sweater, a good two sizes too big for him, and skinny dark denim jeans. Leslie looks great, as always, in a short black sweater dress with a thick brown belt notched tightly at her waist. I'm standing there in an oversized men's t-shirt. I feel like shit.

They both look at me, expectantly.

"You guys look great," I say, flatly, walking into the bathroom and shutting the door on them. I can hear them both shuffle around outside the bathroom door.

"You guys can hear me peeing right now, can't you?" I ask.

Silence.

"I know you guys are standing right outside the door," I say, in a dead tone.

"We're worried about you, Finny," Frank says.

I flush and wash my hands and open the door again to their same expectant faces.

"I'm going out for some air," I say, walking past them.

"Finley, you forgot pants," Leslie says.

"Correct, Lez. Two points," I reply, continuing my descent down the steps.

I glance into the living room and see Mitch and Julie cozied up on the couch. *Good for fucking them. I bet she can have babies too.* I sneer at them and turn to walk out the front door.

"For fuck's sake Finley, you don't have any trousers on! Or shoes!" Frank barks from the doorway, but I ignore him.

The brisk fall breeze on my bare legs feels sensational. I luck out to no traffic on the road and walk across to the skate park.

"Damn it, Finley!" Leslie shouts at me.

They both run across the street after me and I stand at the gated entrance into the skate park, threading my hands through the chain link fence and pulling back as hard as I can. I can feel the cold metal cut into my hands and I relish in the pain. It's a small, microscopic break from the pain in my heart.

"For the love of God, Finley. This is ridiculous! Get back inside, now. That t-shirt barely covers anything on you!" Leslie scolds.

I shake my head and turn to look at her and Frank. Their expressions are so concerned and visibly upset that I glare back at them.

"What do you guys have to be upset about? You have no

worries. Nothing. Your lives are carefree right now."

"I don't know about that," Frank says. "Cos I'm currently chasing down a leggy brunette who is wearing nothing but a thin white t-shirt, and I'm fucking gay! I'd say this is a bad fucking Tuesday for me!"

I shake my head back at Frank, not amused.

"Finley, I know Brody left and I'm so sorry, honey. But you have to come inside," Leslie says, approaching me with her hands.

I jump back from her.

"Don't touch me. Don't…just don't. I can't take any comfort right now, Leslie. I don't deserve it. Comfort right now…comfort will…*wreck* me," I say, my lip trembling.

"You should be wrecked right now, Finley. You've had a crap hand dealt to you and shit…I don't know," she says, running her hands through her auburn bob. "Damn! You're only human, Finley! There's only so much you can take. I guess I'd rather see you wrecked right now than running around outside half naked, acting all cold and detached. This isn't my Finley. My Finley is warm, and funny, and emotional. I need you to let me help you, Finley, because I can't fathom how you…I can't…" she stops, tears forming in her eyes.

I shake my head back and forth and blink hard with a big puff of air bursting from my chest. My vision of Frank and Leslie blur as my eyes fill to the top with tears.

"Can't what? Have a baby? Children? I lost him, Leslie!" I cry out loudly and squeeze my eyes tight, allowing the unshed tears to fall out.

"I screwed everything up and I lost him anyways. I can't have a baby. I can't have Brody. I can't fucking let you help me!" I scream, crumpling onto the ground.

Frank and Leslie rush over and kneel beside me, their hands hovering over me, unsure if they should touch me.

"I don't give a toss what you think you can't handle right now, Finny," Frank pulls me into his arms and hugs me hard, stroking his hand down the back of my hair.

"I just don't understand," I cry, in a squeaky raspy tone. "I don't understand why this is happening."

Leslie's arms band around me next and I feel her shaking, silently crying along with me. I feel Frank's hand slip under my legs and he lifts me and carries me back toward the house. I bury my face into his comforting cinnamon smell, unwilling to look around and see how many people are watching me right now.

"Frank," I say his name, crying, as he deposits me onto the couch in the living room. His bright green eyes look so sad and despondent. I feel terrible for causing that look on his face. Mitch and Julie jump up out of the love seat right next to the couch and I look at them, completely embarrassed. Without a word, Mitch leaves and comes back in with a hot cup of tea and Julie covers me with a fuzzy blanket.

"We need comedy...*I Love You, Man,* it is," Leslie says, smiling at me and rummaging in the DVD case by the fireplace.

"I'll go make popcorn!" Julie cheers.

"Guys," I croak. "It's morning."

They all pause to look at me.

"Pancakes then?" Julie asks.

"Stuff that," Frank says, "make the popcorn, Jules. Add extra butter and bring the chocolate too. Who gives a toss what time it is? Mitch, take that tea and shove it up your arse…or go make it an Irish coffee. On second thought, that might be easier. There's Whiskey in the cupboard," he finishes, and sits down on top of my feet, rubbing my leg soothingly.

Mitch heads back into the kitchen for the liquor and I smile kindly at my new little family. I attempt to let the funny words of Paul Rudd drown my heartbreak, even if it is for just a couple hours.

CHAPTER TWENTY-NINE

Leslie, Frank, Mitch, and Julie all keep me company for the rest of the day, stuffing me full of comfort food and liquor. After a lot of convincing, they let me go to bed early because I told them the crying has taken a lot out of me.

In reality, I just feel like crying again and don't want them to witness it.

The next morning is worse because I wake up and feel like it all could have been a bad dream. I feel like I could look up and see Brody coming back in from the bathroom. But I know it's not true.

I pull up his contact and send him a text.

Finley: I just need to know if you're home or if you're okay?

After what feels like an eternity, I hear my phone beep and my heart races as I rush over to it.

Brody: Home.

My heart aches at the one word reply. I can't help myself, so I send one more text.

Finley: I miss you.

I know he won't reply. He hasn't replied to my hundreds of other texts and voicemails. I have work to do today anyway, so for at least a little while I have to attempt to be functional.

After a steaming hot shower, that I cried most of the way through because all it did was make me think of Brody, I get myself dressed in a hoodie and jeans. I have a conference call with Val today and I need to get my shit together.

"Finley?" I hear Leslie's voice call through my door.

"Come in," I reply.

She walks in wearing her flannel pajamas. She's holding two coffee mugs. I half smile at her and sit crisscross on the mattress. She hands me my black coffee and tucks in right beside me, letting her knees touch my leg. I know she needs the contact with me right now to help her gauge how I'm doing.

"I'm okay, Lez," I say, blowing into my cup.

"That was so scary, Finley," she says, with a serious face.

"I'm sorry. I just...I don't know," I say, looking down sadly.

"I hated feeling like," she pauses, "feeling like I wouldn't be able to get through to you."

"I'm sorry I did that to you. I'm sorry for a lot of things," I say.

"Don't be sorry, just give me the cracks, babe."

"Ahhh, the cracks. The cracks," I harrumph, into my mug.

She sits, silently, waiting for me to continue.

"I messed up, Les. I messed up so, so bad. Brody didn't care whether or not I could have a baby, he just cared that I thought so little of him. He couldn't believe I thought he'd leave me over it."

"Why *did* you think that, Fin?" she says, rolling from her knees onto her hip.

"I don't know. I'm still trying to figure that out." I look up at her feeling a sting in my eyes, "I'm fucked up in the head, I guess!" I say, smiling, tears now running down my face.

Leslie sets her mug down and lays her head on my lap, her auburn hair splayed out on my jeans.

"We're all fucked up, Finley. Frank hasn't had a functional relationship with anything but magazine porn since I moved out here. Mitch and Julie don't speak to any of their family anymore…and I'm pretty sure Mitch has a drinking problem. I have dance-gasms on stranger's legs at clubs."

I smile sadly at her.

"You and Brody are the closest we've seen to anyone having their shit together. This fight you two had didn't alter our opinions of that. You guys are amazing. We all have our shit. You just have to stand tall and figure it out eventually I guess," she finishes.

"I don't know, Leslie. I was literally on my knees, and he looked at me with so much hatred. So much anger. So much…hurt," I swallow hard.

"You came out here for a reason, Finley. It wasn't random. This…" she says, sitting up and looking me in the eyes, gesturing back and forth between our chests, "was no mistake, hon. I adore you. I always have. Frank even adores you. I've never seen him warm to someone like he warmed to you. That can't be a mistake."

I sigh heavily, swiping at the tears escaping my eyes.

"You just need to figure your shit out before you can even begin to take Brody's hurt away," she says, patting my leg.

I nod, soaking in her words. "I just know I don't want to love anyone else, Leslie."

"No shit, Sherlock," she smiles, and I laugh, with more tears dropping onto my lap.

"I fucking love you, Lez," I say, seriously.

"I fucking love you, Fin," she replies, and hugs me tightly.

When she leaves I hear a text notification on my phone and my heart leaps with hope that Brody may have replied.

Cadence: CALL ME!

I sigh and press *Send* on her contact.

Without even saying hello, Cadence starts in on me, "George got a text from Mark that he just picked up Brody from the airport! Early!" she barks into the phone.

"Cadence, I'm not in the mood for a lecture."

"I didn't tell him where you were for you to break his freaking heart, Finley!" she chastises me.

"I didn't break his heart!" I explain.

"Then why is he home already, Fin? He was barely there. He probably spent more time on the damn plane than he did in London. What'd you do?"

"I didn't do anything, Cade. I…" I pause. "I just told him the truth."

"That dickhead actually left you because you told him you can never get pregnant?" she shouts, into the phone.

"No," I say, defeated. "It's not like that."

"Then explain please, because I am way too pregnant to have my emotions toyed with like this, Finley."

"I told him the truth, that I can't have a baby and that the reason I left him was because I didn't want him to leave me," I say in one breath.

"Oh God, Finley," she says.

"What?" I cry, "It's the truth, Cadence!"

"Yeah, but jeez…you didn't need to say it like that, did you?" she says, with her typical big-sister tone.

"It needed to be said, regardless. I've been living with this freaking poison in my body and I had to get it out. I had to tell him," I reply.

"How did he take it?" she asks.

I laugh, haughtily, "Um, not well."

"Gosh, Finley. I'm so sorry," she says, in a kinder tone now.

"It's the shit-hand I'm dealt. I gotta deal with it, I guess."

"It is a shit hand. It's going to work out, though. I know it," she says, confidently.

"I don't think so, Cadence," I reply. "You didn't see his face."

She doesn't say anything back.

"How are my M&Ms?" I ask, desperate to talk about something else for a while. I fondly refer to my three nieces as M&Ms because all their names start with the letter M, and it's so much easier than spouting out all three names.

"The girls are good. They miss their Auntie. We're still Skyping tonight though, right?" she asks.

"Of course, I wouldn't miss my weekly date night with my nieces. How are you feeling?"

"Good! Getting achier the bigger I get, of course, but my due date is coming up so I know that's to be expected."

"Well, I'm saving up all my freelance money from Val for a trip home to meet my first nephew. And Frank doesn't seem to want to take any rent from me, so I think I should be able to swing it."

"Good, good," she replies. "So, what is your plan with London and work and everything?"

"I don't completely know, I guess. But I'm pretty sure if I wanted a job with *Faith's Miracle Jewelry*, I'd have it. The owners kind of love me. And I kind of love them." I smile, picturing them at their dining room table.

"Don't talk about moving out there forever. I'll start bawling. I'm way too hormonal to think about that," she says.

I laugh, "Okay, well, I got Val calling me soon, so I better let you go."

"'Kay. I love you, Finley," she says, and I hear her voice crack on the other line.

"I love you, too, Cadence. But hey, are you okay?" I ask.

"Yes, I'm fine. I just miss my baby sister, I guess. Hormones, remember?" she says.

I laugh and we hang up and I ache for the comfort of my sister's house, hugs, and conversation. Cadence is always tough on me, but I wouldn't want her any other way.

CHAPTER THIRTY

My conference call with Val goes really well. She is extremely pleased with my assessment of *Faith's Miracle Jewelry* and wants me to head back out to the country to go over our offer with them. This is more of a sales job and I'm nervous about having to discuss the specifics of money with this family that is so incredibly kind. But Val assures me that they love me, and if I'm just myself, they'll gladly sign on the dotted line.

It's been four days since Brody left and I'm still no closer to having my issues figured out. The thing that perplexes me the most is why I thought so little of him. Why did I think he wouldn't want me without a child?

I stare at myself in the mirror on the back of the bathroom door. For today's meeting, I selected my black pencil skirt with ankle boots and an aqua chiffon blouse. I thought the color would make my face look livelier than it feels. I think I thought wrong.

I clomp loudly down the stairs with my black satchel over one shoulder, and swing open the door to a surprised Liam, appearing to be mid-knock.

"Liam," I say, shocked to see him here.

He looks past me, nervously, and says, "Hey Finley, I'm just here because I forgot my DVDs the other day. I'm sorry...I'm not trying to be weird, I didn't even know if you'd be here. Frank said I could pop by today."

I shake my head, "No, no, it's fine. It's not weird."

He awkwardly stuffs his hands into his jean pockets.

"Are you off today?" I ask, not knowing what else to say.

"Yep, I had some stuff to take care of with my parents, so I'm off the rest of the week actually."

"Oh..." I nervously fidget with the strap of my satchel.

I haven't seen Liam since the night I told him that Brody was it for me. Seeing him now doesn't change that fact, but I feel a huge sense of sadness thinking back to the euphoric feeling I had when Brody showed up that night.

"How are you?" Liam asks, staring down at his shoes.

"I'm fine...okay," I reply, not wanting to lie to him.

"Things okay?" he asks, looking up into my eyes for the first time.

I shake my head and briefly roll my eyes.

"You don't want to know," my voice cracks.

He takes in my emotional expression and hesitates a split second before stepping closer to the doorway.

"Do I need to fix something again?" he asks, with a pure,

wonderful sincerity in his eyes.

I slouch my shoulders and exhale a huge sigh.

"Oh, God, Liam. You're too nice of a guy."

"Finley," he begins, looking straight into my eyes. "I care about you. Just talk to me."

"Brody's gone," I walk out the front door, closing it behind me. I'm not going to lie to Liam. He doesn't deserve to be brushed aside like yesterday's news.

"I finally told him all the crazy crap in my head and he's gone. He had a right to leave. I'm a horrible, awful person." I finish, locking the door. I shuffle over to the top step and sit down.

"I can't cry about this anymore, I've cried too much. I've screwed up too much. I just need to stop, already!" I finish, dropping my head into my hands.

Liam sits down next to me, keeping a good foot of space between us. I don't feel a single ounce of sexual tension between us anymore. It feels like a friend talking to a friend. Thank God for that because I can't handle much more right now.

"Does this have anything to do with that bullocks comment you made to me at the tarts and vicars party, about you not being worth it?" he says, turning slightly toward me.

I nod my head, unable to meet his eyes.

"My guess is Brody didn't appreciate your assessment of yourself."

I nod my head again. "Or my assessment of him," I finish, looking over to the skate park.

"Yeah, us blokes are funny creatures like that," he says, and I turn to look at him. "We don't appreciate being doubted by the woman we love."

I look deep into his warm brown eyes.

"I feel like it's too late for me to fix it, Liam," I say, feeling my eyes prickle with tears.

"Good thing you're talking with the King of Fixing," he says, smiling playfully at me.

"So, what do you suggest?" I ask, pinching my eyebrows and praying for a miraculously easy answer to come out of Liam's mouth.

"Fix yourself before you try to fix your relationship," he finishes, with a simple shrug.

Well shit. That's absolutely no help.

As if reading my mind, Liam laughs, "Finley!" he says, throwing his arm around my shoulder in a playful way. "You've got to give yourself more credit. You can figure this one out…I'm sure of it."

I smile for what feels like the first time in days, and lean my head on Liam's shoulder. He really is a fixer. Just feeling his presence again, stirs something inside of me I thought was long gone. *Hope.*

CHAPTER THIRTY-ONE

The fresh country air is a welcomed change as Mr. Adamson picks me up at the same spot he picked me up before. His mustache looks shorter today as he hugs me hello, and I can't help but smile at his butterscotch scent. The drive out to the country is quiet. Talking isn't quite as easy for me today, after Liam made my brain hurt, but thankfully the silence seems comfortable, and Mr. Adamson doesn't seem to mind.

Mrs. Adamson and Sheila are both standing in the front yard, waiting for my arrival. Mrs. Adamson nearly jogs up to the door to open it and pulls me into a hug. I fight back the tears at the maternal-comforting feeling that comes over me.

"Finley, love! We are so happy to have you back so soon!" she says, squinting slightly at my watery eyes, but choosing not to address them, thankfully.

"Nice to see you again, Finley," Sheila says, walking over and hugging me. "We're really excited to see what your company has for ideas."

"And we're so happy we get to hear all about it from you, and not some stuffy salesman," Mr. Adamson says, coming up behind us.

They lead me inside to the dining room again. I nervously set up the power point proposal I have on my laptop.

***

An hour later, they are signing on the line, and I'm thrilled with my first sale, and the idea of Val's company being an integral part of their growth. I'm certain that *Faith's Miracle Jewelry* is in good hands. They deserve this so much.

"Finley, love. I want to show you my garden out back before you leave. It's my pride and joy, you know," she says, brushing her long white hair back behind her shoulders.

"Oh yes, my mother's roses are well known in town," Sheila says. "People actually come out just to visit her garden."

"Sounds great!" I say, and Mrs. Adamson leads me out the back door.

"The roses don't look the greatest this time of year, but they aren't completely gone yet," she says, as we mosey around the winding gravel paths, in their beautifully manicured backyard.

"They look beautiful," I say. "I have trouble keeping a plant alive at all, so this is all amazing to me."

She looks at me, thoughtfully, and nods.

"May I be frank with you, Finley?" she asks.

Mrs. Adamson has an uncanny way of being direct and honest, but I can't help but love her for it. In fact, it's what I love most about her.

"Please," I reply.

"You seem like you're in pain today," she says. "Don't get me wrong, you're being wonderful and professional and kind, but my heart hurts just looking at you, my darling."

"I'm sorry, I…" I start, not knowing what to say.

"Don't ever be sorry for pain, love. Never be sorry for pain," she says, shaking her finger at me, sternly. "Pain is what makes the good stuff good. It makes us appreciate the *wonderful*, Finley!" she says, guiding me around a bend to the next area of mossy grass and trimmed shrubbery.

"What if the pain is what pushed the good away?" I ask, because I just can't help myself. I'm prepared to take advice from anyone, former flings, and new clients. Hell, I'll even ask Frank for relationship tips if I have to.

She looks to be deep in thought. I'm not sure she's even going to reply until she smiles back at me expectantly.

"You know, Finley, there was a very dark time in my life after my miscarriage, before we adopted Sheila. I don't tell many people this, but Mr. Adamson couldn't get me out of bed for many days. You see, I think women, in general…I for one, feel like our lives will never truly be fulfilled unless we rear a child. Unless I experienced pregnancy and childbirth. God made our bodies for continuing the human species, right? Adam and Eve…the garden. If I couldn't do that, then what kind of woman did that make me? What was the point of me anymore? Why would anyone want me?"

I look at her with my jaw slightly dropped, stunned by her words.

"It sounds foolish now. I'm old, so those are ancient thoughts, I suppose. You young children don't even need to have babies and you're happy. Look at Sheila. She's not married, no children, and no desire to have children. She says she's perfectly content having her jewelry be her baby, and that fills me with such pride. I'm proud of the fact that I raised my girl to be so sure of her mind and know what she wants."

"But what if I don't know what I want," I say. Mrs. Adamson doesn't know what I'm going through, but the way she's speaking to me right now, it feels like she does.

"That just makes you *you,* Finley. That makes you special. And a work in progress," she says, tapping her finger softly on the tip of my nose. "A work in progress, like a lot of our jewelry pieces!" she laughs. "But just you wait, when we finish those pieces, they are going to be more stunning than we even could have dreamed."

Without thinking, I reach out and grab her arm, stopping our pace.

"Thank you," I say, with tears in my eyes. I pull her to me and hug her tightly.

She hugs me back and brushes my hair off to the side, the way only a mother can.

"*The most beautiful work in progress I've ever seen,*" she says, pulling away from me and stroking my hair around my face.

We walk around the garden a bit longer, giving my eyes time to dry out and then she takes me back inside so Mr. Adamson can deliver me back to the rail station. As I ride back to the city, I think about everything she said. How I can stop being a work in progress and become happy in my own skin again. I feel a shift happening inside of me. I just have to figure out what I'm going to do about it.

CHAPTER THIRTY-TWO

When I get back to London, I'm just hopping off the tube and walking the two blocks to our house when I see I have a voicemail.

I press *One* and hear my mother's voice.

"Finley, it's Mom. Cadence is in the hospital, honey. There's something wrong with the baby," I hear her voice crack, and a muffling of her phone.

I stop dead in my tracks on the sidewalk, people swerve to get around me.

"I know you're so far away, honey, but Cade said you were saving for a ticket, so we're hoping you can come early. She just keeps saying she needs you here. She wants you, sweetie."

Her voice is full-on crying now and I feel my chest swell with panic.

I hang up and call my mom's cell.

"Hello?" My dad's gruff voice cuts over the line.

"Dad, what's going on?" I ask.

"Hey, kiddo. It's...it's not good, Finley," he says.

"Tell me, Dad!" I reply with urgency.

"I think it's better you just get here. We'll be able to explain it all in person."

"Is Cadence okay?" I say, my voice squealing with a cry I've never heard before.

My dad sighs heavily, trying to compose himself, "She's fine, Finley. I promise."

"What about Baby George?" I ask, a knot forming in my throat.

"There's some complications, Fin. Please honey, we'd really rather talk to you in person. Can you do that for me, kid? Can you do me that favor, please?"

He sounds desperate, so I agree. I hang up the phone and run the rest of the way home.

Coldness prickles over my body as I frantically throw clothes into a small carry-on luggage bag.

"What are you going to do? You don't have a ticket or anything yet, Fin," Leslie says, standing awkwardly in the doorway. "Do you know how expensive a short-notice ticket purchase will be?"

"I have to get home, Leslie! This isn't even negotiable. You should have heard my dad," I start, unable to finish that sentence. "I'll just put it on my credit card. Cadence needs," my voice cracks and my chin trembles as a sob rushes out of my chest. "Her baby..." My voice screeches out into that cracked scary sound again and I close my mouth, knowing I can't say anything more.

Frank enters my bedroom abruptly, "Give me your handbag, Finley."

I look at him questioningly, and watch him trudge over to my bed and grab it without another word.

"I have to go soon, Frank," I explain.

"I know, just give me five minutes, love," he contends, as he exits my room.

I have no clue what Frank is doing but I don't have time to think about it. I need to get my bathroom essentials packed.

"I wish I knew what to say, Finley," says Les. "Your poor sister. I just, I wish I could help you or something. Or I wish your dad would have just told you what was going on."

"There's nothing to help with, Les. I just need to get to Cadence right now. I'm praying it's not a worst-case scenario and they are just overreacting. Maybe the doctor will have it all figured out by the time I get there," I say, not really convincing myself.

I zip up my carry-on and make my way downstairs with Leslie following closely behind. When I hit the bottom of the stairs, Frank is in the foyer with his tablet in hand as he hangs up his cellphone.

"Okay, love. Your ticket is booked and paid for and the cab is only two minutes away. I got you on the next flight out of Heathrow in two hours; you'll be home by tomorrow morning. Your ticket confirmation should be in your email account, so you can just use your mobile at the airport," he rushes his words out in a businesslike manner.

I look at Frank, stunned. "Thanks, Frank. I'll pay you back," I finish, taking my purse from him.

"Stuff that. You're not paying me back a pound, just promise you'll come back to us, Fin-Bin. I mean, I hope your sister is okay and everything. Of course I do, but…" he pauses, looking around the room, awkwardly. "I've kind of grown somewhat attached to you, I'm afraid." He looks down sadly, with one hand on his small hip and the other scratching his frizzy orange hair.

I sigh at the sweetness of his sentiment. He looks up at me with tears in his eyes.

"Frank, what is it?" I reach over and pull him into a strong hug.

Frank sniffs hard, "I'm not crying, I'm just...oh, stuff it. I can't handle all these emotions. You women have ruined me." He pulls back and looks between me and Leslie. "Seeing you rush off to go be with your sister is just a lot for me to process. I'm such a girl now when it comes to these types of issues." He clears his throat, "I'm not trying to make this about me. I'm sorry. I just," he pauses. "I don't have family like you do. You guys are kind of it for me."

I hug him again and Leslie comes over and wraps her arms around both of us. We hold each other quietly until a honk comes from outside the door.

"Give your sister hugs from all of us, and call us as soon as you land," Leslie says, with red eyes.

"I love you guys," I reply, looking at both of their tear-strewn faces.

Frank grabs my carry-on and follows me outside. Leslie stays at the doorway, waving sadly at me, turning away to hide her tears. I take one final look at the house that welcomed me when I needed it most. The house with a purple door that now feels like home to me. The house that, despite it all, I'm not ready to leave yet.

CHAPTER THIRTY-THREE

The flight home is torture. Complete and utter agony. I wasn't sure what I was going to find out when I got to the hospital. While waiting to board the plane, I had called my mom, begging her to just tell me everything and she adamantly refused. So for the whole twelve-hour flight, my mind raced with all of the worst-case scenarios. If my mom won't tell me the details, then has the worst already happened?

Could something be wrong with the baby? Or perhaps there is something wrong with Cadence? I'd read an article once about a woman who got breast cancer while she was pregnant and refused treatment because it would kill the baby. That would be Cadence. Being a mother was her whole entire life. She'd gladly lay down her life to save the life of any one of her three girls or the precious baby boy she was carrying. I can't even comprehend what that news would feel like, so I just tried to focus on the plane ride.

Both of my parents are waiting for me outside of the airport when I come outside. The familiar Midwest air is in no way comforting when I lock eyes with them. They look older and tired. I'm not sure if it's from my time away or from the stress of the current situation.

My mom rushes over to hug me and begins shaking into my shoulder.

I pull back, looking into her large, round aqua eyes.

"Mom, what?" I ask, worried sick now.

Her hair is tied back into a messy ponytail at the nape of her neck, and she looks like she hasn't slept in days.

She shakes her head, regretfully, "It's not good, Finley. It's not good." She bursts into a sob, screwing up her face to try and get her emotions under control.

"Jesus, Mom. Tell me!" I cry.

My dad comes over and places a comforting hand on my mom's shoulder while she continues to try and speak but can't find the words. She looks at my dad with a surrendering nod of her head and cries into his shoulder.

"Cadey lost the baby, Fin," he says, in his deep baritone voice.

I pull my head back slowly, looking him directly in the eyes. Flutters of life and people blur in my peripheral vision as the gravity of the news settles in my brain. My dad didn't just say that, he didn't. He continues to watch me somberly, his chin twitching under his dark brown goatee.

"Cadence lost her baby?" Cadence lost her baby. Her. Baby. I hunch over and cover my eyes and face with my hands as my face crumples beneath them.

"No!" I cry, ripping my hands away from my face and looking at my dad, accusingly. "Her little boy?" I question, a cry erupting from my mouth again. Why did I have to say that? Why did I have to say little boy? I just have to realize the situation in another way to fully comprehend this news.

My dad's steadfast strength crumbles at those words and he blinks his red eyes several times in response to the tears coming out of them. He nods his head slightly in confirmation.

I look over to my mom who has completely lost it now. What the hell? Even though I had a twelve-hour plane ride to prepare myself for this, I was in no way prepared for the baby to be gone. I just thought someone was sick or there was a complication. Kansas City has a good hospital. I was certain they would be able to fix whatever was wrong.

I drop my purse on the ground and turn from them, walking a few steps away for some air. This can't be happening. It can't! How could she lose the baby? Her little boy she's been praying so hard for? This was their last chance. Their last time. George said they could try one more time for a boy, but if it didn't happen he was ready to accept that his lot in life was to be surrounded by beautiful women.

My sister is beautiful, too. Cadence is even more stunning in her pregnant form. She was made to have babies. She and her three girls are all blonde, unlike the rest of my brunette family. Like mother, like daughter. Her three little girls were gorgeous, blonde, living, *thriving* proof of my sister being born to reproduce.

As the image of my three nieces pops into my head, I squat down on the sidewalk and cover my face to conceal the sobs that are now erupting from my mouth.

"Oh my God! My M&Ms! How are they going to handle this?"

My mom squats down beside me and wraps her arms around my back, crying. How is my family going to get through this? How is a tragedy like this possible? It isn't supposed to be hard for Cadence. I thought I had taken the entire bad juju away from my family with all my fertility issues. No family should have to endure an infertile daughter and a daughter who suffers a pregnancy loss this late into her third trimester.

My dad bends over in front of me offering his hand, "Let's get in the car ladies, we don't need all these damn people looking at us right now." He ushers us to the car and my mom slips into the backseat with me, continuing to hold my arm close to her the whole way to the hospital.

CHAPTER THIRTY-FOUR

As I follow my mom and dad through the hospital to the postpartum wing, my mind is numb. They explained to me in the car that the placenta had detached inside of her and they couldn't get the baby out in time to save him. She was nearly thirty-seven-weeks along and had no signs of bleeding or complications. The doctor informed her and George that in rare cases, there can be something called silent placental abruption where there are no symptoms and things like this just happen sometimes. They had to do an emergency c-section.

The torture of the situation is that at thirty-seven weeks, she was considered full term. Definitely far enough along for him to have survived if they would have delivered early. But I guess everything happened so quickly, they didn't realize anything was wrong until it was too late and baby George had already passed away inside of her. That part was impossible to think about.

My mom and dad stop outside of a patient's room. Pinned prominently on the door is a golden, laminated circle. My heart compresses as I glance at other patient's doors with nothing on them.

Did that indicate a halo? Like an angel halo?

The door opens before we get a chance to knock and George comes out. He looks so defeated. I want to reach out and hug him instantly, but my emotions are definitely not in check and I'm afraid if I hug him, I'll start sobbing on him. He doesn't need to be comforting me right now. His eyes look up from the floor and he glances at my parents and then to me.

"You made it," he sighs, looking slightly relieved.

"I did," I squeak, my chin trembling.

"She's getting in the shower right now but she told me that she wants you to come in right away, no matter what," he says, feebly.

"George," I look at him pleadingly, taking in his appearance. He looks crushed but still the same, big, cuddly George I remember.

"Come here," he replies, opening his arms to me.

I rush into his arms and my head hits his soft chest as he hugs me tightly, sniffing occasionally. George is like a brother to me. He has the familiar smell of their house on his shirt and I relish in the comfort of his embrace and that particular scent.

For years I had been stopping by their house to play with the girls. Cadence was ten years older than me and started having babies when I was still in school. Their oldest is 14 now, so there were many years when it was just me and their family hanging out. George never seemed to mind me tagging along and we've grown very close over the years. We would gang up on Cadence whenever she would go into a tailspin about Lord knows what. George and I made it our personal mission to break her down when she got going on one of her famous fits. She hated it; we loved it. It was our thing. But while we were very close and comfortable with each other, we never had to go through any situation like this.

"She's been worrying about your flight, so you better get in there and let her know you're here," he murmurs into the top of my head.

"Okay," I look up at him and back at mom and dad for encouragement.

They look at me with sad expectant eyes and I will myself to be strong as I place my hand on the doorknob.

"She won't let me touch her, Fin," he announces, before I open the door.

I look back at him, squeezing my brows together in silent question.

"Since the surgery," he starts, "she won't let me touch her."

He looks at me with desperation in his eyes and I nod in response, placing a reassuring hand on his chest. He grabs my hand and holds it tightly against his fluttering heart, "I need her back, Finley," he whispers, with a pain in his eyes that makes my knees buckle, "*I need to hold her.*"

I nod again, and with a large sigh, I enter the room. It's dark, except for one small lamp above the bed that casts a warm glow onto the head of the bed. The bed is a standard hospital bed and there's a pullout couch along the far wall with rumpled blankets and pillows strewn everywhere.

I hear the lull of the shower in the bathroom and make my way toward the door. I knock loudly, "Cade? It's me."

"Finley?" she croaks.

"Yeah, can I come in?"

"Yes!" I hear her gushing air out in between quiet sobs, trying to compose herself.

She pokes her head out from the shower curtain. Her dirty-blonde hair is stuck down to the sides of her face and her eyes are red and blotchy.

"Were you crying in there?" I ask, with a trembling chin.

"Yes!" she sobs hard, her meager resolve shedding before my eyes. "The shower is the worst, Finley! I was doing okay until I stood under this water. I can't stop thinking about him!" she wails, loudly, as her shoulders hunch over, violently shaking with her cries.

She looks so broken that without thought, I push the curtain back and hug her hard. Her naked, wet body soaks me along with the spray of the water. I don't care that my sister's naked right now. I don't care that I'm fully dressed. She is shattering apart in front of me and I need to hold her as much as she needs me to hold her.

"Finley!" she cries, putting her hands up in refusal at my entry into her shower.

I press her arms down to her sides and clamp my arms around the tops of hers in a tight embrace.

I feel her chest heaving against my forced clinch. After a moment, when her breathing slows, she cries out loudly, "I can't stop seeing his perfect face in my head! He is so beautiful, Finley!"

I release one of my hands from the tight grip I had forced behind her back and rub it down the back of her wet head, blinking against the spraying shower stream bolting onto my face. I don't want to move her, so I just breathe through the stream as best I can.

"He has brown hair Fin, like yours, and George's!" she continues, shuddering in my embrace, "I don't understand, Fin. I don't understand! I just want to close my eyes and go to sleep and have him still be alive and wiggling inside of me again. I'm so close to when things were okay. It was just a few days ago, Fin. A few days ago, things were fine! It's right there! I can almost touch it!" she cries into my shoulder.

She slinks out of my embrace and slowly lowers herself to the ground, hugging her legs and rocking back and forth. "My body, Finley. My body! It's like it's still pregnant. I swear I can still feel him moving in me," she looks up at me, disbelievingly.

I turn and slide down the wall beside her, wiping the water out of my eyes and pushing my wet hair from my face.

"I have this big belly still, and these painful breasts with milk coming in, and this painful incision, Fin. But I have nothing to show for it. Nothing!" She shrieks, crying into her kneecaps and tipping herself back, sitting on the shower floor, leaning on the concrete wall next to me. "My body is mangled to nothing and I don't even have a baby to kiss it all better."

Finally, I feel compelled to respond, "You do have something to show for it, Cadence. You had a baby, a beautiful baby boy. He didn't live," my voice cracks. "But you birthed him. He is yours. Forever and always, he is yours."

"Finley!" she looks at me, still sobbing. "I didn't know I could ever hurt this much."

"Me neither, Cadence. Me neither," I reply, shaking my head and staring forward at the water circling the drain. "I wish I could just fix this, Cade. I wish I could turn back time for you and make this not happen. I wish I could have been there when you needed me. I wish there was something, anything, I could do now," I say, squinting up into the shower spray coming down near us, willing myself to shut up because I know I'm rambling.

She looks at me with wide, puppy-dog eyes, "You're here. That's enough, Fin. You're what I needed," she says, and then nods encouragingly at me.

My heart breaks, looking at her tearstained face, her wet hair and her tiny frame grasping onto her legs like her life depends on it. She looks so young and destroyed. So different from the sister I grew up with. Cadence is so much older than me and has been helping me through all my melodramatic crap for the majority of my life. It's rare that I'm ever a shoulder for her to cry on. She always had her life together. George and Cade were high school sweethearts and married young. She had her oldest daughter, Megan, at only 21 years old. It was that easy for Cadence. She wanted to be a mother and she became one. It seemed like that's how the majority of Cadence's life played out. I was always the screwed up little sister who didn't do things the normal and traditional way.

She was a huge buffer between me, Mom, and Dad when they were upset with Brody and me for not wanting to get married. She was the fixer in our family and was always able to help Mom and Dad understand me. They knew Cadence and I were close, so if Cadence told them I was okay, they took her word for it and tried not to meddle as much.

The girl chewing on her knuckle right now as water rolls off her skin, is not the sister I grew up with. Cadence has just endured one of the most tragic things a person can imagine, and here she is, telling me that *I* was all she needed right now. Despite her meager appearance, she is still managing to make me feel stronger than I ever believed I could be.

"I love you, Cadence. I madly and truly love you." I wrap my long arms around her bawled up form, and continue crying with her for a while until George's voice breaks our bubble.

"Uhhh, hello?" George says, tentatively, from the cracked door.

"George?" Cadence replies.

"What happened to Finley?" he questions, coming into the bathroom.

"She's in the shower with me."

"Oh, God! Crap! I'm sorry, I'll leave!" he says, rushing quickly out the door.

"She's not naked, George. It's fine!" Cadence calls back to him. "But she might need some dry clothes." She half smiles at me, wiping my hair back from the side of my face the way only an older sister could.

CHAPTER THIRTY-FIVE

I help Cadence out of the shower and dry her off. I catch a glimpse of us in the mirror and cringe at the horror of how we both look. I'm fully clothed and completely soaked, with makeup running down my face; Cadence looks pale and wobbly as I use a towel to dry her hair for her.

George knocks again, "I have Finley's suitcase, am I okay to come in?"

"Yes," we reply, in unison.

George opens the door and takes in the sight of his wife wrapped in a towel and me in my soaking wet clothes.

"Are you guys okay?" he asks, looking sadly between the two of us.

Cadence looks at me with a small affectionate smile and then walks over to George and lays her head on his chest, prompting him to wrap his big arms around her. He closes his eyes and I swear I can see the pain and grief in him float off his body and into the steamy shower air.

I smile at the beauty of them, with tears in my eyes. George looks up to me with wide eyes and mouths a silent, "Thank you."

CHAPTER THIRTY-SIX

I plan to stay at Cadence and George's house for the next couple weeks. Mom and Dad understand completely and are grateful I'm there to help her and be with the girls.

The grief comes in waves for Cadence. One minute she looks good and strong, staying busy and moving a lot to help speed up the healing from her surgery. Then the next minute, she gets a far off look in her eyes and tells us she needs some air. Every time she puts her shoes on to go for a walk, I ask if I can come, and she always says no. It breaks my heart because I just know she's out there crying by herself, and yet, I can't force myself on her.

George is home with all of us, too. He's working a lot on his laptop, so I offer to take the girls to school and pick them up every day. Whenever I look at him, though, he almost always has his eyes on Cadence. From what I can tell, he's doing a lot more Cadence-watching than actual work.

My M&Ms each deal with the loss in their own way. Maya is five and seems to understand it but isn't overly emotional about it. However, she keeps going up to Cadence's tummy and rubbing it. Watching Cadence's reaction to that is like a cruel and unusual punishment, but I can't help but smile at the beauty of Maya's innocence around the whole situation.

McKinley is nine and seems to be pondering where baby George ended up, which sparks lots of interesting explanations of heaven, like who goes to heaven, and how you get there. I end up answering a lot of those questions because McKinley has attached herself to my hip the whole time during my stay. I can tell that of all the girls, she's missed me the most and is making up for lost time.

Megan took Baby George's passing the hardest. At fourteen years old, she's emotional, so having hormones raging in her body with puberty striking, is of no help. I think she feels some guilt, too, because prior to losing Baby George, she complained about her sisters a lot. Since Baby George has passed, I notice her actively seeking out her sisters to play with them. She even tolerates more of the kid toys and games the younger ones enjoy. A big change from her typical iPod and iPhone solitary confinement she always lived in before. I'm thankful because I know Cadence is noticing. When I see her watching them, I see that old, memorable light in her eyes I thought was gone forever.

There's extra work around the house, too, because we're all helping prepare for the memorial service that Cadence and George are having for Baby George. They opted to have him cremated, which I know couldn't have been an easy decision. Cadence opened up to me about it one night and said she just couldn't imagine his tiny, perfect body buried in the ground, an arm's reach away from holding him.

We've been home for three days now and I'm helping Cadence look online for special music to play at the ceremony in a couple days. We all hear a knock on their front door. Cadence and George live on a small acreage, so they don't get many knocking visitors. Most people that come here know them well enough to just walk in.

A moment later, George walks back into the living room followed by Brody. My heart drops at the sight of him. I'd be lying if I didn't think about driving into the city to see him half a dozen times or more. But I always stopped myself because now wasn't the time for my relationship bullshit. Cadence, the M&Ms, and George need me here and that is a rarity. They've been helping me for years, so it is all I can do to return the favor.

Seeing Brody standing there in his faded blue jeans and loose flannel shirt sends familiar flutters in my lower belly. He looks as good as always. My heart silently breaks at the idea that he isn't as affected by our break up as I am.

"Hey, Cade," Brody says, striding into the living room to Cadence who's sitting on the couch next to me.

Cadence stands up slowly, cautious of her c-section incision and gives him a long hug. I can smell the familiar scent of Brody. *Clean, fresh, perfect.*

"I wish I knew what to say," he says, pulling away and sweeping his hand through his now shorter curly brown hair.

"Yeah," Cadence replies, with a sad look. "Nice of you to stop by," she says, looking a bit emotional again.

"I, uh...I brought gifts for the girls, but they don't have to open them now if they're in bed," he says, awkwardly, holding three pink gift bags in his hand. "I meant to get here earlier, before they went to sleep."

"Of course they can open them now, I'm sure they aren't asleep yet. They'd love to see you," she says, looking to George.

George leaves the living room to go bring the girls downstairs. We had just put them to bed a few minutes before Brody's arrival. Nighttime procedure was a mess every night. The girls were always getting into trouble for playing in each other's rooms and not sleeping.

"Hey, Brody," I say, pulling at the strings of my hoodie, awkwardly.

"Hi, Finley," he replies, barely looking at me. *Damn him.*

The girls come sprinting into the room and light up at the sight of him.

"Brody!" the two younger girls bound into him with huge hugs and smiles.

Megan stays back by the wall, tucking her long blonde hair behind her ear.

"Hey, Megan," Brody says, looking at her while ruffling the hair of the two younger girls.

"Hey," she replies, looking a bit shy. Gosh, she's so beautiful. When she figures that out, she'll never be shy again.

"I have presents!" he says, tweaking his eyebrows up and down at Megan. Megan stifles a small smile.

McKinley and Maya grab a bag each and Brody hands one off to Megan, who finally comes further into the room and sits down on the floor. They all dig into their gift bags and pull out individual bags of M&Ms and start giggling.

"Can we eat some, Mom?" Maya asks, looking over to Cadence.

"You can have one small handful each, and that's it. Small!" she adds, while they rip open their bags.

Brody always brings M&Ms to the girls, ever since he discovered my nickname for them. My heart aches at the familiarly of his gesture.

"There's more in there," Brody says, sitting down on the floor next to Megan.

They all reach into their bags and pull out several cellophane-wrapped packages of baseball cards. I stifle a laugh as they all look at him with confused expressions.

"My brother gave me my first set of baseball cards and now I have hundreds and hundreds of them," he says, raising his eyebrows dramatically to Maya.

"What does that have to do with us?" McKinley asks. God I love her, she is just so brutally honest with her questions. I wish it came that easily for adults.

"I think," Brody begins, looking up at Cadence, cautiously, "Your baby brother, George, would have liked it if he had big sisters cool enough to have their very own baseball cards. So these are something you guys can keep to help you always remember you have a brother, even if he's not here with you every day."

The room falls quiet. I'm surprised to feel tears running down my cheeks. Cadence's soft sob breaks the silence.

Brody looks up with a worried expression and Cadence nearly falls on top of him, hugging his shoulders, tightly.

"Damn it, Brody," she cries into his shoulder.

He looks up to George, clearly concerned. George smirks and nods his head.

Cadence sniffs loudly and stands upright again. "That is so, just so...perfect."

The girls murmur quick thank yous and open their baseball card packs and begin bickering over whose are better. Brody stands up and George shakes his hand and pulls him into a half hug, slapping his back the way guys do when they don't want to appear too emotional.

Megan stands up with her head lowered and crashes into Brody, squeezing him around his waist, tightly burying her face into his stomach. George half smiles watching her, and she releases Brody and rushes over to hug her dad.

I sniff once and wipe my face, standing awkwardly.

"Can you stay for a drink, Brody?" Cadence asks.

He looks over at me for a brief second, and replies, "Uh, sure. I can have one, probably."

Cadence heads into the kitchen and starts opening a bottle of wine.

"That was…" I shake my head, unable to finish the sentence.

He shrugs back at me and looks down at Maya and McKinley playing on the floor. George tells them it's time for bed again and that they can take their cards with them. That seems to appease them and they head off after saying thanks again and giving Brody another hug.

"How are you?" I ask, with a small frog in my throat from all the tears I'd just shed.

"I'm okay," he replies, looking at Cadence in the kitchen. "Need help opening that?"

And just like that, he's gone. My heart aches at the coldness in his demeanor. I don't know how to break through this huge shield Brody has built up with me, but I know I need to try.

George joins Cadence and Brody in the kitchen as they pour red wine into four glasses.

"Come here, Fin," Cadence says, obviously trying to convey a message to me.

I go into the kitchen and we all settle ourselves on the barstools that wrap around the kitchen area. Brody, George, and Cadence speak about the memorial service coming up, and everything they need to do to prepare for it.

"Actually, Brody, I was wondering if you'd be willing to help Finley with the girls tomorrow. She's bringing them into the city to buy them all new dresses for the service and she promised to take them to see *Frozen*…again," she laughs, nervously. "I'm worried she's going to be in over her head with all three of them alone all day tomorrow. George's and my parents are coming with us to the funeral home, so they can't go with her."

Smooth, Cadence. Real smooth.

Brody smiles kindly at her and clears his throat, "I, uhhh."

"You're the only one in the city I can think to ask that the girls actually like!" she smiles, brightly.

While I'm horribly uncomfortable with my sister's shameless matchmaking skills, I'm happy to see her speaking animatedly about anything again. She looks like the old Cadence.

Brody purses his lips into a smile, "I could probably handle that."

"Great!" Cadence exclaims.

"You'll probably like *Frozen*, Brod," George chimes in. "Seriously, I love it. The girls make me listen to the soundtrack in the car all the time. It's good. I'm not ashamed."

Brody smiles and stands up from his seat. "No problem, I probably should be going though."

"Can I walk you out?" I ask, nervously.

He nods without expression, hugs Cadence goodbye, and shakes George's hand.

We walk down the hall to the front door and Brody holds the door open for me to pass through. I tuck my hands into the front pouch of my hoodie and shiver at the cool, nearly-winter air.

He comes to a stop beside me and I take in his face, illuminated only by the soft yellow porch light.

"You look good," I say, unsure where to start.

He sighs, heavily, "Finley, let's just..."

"Don't, Brody. Don't just act like we can be friends and pretend nothing happened."

"I'm not trying to, Finley. I'm just trying to," he pauses, looking down and scuffing his boots on the porch, "Survive, I guess."

"Me too, *Brody*. This isn't easy for me, you know. You ripped my heart out when you left that night," I say, stepping closer to him to force him to look me in the eyes.

Instead, he takes a step back and turns away, laughing slightly.

"Oh, believe me, I know. Leslie called me the next day and gave me all the details. She raged my ear off for a good ten minutes. Then Frank got on the phone and I had to hear it all over again. He has a real colorful way of talking, let me tell you," he finishes, turning to look at me again.

I shake my head, not sure how to respond to that. I love my friends, but I'm not sure I needed Brody to know what a mess I was the day after he left.

"And what pisses me off," he says, turning to face me again, "Is that you weren't the only one whose heart was ripped out that night,

Fin."

"You didn't even give me a chance to explain!" I start.

"Explain what? Explain that I've done nothing but love," he breathes heavily, composing himself, "Love you like *crazy* for the past five years, and yet you thought so little of me, that the minute things got rough..."

"I don't know what I was thinking, Brody!" I exclaim, grabbing his face, forcing him to look me in the eyes.

He shoots daggers down on me. "You could have given me a chance first, Finley. I deserved a chance to prove you wrong."

"I know!" I cry, tears forming in my eyes. "You think I don't know that now? You think I don't know what a colossal mistake I made in doubting you? In doubting your character? It's the biggest mistake of my life. And now I just have to live with it and watch you...watch you..." I can't finish that thought.

He shakes his head free from my grasp.

"Watch me what? Watch me find someone fertile and play house with another woman? That's what is so mind boggling to me, Finley! Who *are* you right now?" he admonishes.

"I get it now, Brody. It was all me! All of it! I couldn't get past it, for myself. I went through all these scary tests, and then the doctor said *adoption*, and it was like the wind got knocked out of me! To know that I can't do this basic human nature thing with my body...it broke me, Brody. I was *broken*."

"So you turned me into your scapegoat by pegging me as the villain in your messed up mind. *You* broke us, Finley," he finishes, with a sneer. "But don't worry, I'll be there for those girls tomorrow. And I'll be there for the memorial service on Saturday, because contrary to what you may think, I'm *not* a piece of shit."

Before I can say anything else, he stomps off to his truck and I'm left alone on the porch. Alone with my thoughts, alone with my pain, alone with my massive, massive mistakes, and a seriously dwindling amount of hope.

CHAPTER THIRTY-SEVEN

The M&Ms are extremely excited for our day together because they get to skip out on school, and that's better than Christmas to them. We drive into Kansas City to shop and I appreciate the distraction from my thoughts and the sadness that is engulfing me. There's just too much rolling around in my head right now. Cadence, Baby George, Big George, and now Brody. It's too much.

My lightness is short lived because we're headed to the movie theater where Brody is meeting us. After we park, I grab McKinley's hand, Megan grabs Maya's hand, and we make our way to the theater entrance. Brody is waiting for us in the lobby, looking great in a long-sleeve half-button grey shirt and jeans. His sleeves are pushed up slightly on his forearm, revealing his dark arm fuzz and I have to physically restrain myself from reaching out and stroking his arms.

I'm not ashamed to admit that I tried a little harder on my appearance today, hoping Brody might take notice. I'm not disappointed when I see his eyes run up the length of my body. I'm wearing my black leather leggings that have sheer wrap-around cutouts on the thighs. I paired them with a cream-colored top that drapes off the side, revealing a lot of my shoulder.

"Hi," I say, coming up to him.

"Hi," he replies, eyeing the exposed skin along my collarbone and arm.

"Did you get our tickets?" McKinley asks.

"Not yet," Brody laughs, "I just got here."

He grabs McKinley's arm and pulls her into him, ruffling her hair. She whines and attempts to straighten it and we head over to the ticket counter.

After arguing over who is going to pay for the tickets, I give in and let Brody buy them, as long as he lets me pay for the concessions. I hate this argument. It feels so formal and awkward, not at all like we used to be.

We get two large popcorns and two large pops to split between all of us. Brody causes all the girls to giggle when he flashes them the M&Ms he's stashed away inside his jacket.

He's so good with the girls, so natural. Just seeing him with them reminds me of all that I ran from and what I would have never been able to give him. The familiar ache in my heart returns and I turn away from his watchful eyes to conceal my thoughts.

"Finley, I need to go to the bathroom," Maya says, as we settle in our seats waiting for the previews to start. I'm so far away in my own thoughts that she has to repeat herself three times before I register what she's saying to me.

I get up and lead Maya past McKinley and Megan, just when I go to pass by Brody, he reaches out and grabs my wrist.

"Hey, are you okay?" he asks, concern on his features.

Yesterday, I would have killed for him to look at me like that. I've been dying for him to call me and check on me, care about me, anything. Now that I have it, I don't think I still want it.

"I'm fine," I say, and shake my head, following Maya out of the theater to the bathroom.

As Maya does her business, I look at myself in the mirror and I feel ridiculous. Here I am, dressing up for a man I'm trying to win back, when I know damn well he'd be a thousand times better off without me. Brody is perfect. He's great with the girls. He is meant to be a father. He will be the perfect father to someone…someday. I'm being selfish trying to win him back. I silently chastise myself as I pull my collar up to cover my bare shoulder.

When we come back into the theater, Brody eyes me, warily. The previews start, and he doesn't get a chance to ask me any more questions. I'm thankful for the dark theater and the nearly two hours of solitude I have to get my thoughts together, but I feel Brody's eyes on me throughout the film.

After the movie is over, I barely look at Brody as he walks us all to the car. I shut the last door once all the girls are safely in their seatbelts, and walk around the back of the car, nearly running into Brody. His face is covered with concern.

"What is it, Finley?" he asks, firmly.

"It's nothing," I say, plastering on a smile but refusing to look him in the eyes.

"Don't give me that. What is it?" he asks, looking at the girls in the car.

I look in quickly too, and see they are all back on their electronic devices they brought with them for the ride down.

"Come on. You wanted to talk last night and now you have nothing to say?" he says.

"It doesn't even matter anymore, Brody."

"Then why don't you tell me, if it doesn't even matter?"

I shake my head again.

"Just fricken' say it, Finley. I don't just…I don't just stop caring about you, you know. You owe it to me to at least be honest," he says, grabbing my arm with his large hand.

I look deeply into his blue eyes, "It's just that…this is all for the best, Brody."

"What's for the best?" he asks, furrowing his brow.

"You're *great* with kids," I half laugh, half cry, because the insanity of the juxtaposition I feel is beyond comprehension.

"Seriously Brody, you're wonderful with those girls! My M&Ms." My eyes well with tears. "You deserve that, Brody. You deserve to have your own M&Ms."

He shakes his head at me, but I can't decipher what he's thinking.

I shrug my shoulders and move past him, and he stops me by my arm that he's still holding on to.

"You can't…you just…you can't just say that stuff and walk away, Finley," he says, turning his face to look at me, his eyes red.

"I mean it, Brody. I was right in leaving you. You didn't deserve to be my scapegoat. I was lying to myself about why I left. It wasn't your feelings that scared me, *it was my own.*"

I sniff once and look him in the eyes again.

"It's just too much to live with this regret of not being able to give you what you so crazily deserve," I finish.

He turns his body to face me fully again. "Don't I deserve you?" he says, confusion all over his face as his eyes rove over mine.

My chin trembles as I fight back the cry growing inside me. "You deserve better, Brody. So, so much better," my voice cracks and my reserve falls.

He shakes his head, rapidly, back and forth.

"No. No, *fuck that*," he growls, and slams his lips to mine.

I gasp against his mouth, surprised at the brute pressure of his mouth. My salty tears slip from my eyes and mingle in between our lips as he attempts to kiss the pain inside of me away. His kiss feels possessive and passionate…needy and achy. It's all I wanted him to do to me last night. This is Brody. My Brody. I love him. I love us. But I can't do this to him. I can't take his life away from him. A man like Brody is worthy of everything he wants in life. And I know I can't give him that.

I regretfully break the kiss, quickly, and cover my mouth, shaking my head at him. Before he can say anything, I turn and run around the car and hop into the driver's seat.

Megan is eyeing me cautiously from the passenger seat.

"Are you okay?" she asks.

I nod my head, dropping my hand from my mouth, unable to speak because I know if I do, I'll just cry.

"Are you sure you want to drive away right now?" she says.

I look over to her, my jaw slightly dropped, and then start the car and leave.

CHAPTER THIRTY-EIGHT

I get ready for Baby George's service with a numb, foggy feeling over me. Crying today is a given. I'm going to be watching my sister spread the ashes of her baby over the Fourteenth Street Bridge, just outside of town. It's where she and George had their first kiss when they were young children, dreaming of a life together. I'm sure they never envisioned doing something like this in that special spot, but they both agreed it was the best place to have the service.

My dress is a simple knee-length fitted black dress with a scoop neck and short sleeves. My sister wanted something loose to hide her stomach because it hadn't bounced back to its original form yet, so yesterday when we were shopping for the girls, I found her a pretty, long flowing maxi dress I knew she'd approve of.

"Knock knock," I say, entering her master bathroom with a small package that came in the mail yesterday.

She's sitting on her stool in front of her vanity mirror. Her blonde hair is in a messy bun at the nape of her neck and she looks like she's in the process of doing her makeup.

"Can I help?" I ask.

She nods, silently.

I set the box down and sit up on the counter in front of her. I lean in to apply some eye shadow and tears slip out past her eyelashes. I pause, and her eyes flutter open, looking red and puffy.

"Cadence," I say, my voice cracking at the pain and anguish in her eyes.

She squeezes her eyes hard, and more tears spill out.

"I just keep picturing him, Finley. His soft pudgy cheeks, his beautiful brown hair," she says, grabbing one of my loose brown locks hanging in front of my shoulder.

"Do you regret cremating him?" I ask.

"No," she shakes her head. "I don't. I can picture him here," she says, pointing to her head. "And here," she points to her heart, her chin trembling wildly. "Those images are more beautiful than any funeral home could have made for me."

I nod and my eyes well with tears.

She sniffs hard again and forces a pained smile at me.

"How about no makeup?" I ask.

"Great idea," she stands up and pulls me in for a hug.

"Are you going to tell me what's in the box, or do I have to figure it out myself?" she asks, pulling back and sniffing.

"It's for you. Open it," I say, handing it to her.

She opens the small black jewelry box and gasps when she sees what's inside.

As soon as Cadence was released from the hospital, I called Mrs. Adamson about making a necklace for her. I wasn't sure if she and Sheila would have the time or resources to make one quickly enough, but she expedited the shipping, and it arrived yesterday, just in time.

Cadence's hand touches the beautiful silver cross that has intricate pressed detailing around the edges, and one light-blue stone at the top. She feels the layers of thin, shiny, silver wires in the shape of angel wings fastened on the back. Engraved across the cross are the words: *Mommy's Angel.*

She looks up to me with tears falling down her cheeks, "Finley."

I smile at her.

"It's the most beautiful thing I've ever seen," she cries, and hugs me hard with the necklace clasped tightly in her hand. "I love it."

I hug her hard and then pull the necklace out of the box and fasten it behind her neck, "You ready?"

She takes a deep breath, touches her necklace on her chest and links her arm with mine as we head downstairs to George and the girls.

The day is chilly and overcast and there's about twenty people all huddled near each other on the Fourteenth Street Bridge. It's a rural part of town, so traffic shouldn't be an issue. George and Cadence only invited close family and friends. McKinley is grasping my hand, tightly, and in her other hand are her baseball cards. I smile when I see that all three girls brought them with.

Maya is climbing on the curb by the bridge and Megan is holding George's hand. Cadence looks flustered and nervous and my mom is clutching her arm tightly to try and calm her nerves. My dad is standing near all of them, looking stoic as ever.

I'm not surprised to see Brody walking up in his tailored grey suit. I knew he'd be here for Cadence, George, and the girls. His eyes meet mine and he half smiles at me. At first, I think he's going to come up and stand by me, but he stops himself and stands awkwardly behind some of George's family. I'm grateful for that because I know that the closer he gets to me the harder it will be to push him away. Especially today.

The pastor quiets everyone down and begins the service with some scripture. He then says a few words about George, Cadence, the girls, and then Baby George. My sister is crying freely, and I'm sniffing loudly as tears run continually down my face. I can feel McKinley's eyes on me several times throughout the service and I squeeze her hand a little tighter in response, each time.

"And now, Cadence would like to say a few words," the pastor announces.

This is news to me; she hasn't mentioned speaking at the service at all. I wonder if this is what she did on all of her walks.

Cadence places her hand on the rail of the bridge and clears her throat.

"I'm definitely not a poet, so don't judge me too harshly. This is just something I needed to get out of me before we say goodbye."

She unfolds a white sheet of paper.

"I've titled this poem:

Postpartum, With No Baby

**I have memories of flutters down below.
Ultrasound pictures of growth and more.
Doppler heart rates streaming loudly,
sighs of relief as progress shows proudly.
I am postpartum, with no baby.**

A BROKEN US

I have visions of lying on my back.
Concerned white masks staring back.
I place my hand on my small bulge,
stroking finally the boy I once indulged.
I am postpartum, with no baby.

I have strange stretch marks and new scars.
Bruises on veins from multiple IVs.
Rashes from tape the doctors used.
Yellow streaks from surgical goo.
I am postpartum, with no baby.

I have swollen breasts and leaking nipples.
Tender cleavage and blue veins streaking.
I wear tight bras to prevent the milk
I produced so easily in pregnancies past.
I am postpartum, with no baby.

I have hot flashes and cold shivers daily.
I have sad times, mad times, and even some happy times.
Cramps and twinges internally,
reminding me of what used to be.
I am postpartum, with no baby.

I have a swollen belly that's bigger than before.
No pants that will button, this I can't ignore.
Maternity clothes are all that fit,
despair at the cause of all of it.
I am postpartum, with no baby.

I have sympathetic glances and comforting strokes.
All from loved ones who want to cope.
Cookies, texts, and casseroles.
Cards and gifts to help console.
I am postpartum, with no baby.

> I have confusion on what to pray for.
> Because it all came easy, three times before.
> I begin to wonder, what's the point?
> When God will surely disappoint.
> I am postpartum, with no baby.
>
> I have a husband who's given me his love.
> In times of grief, loss, and all of the above.
> Sometimes I wonder how he's handled it,
> watching in agony as our nightmare hit.
> I am postpartum, with no baby.
>
> I have three daughters I love with all my heart.
> They are my everything, and I swear to never part.
> I shall give up on the dream of having a boy,
> to be the Mother to three girls who give me the most joy.
> I am postpartum, with three miracles.
> And *one* angel."

Cadence smiles beautifully as she finishes, and Megan rushes up to her and wraps her arms around her. George comes over and hugs both of them and we all attempt to quietly control the sobs inside of us on this quiet bridge.

A warm hand runs down my arm and clasps my free hand. I look over and see Brody standing beside me with red eyes. I squeeze his hand back, tightly, and then squeeze McKinley's hand tightly as well.

As the pastor wraps up the service, George's Dad brings five blue balloons up to where George, Cadence, Megan, and now Maya, are standing. McKinley releases my hand and runs up to join them.

Brody's arm bands around my back as the girls, George, and Cadence release the blue balloons into the sky. They then sprinkle the ashes into the creek below the bridge.

Everyone hangs out for a while, hugging and talking. Brody goes up and gives all three girls a bag of M&Ms and smiles sweetly at Cadence. Cadence smiles back and hugs him for a long time. I see her whisper something into Brody's ear and his expression turns very serious.

CHAPTER THIRTY-NINE

After everything is cleaned up, Brody asks me if he can drive me back to Cadence's house. I nod in acceptance, unable to come up with a legitimate reason to say no.

As we wind through the gravel roads, away from the bridge, Brody reaches out and grabs my hand, pulling it to his lap. I look down at our hands and feel sadness at the comfort of his hands holding mine.

"You okay?" he asks, softly.

"Yeah, that was intense, but gosh, Cadence is amazing," I reply, incredulously.

"Yeah, she is. I think she looked almost peaceful after it was over."

I shake my head. "Amazing."

"So what's your plan now?" he asks, looking over at me with his wide blue eyes.

I search his face, looking for signs of where he's going with this but I don't see any.

"Back to London, I suppose." I pull my hand out of his.

He nods, "I figured."

He figured? I have no clue where this is going, and the longer we drive, the smaller his truck begins to feel.

"Gonna continue working for Val over there?" he asks.

I shrug, not really feeling like talking about work right now. "Uh, yeah. I guess."

"It's good money, right?" he says.

Seriously, is this truck shrinking?

"It's fine," I reply.

"If Frank continues to refuse your rent check, it should be pretty easy to live over there, right?"

"What?" I ask, confused with why the hell he's asking me these questions.

Feeling suddenly hot, I roll the window down and lean my head out, craving the fresh air.

"It'd be cool, too, if you could work directly for that jewelry company. They seem to like you enough," he says, perfectly calm.

"Can you just stop?" I reply, loudly.

"Stop what?" he asks, looking at me, confused.

"Stop asking me all these dumb, normal questions, like this is totally normal for us. You know what, just pull over. Pull over right here," I say, as we approach a small wooded area with large trees covered in bright orange leaves.

"What's wrong?" he asks, sounding alarmed.

"I need air!" I say, as I leach the car door open and get out, walking unsteadily in my heels, deeper into the little forest area.

Brody hops out and follows behind me.

"I was just curious," he says

"Enough, okay?" I say, swerving around to face him. "I can't take this, Brody. I can't take you acting like you don't give a crap that I'm going to be in London, and you're going to be here, and we're just going to go our separate ways, and do our separate things from now on. This day is depressing enough." I turn around and duck beneath a tree with low-hanging orange leaves.

"I do give a crap," he says, grabbing my elbow and pulling me backward into him. "I care like crazy, Fin," he breathes into my ear, his hands on both of my arms, holding me tightly against him.

My chest rises and falls with his close contact.

"Brody..." I start, my heart aching at his wonderful touch.

"Just let me say this, Finley," he says, turning me to face him while continuing to hold me by my arms.

"When you said what you said back in London, about me leaving you because you can't ever get pregnant...that ruined *us*, Finley. It ruined everything we were about."

"I know, Brody! And I can't tell you how sorry I am for that," I say, defensively, not wanting to listen to this anymore.

"I know you're sorry. But I'm even sorrier. I'm sorry I didn't show you that *you* were more important to me than *us*. *You,* Finley, are everything to me. I am nothing without you. I don't care about loving us anymore. Don't you see that? I want to love you, and you alone. Because if I don't have you to love in my life, then I have nothing, Finley. You're it for me. Can't you see that?"

Tears fill my eyes. Seriously, how do I even have tears left?

"Brody, I can't be with you. You're going to be an amazing father someday and I can't take that from you. Don't you see how that could ruin whatever it is we have? I'll resent myself, Brody! I will! I'll hate myself for not giving us an *us baby*."

"Finley," he groans, and tucks my hair behind my ears. "I don't give a shit about having an *us baby*. You're what I care about. For all I care, I'll be the best fucking uncle the M&Ms and the world have ever seen!"

I laugh at that.

"I'm serious, Finley. Those girls fulfill a lot for me. If you'll have me, I'll be an uncle to the best three girls in the world, with the woman I've been dreaming of my whole life."

"Brody, I've changed so much these past six weeks. I love London. I love being near Leslie…and Frank even."

"That's fine!" he rushes, and kisses me quickly on the lips. "I'm where you are, babe. I'm with you. Forever. I'll live there, too. Or we'll get our own place, right next door if you want. I don't care. Can't you see that, Finley? Can't you see how badly I need you?"

"I need you, too!" I cry, my reserve crumbling.

"Then stop *fighting* this," he says, and smashes his lips into mine, squeezing his arms around my waist, my hands resting on his chest.

"Brody, wait…" I pull back, but then look at his lips and think better of it. I pull his face against mine again, threading my fingers through his beautiful curly brown hair. His beautifully familiar hair.

I push him away again. "I need you to be clear on this Brody. I can't have a baby. Ever."

"I don't care. We'll adopt!" he laughs, kissing my nose. "Or we'll foster, or we'll just rock the auntie and uncle titles and travel the world together and never have children. I don't care, Finley. Just as long as it's all…all of it…with *you*."

"We'll figure it out together?" I ask, one more time, scared out of my mind at the possibility of losing Brody again.

"Yes, baby. Together," he says, kissing me again and pulling back to murmur against my lips. "Life is too precious to spend another second away from you, Finley. I love you, baby. I'll love you forever."

"I love you, Brody," I breathe heavily against his face. "I promise I will love you fiercely and forever," I say, staring deeply into his eyes.

"That's all I'll ever need," he whispers, against my lips.

I grab his face again and connect our lips in a hungry, desperate kiss. Brody grasps my face in his hands, reverently consuming my entire mind, body, and soul. This is a kiss to end all kisses. I'll never be the same after this kind of kiss. And I never want to be.

I need to feel complete with Brody. I need to feel like I'm enough. Enough of a woman for him to love me through it all. Brody gives me that feeling in spades. It was my own issues and insecurities that made me doubt what we had before. I had to grieve the loss of being able to have a child, and accept the idea of only having Brody. Brody is all I want, and all I need. And amazingly, I'm all he wants, and all he needs. I'm enough. *I am enough.*

THE EPILOGUE

Call me crazy. Call me stupid. Call me naive. But I really, honestly, and truly, never saw this day coming. Not even when I first met Brody and felt all the warm fuzzies a new relationship makes one feel. It just never was a part of our plan. It didn't seem like a part of our future.

I. Was. Wrong.

The intense joy I felt when Brody got down on one knee and asked me to marry him at Christmas time, was similar to the exhilaration I felt the time I jumped off a forty-foot cliff into a river in Colorado. It was exciting and terrifying. The adrenaline and pure happiness those acts evoked, was like, the best kind of high.

The fact that it was the most beautiful ring I'd ever seen was just an added bonus. Brody bought me a huge blue sapphire with tiny white diamonds wrapped around the stone and the thick platinum band. The blue reminded me of his eyes every time I looked at it. It was non-traditional and one-hundred percent me. I found myself surprised at the pure pride I felt having a ring on that particular finger.

Brody and I made up after Baby George's memorial service and we immediately made big plans for our future together. We'd fallen into a new, wonderful version of normal. We agreed that we would wait to decide what we wanted for our future in regards to having a family because we had plenty of time ahead of us and we knew without a doubt, we were in this together. Our immediate future plans were on hold until after the holidays. We just needed time to reconnect and talk through our feelings before we worried about where we were going to live.

I smile every time I think of Brody's proposal. He caught me completely off guard, dropping down to one knee at my sister's house, in front of their Christmas tree. I didn't know what the hell was going on until I saw him fumbling awkwardly inside his pocket.

He pulled out a small, velvet jewelry box and said, "A wise woman once told me, in no uncertain terms, *Put a ring on her finger or your ass is grass,* and that's exactly what I'm doing."

I laughed as I heard the M&Ms gasping at his curse word. Cadence joined me in the laughter and I looked over at her and saw instant happy tears. That sounded just like Cadence. Her tears cemented the fact that Brody was actually proposing to me right now! George watched happily, and I looked back at Brody with an incredulous look.

Thankfully, he saved himself from that horrible proposal speech by saying, "Luckily, it was already a part of my plan." And he flashed his eyebrows flirtatiously at me.

Because I'm an idiot, and don't think before I speak, the first words out of my mouth after he asked me to marry him, were, "Brody, we don't have to!"

His face was horrifying. He looked like he wanted to kill me, but was restraining himself. I'll never live that one down. *We don't have to? Gosh, how big of a jerk am I?*

However, I don't regret saying those words to him at all, because I can still vividly remember his epic response.

"I know we don't have to, Finley, but I want to. I want to love you and cherish you for the rest of my life. I want to see this ring on your finger, and know that you are mine and I am yours, and that together, we will figure things out."

Tears filled my eyes as my skepticism crumbled beneath his beautiful words. I cried out a yes, and dropped to my knees, hugging him like I'd never hugged him before. I never thought a proposal from Brody would make me so happy, but hearing him ask me, and seeing that ring and the pride and joy on his face as he placed it on my finger, was overpowering.

I wanted to marry this man. I wanted him to refer to me as his wife. I wanted to refer to him as my husband. It felt like a final puzzle piece had been placed.

After we got engaged, the biggest change in our relationship was our move overseas. Brody was the one to suggest it, and I was shocked and thrilled. I always took him as a Midwesterner for life, and I knew he loved his job. But he told me that he meant it when he said we'd figure our lives out together.

A week after the New Year, we put our house up for sale and sold most of our furniture and possessions on *Craigslist*. It was surreal, boxing up all of our keepsakes and shipping them off with a London postcode on the box.

Frank was elated when I told him I was moving back to London with Brody. He said we were welcome to stay as long as we wanted and that he loved having extras in his house. Especially extras that looked like Brody. I told him that there wouldn't be any more peepshows if I had a say in it, and he told me in no uncertain terms to *buggar off*. The cheeky bastard.

The biggest excitement that further secured our move to London was when Mrs. Adamson offered me a job at *Faith's Miracle*

Jewelry as their fulltime marketing representative. The second the offer came out of Mrs. Adamson's mouth, I, albeit unprofessionally, squealed with excitement. She laughed kindly through the phone, obviously pleased with my eagerness to come back to London and work for her. My official title will still remain under the umbrella of Val's company, because a job transfer is a lot easier to manage in terms of living in a foreign country.

I felt awful leaving Val, but she told me she saw it coming when I first left. She also said she was going to keep me busier than I could handle with extra freelance work, and I smiled and hugged her tightly. I owed a lot to Val. Not only did she teach me everything I knew, but she connected me with the best employers I could ever have hoped for.

Brody's job situation was still up in the air. The fact that we were getting married was making things a lot simpler, though. He said he'd start seriously job hunting after the wedding once we were all settled. Thankfully, we had a decent little nest egg saved up, thanks to the big profit we made on our house sale, and since we sold most of our furniture. Not to mention, Frank's continued refusal of accepting rent payments.

When we arrived at the house, all of our shipped boxes were in the master bedroom down the hall from the living room. Apparently, Frank had called his parents to ask them if he could rent out their room and they were surprised he had left it empty all this time. Brody and I were pleasantly surprised to walk into a gorgeous, fully furnished master bedroom with a master bathroom attached to it. It felt like a honeymoon suite we got to live in 24/7, dual shower heads and all. However, Brody and I missed our tiny purple twin mattress on the third floor. We may have missed it enough to christen it again…a couple of times. Four times, tops.

Brody adjusted really well to living in London. He and Leslie were already friends and he seemed to be developing some sort of weird *bromance* with Mitch that we all made fun of constantly. Brody introduced him to the TV show, *Breaking Bad*, and ever since then, they were nearly inseparable. All I had to do was say purple sheets and Brody would drop whatever he was doing with Mitch and come running.

I saw Liam about a month after Brody and I moved to London. He stopped by with Theo one Sunday afternoon. It was awkward and nerve-wracking at first, but he seemed genuinely happy for me and Brody. He actually shook hands with Brody and the two of them appeared to be able to tolerate each other. After the whole Jake fiasco in college, I would have never guessed Brody would be able to be cool and normal with Liam. But Brody and I really had come a long way. We were maturing together, and with that, came a newfound confidence in our relationship. I knew Brody wasn't going anywhere and he knew I wasn't going anywhere. We loved each other, through and through.

Liam told me he was glad I found my very own fixer, and I thanked him for being a great friend to me when I needed it most. The girl who ends up with Liam will be incredibly lucky.

***

The waves crash against the beach outside and I walk carefully over to the patio to enjoy the view. We chose Mexico to get married because it's quick and easy. We waited until later in the spring to ensure that my sister was feeling one-hundred percent recovered and could fully enjoy the day with us.

The color of the aqua water crashing onto the white sandy beach is simply stunning. I can't believe in fifteen minutes I'll be walking down the sand to Brody. *My husband.* I reach down to touch a *Faith's Miracle Jewelry* piece that Mrs. Adamson made for me especially for this day. Mr. and Mrs. Adamson and Sheila are even down here in Mexico for the big day, and I am excited to celebrate with them.

The necklace they made me has blue stones in an antique silver lattice setting. She told me it was my something old, new, and blue. My niece, Megan, loaned me a beautiful white flower hairpiece for my something borrowed. My long brown hair is curled, and pinned over to one side down the front of my shoulder, and her flower is the perfect accent. She blushed a fierce shade of crimson when I asked her if she thought Brody would like it.

"Oh, Finley," my mother says, gasping as she walks into my hotel suite. "I've never seen a prettier bride. Don't tell your sister," she says, hugging me and trembling slightly from the silent tears she's shedding.

"I'm sitting right here, Mom," Cadence's voice cuts through the moment.

"Oh, shut up. This is Finny's day," she says, pulling back and handing me a small bouquet of deep purple calla lilies.

"Dad's waiting downstairs for you, sweetie. Are you ready?" she asks.

I nod, looking at myself in the mirror one more time. My dress is fierce. It's a lightweight, soft taffeta material and has a huge, wide skirt, yet remains beautifully simple. The waistline hugs me in the perfect spot and there's beautiful intricate beading adorned in the deep v-front. The back dips down incredibly low and has thin spaghetti straps that come to the front. *I'm definitely ready.*

My dad smiles approvingly at me when I enter the resort lobby. He leans over and gives me a soft kiss on the cheek. With one more deep breath, we head down to the beach where everyone is waiting.

The song playing me down the beach isle is *I Won't Give Up by Jason Mraz*. As soon as I hear the song, my emotions take over and a small sob erupts from my throat. My dad pats my hand, soothingly, and we pass through two concrete pillars…and then, *I see him.*

Brody looks simply perfect in his light linen trousers and white button-down shirt with a few buttons undone. I blink my eyes, rapidly, trying to clear them so I can see his face better. His brown, curly hair is slightly longer, just the way I like it, and his sleeves are rolled up his forearm. His fresh Mexico tan makes him look sexier than I ever remember him looking. I feel my dad pulling me back, preventing me from running down the aisle and jumping into Brody's arms, which is exactly what I want to do. Then again, the other part of me wants to continue walking down this aisle for the rest of my life. The complete look of adoration on Brody's face is something I could stare at forever.

When my dad hands me over to Brody, I reach over and hug him tightly, fighting myself not to kiss him. His eyes are red when I pull away and he smiles back at me like he's the proudest guy in the whole universe.

I don't hear much of what the minister says, except for the part where he tells us it's time for us to exchange vows.

I go first.

"Brody. Today I get to call you my husband. My man," I smile, and two tears slip out. "Thank you for loving me through all my craziness and for seeing me better than I've ever been able to see myself. Only you could have made me feel like the woman I am meant to be and not like the work in progress I really am. Thank you for forgiving me when I didn't see us for the truly special thing we are together. You are remarkable, Brody. You are my absolute world. You have given so much to me, and I promise to give you all that and more. I'll do whatever it takes to continue making you...and us...happy in our marriage. And I promise to be honest and open with you for the rest of my life. I love you."

Brody looks down, wiping tears out of his eyes. The air around us is utterly still as he takes a moment and clears his throat before he begins.

"Finley. My Finley. My forever," he says, with a smile and looks down. "Today I marry you and thank God that I get to keep you. I would have fought forever for you, Finley, and I'm so happy that today I get to call you my wife. I will never need anyone in my life, more than I need you. I will never love anyone in my life more than I love you. I will never cherish anyone in my life more than I cherish you. Finley, I want to travel the world with you. I want to experience life with you. And I want grow and change with you. Together, Finley, if we're together, I will be the happiest I can ever be in my life. And I'll do everything in my power to make you the happiest you can be in your life. You are all I'll ever need in this world. My Finley. My wife."

He gives me a large smile and reaches his hand over to wipe the tears streaming down my face.

The minister says a few last words that I don't bother listening to, and then, we kiss.

Brody takes my face in his hands and claims my mouth the way he's always done. He holds my face like it's his most prized possession, and rubs his thumbs on my cheeks, soothingly, while he deepens the kiss. My hands ball up his shirt as I attempt to maintain some semblance of control in front of our family and friends.

We pull apart, and smile at each other as we hear the loud cheers of Frank and Leslie over everyone else. We look out to all our friends and family and smile proudly at everyone that's watched us on our journey. Our journey of changing *us* to *you*, heartache to hope, and broken love, to *our* love.

THE END

THE ACKNOWLEDGEMENTS

A huge thanks to my editor, Heather Banta. You truly are wonderful at what you do and I'm so grateful I got to work with you again. I honestly don't think I could do all this without you. Thank you for not yelling at me too much for throwing too many "justs" in a sentence or for making into in to two words. There I go again. Or for using CAPS too much. You tolerate me and I appreciate you. And sorry I like the word "familiar."

Thanks to my plethora of beta readers and proof readers that helped grow and develop these characters into real people that I'm sad I can never sit down and actually hang out with. Seriously, Frank would be so much fun. To my "Sioux Falls Mom," Becky, my sister Abby, and my bestie, Ashley, thanks for going on this journey with me, chapter by chapter. Your time and input on my story and characters really helped mold this into something I am very proud of.

Big thanks to all the book bloggers out there that donate their time to help indie authors, like myself, get our names out there. Your jobs can be thankless at times, but I promise you, we see what you're doing and we are super duper appreciative. In particular I want to thank, Angela Pratt from ifeeltheneedtheneedtoread.com and Patricia Green from roomwithbooks.com. Both of you have been extremely generous with your time for me and I can't thank you enough.

And last, but certainly not least, thanks to my family for their support of this writing gig of mine. I had no idea what a true passion this would turn into. I know, without a doubt, that I couldn't do it without the support of my husband, Kevin, and my little peanut, Lolo. Thank you guys for being all the inspiration I need to continue pursuing my dream.

And as always, shout out to my angel babies that will forever hold a special place in my heart. Not a day goes by where I don't think of each and every one of you. You and Lorelei were my inspiration to start writing and it amazes me still that you are able to give me such a tremendous gift when your lives were so short. I love and miss you all. I'll see you someday.

FOR MORE ABOUT THE AUTHOR

www.amydawsauthor.com

www.facebook.com/amydawsauthor

www.twitter.com/amydawsauthor

Check out more novels in the London Lovers Series, available at all major retailers!

#1 Becoming Us

#2 A Broken Us

#3 London Bound

#4 Not The One coming soon

Also, a Memoir by Amy Daws:

Chasing Hope

A mother's story of loss, heartbreak, and the miracle of hope.

Sign up for the Amy Daws newsletter to stay informed of official release date announcements!

www.amydawsauthor.com/news

If you enjoyed this book, please consider
taking the time to post a review.
Reviews are extremely helpful to authors
and there is no better way to
thank them for their hard work.